"*Charlie Four Kilo* allows the reader culture. Hard-hitting, humorous and a compelling storyline that leaves the

Advanced Clinical Nurse Practitioner

"A genuine page-turner and an amazing insight into the challenges faced by Veterans. Rich vividly reveals how dangerous and stressful the criminal world is"

- Lt Matt W (Royal Navy)

"First few chapters get you hooked and are light-hearted, but nothing can get you ready for what happens next. Beyond belief, frightening, scary but most of all a can't put you down read. Brilliant."

- Dave Nich

"This book is simply a great read that has a mixture of humour, fear, psychological trauma and near death experiences. It encapsulates that organised crime is like any other business with its high and lows except that legitimate businesses don't have the law knocking at the door. A must-read."

- Maj (retd) Cormac Doyle ARRC. BSc Dip He MH RMN CPN EMDR CEO The Bridge Charity.

"Try and keep a steady pulse. This is a nerve-jangling account of redemption. *Charlie Four Kilo* is a remarkable story told with honesty and integrity."

- Chris Nott, Author of "Call Sign Chopper", www.CallSignChopper.com

"This is a fast-paced gripping tale of life in the darker side of society. Succinct and to the point it keeps you locked in. I could feel the tension in the characters jumping out from the pages. A must-read!"

- C. Ollis

Charlie Four Kilo

Rich Jones

Published by iink Media in 2020

Copyright © Rich Jones

Author Rich Jones' back cover photo courtesy of Yon Alexanders

First Edition

The author asserts the moral right under the Copyright, Designs and Patents Act 1988 to be identified as the author of this work.

All Rights reserved. No part of this publication may be reproduced, stored in a retrieval system or transmitted, in any form or by any means without the prior consent of the author, nor be otherwise circulated in any form of binding or cover other than that which it is published and without a similar condition being imposed on the subsequent purchaser.

Paperback ISBN: 978-1-80031-541-9
Ebook ISBN: 978-1-80031-540-2

www.iinkmedia.com

iink Media

Thank you...

...to my loved ones who stuck by my side

...to my new-found friends that have supported me without judgment

...to the veterans who served and those that are still serving in Her Majesty's Armed Forces for being prepared to make the ultimate sacrifice

...to all the military organisations set up to support us in our time of need

...to SSAFA who have gone above and beyond to support me and my family. They deserve a 'special thanks'.

"In every generation, men are born who, in their heart of hearts and the blood of their bloods, are warriors; but, when there are no more wars to fight, what must these men do, these men?"

Unknown

Contents

1. ROAD TRIP 1
2. A WALK IN THE WOODS 6
3. OUT OF THE FRYING PAN 15
4. INTO THE FIRE 28
5. FULL OF SHIT 37
6. ALFIE 51
7. REBUILDING THE BUSINESS 1 67
8. DARK TIMES ON THE HORIZON 90
9. THE BUTTERFLY EFFECT 109
10. DARK TIMES 129
11. THE BOY 148
12. THE NEW FIRM 155
13. NOT EASY MONEY 166
14. MAN DOWN 174

GLOSSARY 187

1. ROAD TRIP

It's fair to say that at some point in our lives most of us would have woken up in what can be considered as unfamiliar surroundings, maybe a serious night on the piss or you've crashed out on a mate's sofa after a heavy smoke, you may have even got lucky. Now take Murray for example, he really hasn't got a fucking clue where he is; in fact, he can't even remember how he got there. Now under normal circumstances, this can be considered as embarrassing, but he knows this is different, how does he know? He knows this because he's been gagged, his hands and feet are cable-tied behind his back, there's a rope leading from his hands securing a stinking hessian sack over his head which is also tied behind his back. So an accurate description would be, he's been trussed up like a fucking chicken.

He's racking his brains, trying to recollect how he got himself into this predicament, whilst at the same time trying to make himself as comfortable as possible. His left arm's gone to sleep, he has a splitting headache, his whole body aches, his eyes are seriously stinging, his face feels like it's on fire, his nose is snotty as fuck and the sack that's on his head reeks of petrol. What he does know, is that he's moving, so he must be in a vehicle of some sort. It doesn't feel like the boot of a car, because although he can't move, he is partially sat up. It feels more like he's in the back of a van slumped against the side panel. How long has he been out, where is he being taken, who's driving the van, what are their intentions? These are just some of the questions bouncing around in his head.

He's struggling to gauge the passage of time and distance. He's pretty convinced that he's either on a motorway or a long dual carriageway because since he came to, the van doesn't seem to have made any major changes in direction, it hasn't sped up, slowed down or appear to have overtaken anything, indicating that there is a lack of traffic, which could mean that it's possibly late at night or in the early morning hours. One thing that's for sure, wherever he's going, it's gonna be no picnic.

Now when you're in a position like Murray it's very hard to consider the gravity of what might be about to happen, so to have a bit of a cry as you reflect on your life is quite normal. Anyone who's found themselves in this kind of situation will silently agree; of course they won't admit to it because that will make them look weak. But trust me, we're all human and Murray is crying like a fucking baby. He's becoming quite agitated as his nose is blocked – combine that with being gagged, he's beginning to struggle to breathe. The smell of petrol from the sack has brought on the mother of all headaches and the fumes keep spinning him out. On the bright side, if there is such a thing, he is beginning to recollect fragments of how he might have ended up in this precarious position.

He was in his local pub, it was a busy Friday night and he had to take a private call so he opted to go outside to the car park where he could have a spot of privacy; it was raining so he thought he'd plot up in his car to take the call. As he approached the car from behind, someone called his name. Turning, he heard the sound of aerosol being released; whatever it was hit him square in the face and he simultaneously felt his body lock up, spasming as he was hit from behind with what must have been a taser or stun gun, either way there was fuck all he could do anyway. The next thing he remembers was waking up feeling like shit.

As this nightmare continues he's sure he can hear voices coming from the front of the van; he can definitely hear faint music coming from the stereo. At times he's sure he can even hear them laughing. This is very unnerving, whoever has taken him obviously doesn't give a toss; they're sat up in the front laughing and joking and he's in the back, gagged and bound, pissing his fucking pants in fear. Who the fuck are these people? The van begins to slow down, his arse starts twitching and not just a little bit, he's seriously bricking it. He's trying to brace himself for another shot with a taser or a kicking. He feels the van veer gently to the left as it pulls off of the road and gradually stops.

The talking is now a lot clearer but still inaudible. He hears the driver's door open and close, he can definitely hear footsteps approaching the side of the van, he's now almost accepted his fate – whatever happens next is probably out of his control, he just decides that he won't struggle, he'll just go with the flow. He can hear the sound of keys and the next thing is the sound of metal knocking against something and a bit of fiddling around with a part of the van. What the fuck are they doing? Then he hears a familiar sound, the sound of a fuel pump – they've only stopped to fuel up. This sends Murray's thoughts into overdrive; he doesn't know whether to feel relieved or not, whatever his fate might be it has now been prolonged, even if it's just for a short while, but this doesn't stop him thinking how far have they travelled or how much further are they going? The same questions keep going round and round in his head. This headache is unbearable, he's never felt so shit; in fact, if his fate is to be ironed out this would almost come as a welcome relief compared to how he's feeling right now.

The fuel pump stops and he hears the familiar sounds of the nozzle being replaced and the fuel cap being screwed back on. Then there is an eerie silence as they must have gone off to pay the bill. He is now slipping into what can only be described as a dream state. He's cold, really cold, the pain, the suffering along with this headache that just won't subside, he feels as if his body is shutting down but the fact that he's in some serious trouble is keeping him semi-alert. The van door goes again and once again he can hear the muffled conversation of his captors along with the sound of the stereo as the engine starts up. Who are they? They just appear to be far too relaxed considering they have a kidnapped person in tow. This now poses another question – do they do this for a living, that being the case who has Murray upset enough to warrant being taken?

The van pulls away slowly and then starts heading along what can only be presumed as the same road, but he doesn't really know. He keeps replaying over and over in his head what happened the night before and how this came about; he's trying to remember who was calling him before he was taken. Nothing comes to mind but then again he'd had a few drinks and stuck a few lines up his nose, so things weren't exactly one hundred percent in the faculty department and to top it off he is busting for a piss.

Time seems to pass slowly, he can't figure out what's what, is it night, is it day, has he been out for longer than he thinks? One thing's for sure – he cannot hold out any longer to the relentless pressure from his bladder, he finally submits and pisses himself, properly. So now you can add a set of stinking piss-soaked jeans to the equation, how very embarrassing for him. His captors will naturally think this has happened out of fear and not as the result of a full bladder and the lack of appropriate toilet facilities. He may as well have filled his fucking pants with shit in the process, it would have made no difference at this stage of the game and I guess the consolation prize is at least he'll be warm for a few seconds.

Murray slips out of consciousness again only to be woken up by the sensation of the van slowing down. Once again he gets a massive shot of anxiety along with an extremely unhealthy dose of paranoia, a simple side effect of the coke consumed the night before, but these feelings are real and they do fuck you up. The van has definitely taken a turn onto smaller roads, as it's constantly shifting from side to side and nowhere near as smooth as earlier. The same questions again spinning around in his head, but he has no answers. Shortly the van slows right down and eventually comes to a stop. Again he hears the voices up front, the engine is still running, one of the doors opens and he can feel the van shift in weight slightly as someone gets out.

Words cannot describe how Murray is feeling now, this ordeal seems to have been going on forever, the reality is it may have only been a few hours. The van begins to pull away slowly and starts crawling forward but this time onto a much bumpier surface, if he's to take a wild guess he'd say it wasn't a road, not a tarmac one anyway. The van pulls up and someone gets back in, it then pulls off and starts heading down what must be a track of some kind, this is not good. He's now convinced only bad things can come from this. He can't hear the radio anymore, but every now and again he can just about pick up the sound of conversation, no laughing, so he's not sure how to take that – are they getting serious for something?

This part of the journey seems to drag on, the van isn't exactly shifting and it feels slow, very slow. The surface seems to change again and is now even bumpier, the off-road kind of bumpy, he's being thrown around like a rag doll in the back, he's now laid on his side, this just keeps getting worse by the minute. He just wants this to end; he no longer cares how it ends, he just wants it over. He's lying there contemplating his life, thinking of his family and his friends, wondering if they have noticed he's missing yet, probably not though as it's a regular occurrence for him to go on a bender for a few days especially over the weekends. He's not a religious man, but he is having a quiet word with God asking, praying, that if he can come through this ordeal in one piece he promises he'll be a good boy. He's at a point in his head where he's virtually having an out-of-body experience, though it's dark he swears he can see himself slumped over in the back of the van in a foetal position… with cable ties, a sack over his head and piss-soaked jeans.

2. A WALK IN THE WOODS

The van stops, bringing Murray back to the harsh reality of his situation. The engine is switched off, and he hears two doors open and close quietly. He can hear the sound of keys then the sound of doors being locked or unlocked. He can pick up on bits of conversation but again too faint to get anything from it, he is still none the wiser. This situation is so surreal he's definitely past caring, he's all cried out and his pride left the building once he'd pissed his pants. Finally, bringing a sense of relief, the van doors open.

He hears a strong not loud but recognisable voice, "Don't fucking move." Move? Is he fucking kidding? Murray can't move even if he wanted to. The voice he recognises belongs to someone he knows only as the "Russian", though he's not Russian, he is from that part of the world but nevertheless he is known as the "Russian". Murray feels the van drop slightly as the Russian gets in and he can just pick up the flicker of lights, once again he says, "Don't move." Murray can sense that the Russian is close, very close, and a bright light briefly shines through the sack and into his eyes; next thing he realises is he's being grabbed by the head and dragged along the van floor; he drops out of the van and onto the ground. The adrenaline is pumping so much that pain is non-existent. He hears the Russian jump out of the van and again say, "Don't fucking move." The Russian leans right up in Murray's ear, again a bright light pierces his eyes, and whispers, "I'm going to cut your feet loose, don't try running." On that, Murray feels something move between his ankles and snip the cable ties – no sooner than that is done he hears the Russian say whilst chuckling, "Fuck me he's pissed himself." Murray straightens his legs and feels the blood rushing back into them. Mind you, he's still on the ground so he's still far from comfortable.

He can't hear the other person but he's sure there's someone else there. "Stand-up, we're going for a walk," says the Russian. Apart from the odd flash of light from what must be torches it's still pitch black. Murray feels a tug from the rope that's round his neck, he's now being led like a fucking dog. He stumbles and falls over but whoever has control of his lead just pulls it again. Murray awkwardly gets up and tries to walk again, he's only just getting the feeling back in his legs, his left arm is now coming back to life. There is no talking, so Murray tries to use this time to figure out what the fuck is going on. There's no light, so it must still be night, but what night? Friday, Saturday, Sunday – he really doesn't know. It's beginning to warm up; it's only late autumn so it's not freezing by any standards. The ground underfoot feels fairly soft, but not grassy, like mud and it's pretty uneven. He can't smell anything due to the state of the sack that's over his head and his nose is still blocked from the coke.

Murray is having a feeling of serenity; although he knows he's in trouble he's not really thinking about what might be about to happen, he's living in the moment, which is all he can do. He's thinking about where he might be, he can't hear any sounds apart from the faint footsteps of whoever is escorting him on this expedition. They don't even appear to be communicating in any way at all; all he gets is the odd flash of light from their torches. This nightmare is all he can think about and his night in the pub on Friday seems to be a distant memory, although it may have only been the previous evening. He stumbles and falls again, only to be sharply dragged back to his feet, again they continue on their way.

Murray feels his lead tighten once again, only this time the Russian calmly says, "Wait here." Have they arrived at their destination? He hasn't got the foggiest how long they've been walking for, they can't have covered that much ground as it was slow progress. This time the light shines directly in his face and he feels who he can only presume is the Russian grab the sack that's over his head; first he loosens the rope that has been secured around Murray's neck and then slowly removes the sack.

Murray's night vision is all over the place, it's still dark but with the constant flashing of torches in his face he still can't see particularly well, what he can see is two people, one who he knows is the Russian – he can't yet see his face but it's the man's stature – he's tall, around six-four maybe six-five and quite solid. For someone in his line of work he would be. The other guy, and he's assuming it is a man, is very hard to gauge as he is saying and doing very little, the fact that the torches are attached to their heads like miners' or cavers' lights is slightly disconcerting, they must be keeping their hands free for something.

The silent man is standing about ten feet in front of Murray and the Russian is to his rear left, which is troubling because his hands are still tied behind his back and he is feeling extremely vulnerable. It's still dark but regardless of the flashing lights his eyes are slowly adjusting, he can now make out that the quiet guy is dressed in dark clothes but it appears he is wearing a hood or balaclava. Murray is feeling quite indifferent about this as he could be masking his face for a number of reasons, so the jury will remain out on that, for now anyway. The Russian is also in dark clothes but he doesn't have his face covered, not that there's much point as his voice and build give him away anyway, besides he's the kind of character you don't forget, ever.

The Russian moves in front of Murray and delivers a statement, "Right, I'm going to give you some instructions. I suggest you follow them, do you understand me?" Murray acknowledges this with a simple nod, not that he has many choices, because he's still gagged. The Russian calmly says, "If you take a look down at your feet you'll see we've taken some time to mark out a rectangle on the ground." Murray looks down and can just make out the shape in front of him on the ground; it's partially revealed by the torchlight and he makes out basic shapes and images in the dark. The Russian now says, "I'm going to cut your hands loose, don't try anything stupid." Murray feels a sudden snip as the Russian cuts the cable tie around his wrists, finally feeling slightly less vulnerable. The Russian walks a few feet away; returning with a spade, he throws the spade on the ground at Murray's feet. "Dig," he commands. Murray looks at him in utter fear and a semi-state of confusion. "Fucking dig," he says again, this time slightly elevating his voice. Murray is feeling submissive but he doesn't want to be digging his own grave. He continues to gawp at the Russian and the other guy, flicking between the two of them wondering what the hell is happening to him. The Russian backs up and stands next to the other person. Murray can see well enough to make out the details on the other guy's clothes and he can confirm he is wearing a balaclava and dark gloves, the jury have almost finished deliberating, and this isn't looking good.

Once again the Russian barks, "Start fucking digging." As he delivers this worrying demand the silent guy reaches his right hand into the left breast of his jacket and removes a semi-automatic pistol. This is seriously fucking Murray's head up; he's now picturing the jury heading back into the court room with the foreman waving a piece of paper in his hand. Whilst Murray is looking at the Russian in disbelief, the silent guy takes a silencer out of his other pocket and calmly attaches it to the barrel of the semi. Murray now hears the jury state, "You're fucked." The Russian now sounding quite impatient says in a slow yet direct manner, "Dig the fucking hole." No sooner than this order has been issued, the gunman snaps his body into position and sharply squeezes a round off – it hits the ground directly between Murray's feet. In Murray's head, time has just stopped. As the round impacts, Murray looks up at the gunman who is looking directly at him – there is a slight wisp of smoke exiting the barrel. The gunman casually turns his head and looks at the Russian, who doesn't move, he just remains fixed looking at Murray ready to deliver another order. The gunman's position only changes when he bends down to pick up the empty case that was ejected from the breach; however, the gun is always trained on Murray, and apart from this one movement his position remains the same – legs shoulder-width apart with both hands on the gun, he looks back at Murray and raises the weapon, only this time aiming at his head.

Murray picks up the spade and starts frantically digging, he's going so fast there's mud going fucking everywhere, most of it back in the hole it came from. Noticing this the Russian says, "Stop fucking about and do it properly." This falls on deaf ears as Murray continues to dig like his life depended on it, and for all he knows it does. After a few moments Murray calms down and not because he wants to, it's because he's out of breath! He collapses into the partially dug hole, dropping the spade in the process. He's on all fours, desperately trying to get air through his nose but this is proving hard as it's still fucked from the coke.

The Russian walks forward, grabs Murray by the arms and lifts him to his feet, in the same way you'd lift a young child who's just fallen over. Murray is stood on the edge of the partially dug hole and the Russian is stood in it. The Russian leans towards Murray, gets right up in his face, he's close, uncomfortably close, he whispers to him, "Do you want to live?" Murray sobbing uncontrollably nods. "Then do as I fucking say," whispers the Russian. On that, the Russian slowly returns to his position next to the gunman who still has the gun pointing at Murray's head. They look at each other again, waiting for Murray to start the task set before him. Murray decides to start digging, this time at a workable pace.

He doesn't know how deep to dig, so he thinks the best thing is to follow the template that has been laid before him and dig down a layer at a time. Whilst digging what he feels might be his own grave, he can't get over the sound of the gun as it was fired at him; he's never heard a gun fired before, especially one that has been suppressed. He thought it would be a lot quieter but it wasn't, he's trying to figure out why it seemed so loud. Was it a mixture of shock and fear that made it seem louder or was it just that he's seen too many movies that gave him the impression that a silencer would be silent? Either way, it's a sound he'll never forget.

The sun isn't up yet but it's getting light as he can see so much more. He can see that he is in a pretty dense wood, it's an evergreen wood so there are no leaves on the deck, just loads of fine needles. The daunting thing is that the gunman hasn't fucking moved; on the odd occasion he looks at the Russian but that's it. Who is he? The hole is getting deeper now, he definitely feels if he was to lie down it would be deep enough to cover his body – why is he thinking these thoughts? They make no sense, if he is to be killed then why would he want to make it easier for them; he's beginning to feel stupid as well as worried.

The Russian walks up to Murray and says, "Stop digging." Murray doesn't know whether to feel relieved about this or not – relieved that he can have a rest, but shitting himself because of what might come next. "Put the spade down and get in the hole," says the Russian. Strangely Murray complies, he doesn't want to but he's remembering what the Russian had told him earlier about living and doing what he says. Murray is now standing in the hole which is coming up to his knees, he looks at the Russian waiting for his instructions. The Russian then says, "Kneel down and put your hands on your head." Murray does so, then looks up at the Russian but also at the gunman who has now adjusted his position and is holding the gun with just his right hand, but still pointing it at his head.

The Russian's demeanour changes, aggressively he says, "So you think you're a gangster, you want to play like a fucking gangster, this is what gangsters do." The Russian repeats his previous statement; Murray is just looking at them in utter fear, tears pouring, snot everywhere. He's feeling pretty written off, to the point that he will agree to anything in order to survive. The Russian continues to say, "We took you on based on the recommendation that you would be a good customer – are you with me so far?" Murray just continues to sob staring at the Russian who repeats, "Are you with me? If so, nod your fucking head." Murray nods his head. "Good now we're getting somewhere," says the Russian in a slightly calmer voice. He continues gradually elevating his voice as he speaks, "Since we took you on you've been consistently late with the money, you are blatant as fuck when talking on the phone, and whilst we're on the topic of phones when you want something you don't stop fucking ringing. When we need our money you never answer the fucking phone. You turn up to meet our people with a car full of fucking idiots in tow and to put the nail in the fucking coffin we've been hearing rumours that you're telling every prick out there who you're getting your coke from – is this true?" Murray reservedly nods, to this the gunman looks across at the Russian and without warning puts another round down, this time hitting the ground centimetres from Murray's knees.

There's that sound again, as it seems to reverberate around in his head he sees the gunman stoop down and retrieve yet another empty case which he deposits into his jacket pocket. Murray is thinking, 'at this rate he won't have any left for doing the deed, that's almost funny.' The Russian now delivers yet another direct statement, "Okay, here's what's going to happen, you are going to round up all of the money you owe us; once you've paid your bill, you can fuck off back to that useless prick that sent you to us." Murray, now feeling a sensation of relief almost euphoric, nods in agreement with the demands. "You have one week, if you are a day late we'll be back here, if you tell anyone about this you'll be back here along with your fucking sister – do you understand me?" says the Russian in what seemed like a closing statement. Murray again nods in compliance, whilst wiping the tears and snot away from his face.

The Russian looks at the gunman, who nods and lowers the gun so it's held down by his side, the Russian then goes on to say, "Right, here's how it's going to work." He casually walks over and picks up the spade and looks at Murray who is still in a state of semi euphoria. "We are going to fuck off now, and when I say we I don't mean you." In the light that Murray is even alive to hear this he doesn't really care about being abandoned, he just continues to listen to the next set of instructions. "The time now is just after six, you will wait here until seven, I know you have a watch on so don't even bother trying to play fucking games with us," says the Russian, "once your watch hits seven, walk in the same direction that we leave, don't bother trying to catch up just take your time. After a while you'll hit a track, turn left and walk until you see a road, as you approach the road you'll see a wooden post either side of the track – behind the post on the left you'll see a large flat rock, under that rock is your phone sealed in a plastic bag, that's your ticket home." The Russian continues to say, "Do not fuck us about, you have one week as from today, we want all the money by five o'clock Friday evening." The gunman replaces the gun back into his jacket. He looks at the Russian and they both casually walk off, into the woods towards what Murray hopes is his way out of this mess.

Murray slumps to the deck and removes the gag, stretching his mouth and spitting out all the crap that accumulated – he's covered in mud, piss, snot and tears but he's never felt happier. The prayers he said in the back of the van were answered, the only problem is he's gonna have to break his end of the deal for now because the bit about him being a good boy will have to wait until he's paid his bill. He sits on the edge of the hole just contemplating his next move; whatever it might be he's going to have to pull out all the stops, because he usually pisses all the money he has up against the wall playing the big man. Every word that was said is ringing around in his head. He spends the next hour trying to process what has just happened, but there is no processing this ordeal because it's far from over. Once he gets his phone, arranges a lift and starts speaking to his mates then, and only then, might he have an idea of what to do.

Seven on the dot and Murray starts walking. Fortunately the sun is up and he can see the ground pretty clearly, so he can just about make out his kidnappers' footprints, and decides the best option is to follow these. He eventually hits the track which he turns left onto; the footprints disappear but he's pretty sure he's going the right way, as he can hear the sound of the odd car go by in the distance. As he heads down the track, the sound of the traffic gets louder. He turns a slight bend and sees the road and, as luck would have it, the two wooden posts; he quickens his pace and can't help breaking into a bit of a run.

Slightly out of breath he walks up to the post on the left, sees the rock and, as described, he finds his phone sealed in a bag under the rock. Written on a piece of paper is what looks like a postcode; he takes his phone out of the bag and switches it on, hoping that there's enough charge left to make a call. Fortunately the battery is almost full, but there is nothing in the way of a signal. He opts to take a walk down the road just to see if he can pick up a random signal. The fact that he's covered in mud and piss doesn't really occur to him as this is a normal state for him on a Saturday morning. He manages to get one bar of signal, this is barely enough so he holds his position and calls his pal Will. The phone rings continuously, there is no voicemail it just keeps ringing, it had dawned on Murray that it's early on a Saturday morning and pretty much anyone bar his mum would still be in bed or, worse still, not even got to bed yet. He pictures them all plotted up at someone's house, nursing a warm beer and reluctantly trying to sniff coke up a blocked nose.

Murray decides to continue walking along the road. He doesn't know if he's going in the right direction, he just keeps moving and trying a selection of different numbers he has in his phone. The thought does enter his mind to call his mum, but he quickly dismisses this as a bad idea. Eventually Will answers the phone, and Murray starts screaming down the phone at him, "Where the fuck have you been? I've been trying to get hold of you for fucking ages. I need you to come and get me, I haven't got a fucking clue where I am so I'm texting you a postcode, I'll be on that road – text me when you leave." Will enquires what's going on and Murray simply replies, "I'll tell you when I see you," and puts down the phone.

3. OUT OF THE FRYING PAN

Murray has been loitering around on this road for a while; he hasn't received any messages from Will and continuously checks his phone for signal strength which is hovering between one and two bars, enough to receive a text. A half-hour passes and he decides to text Will, "where R U", he waits and has no reply so he texts again, "let me know when you're on the way." Again he has no response so his lack of patience kicks in and he calls Will once again; the phone continues to ring, he tries several times with no luck. He's beginning to understand what the Russian was talking about as he's now experiencing these problems first hand. It's now approaching nine o'clock and still no answer, he continues calling whilst simultaneously sending a barrage of abusive text messages.

Another hour of frustration passes and Will replies, "just leaving now, be with you in 3 hours." Murray texts "3 fuckin hours, why so long?" Will replies saying, "gonna grab some breakfast on route." This infuriates Murray so he calls Will who doesn't answer; he calls again, still no answer. Five minutes pass and Murray's phone rings – it's Will, Murray screams, "It's not a fucking picnic, I've been fucking kidnapped by the Russian and we need to get money sorted fast, get here as quick as you can, we'll get food on the way back, how long will you be?" Murray is told he'll be picked up in just over an hour. Finally Murray settles down, and despite sticking out like a sore thumb he finds somewhere to sit down by the side of the road.

Approximately forty minutes pass, and he can hear a car screaming down the road; he knows it's Will because he can hear the music. Murray is relieved that his ride has finally turned up. The car pulls up next to Murray, only to be greeted by Will and two other people who he hasn't met before. The front passenger door opens releasing a cloud of heavy smoke which has been produced from the joints they've been smoking on route, the passenger jumps into the back and Murray climbs in the front. As he sits down, Will comments on the state of Murray's jeans and asks had he pissed himself, to which Murray just looks at him, and asks, "Who the fuck are these two?". In a blasé way Will says, "Couple of new customers I met last night." Will asks in a slightly confused way, "Where did you say you went last night?" Murray puts his head back in frustration and takes a deep breath; as he exhales, he quietly says to Will, "Turn the music down a bit." Looking perplexed, Will stares at Murray and lowers the volume. As soon as Murray can hear himself think he says, "I've just had an intimate meeting with the Russian." Will still looking perplexed says, "Oh right." Murray trying to remain calm says, "I don't really want to spell it out but we need to have a private chat about a few things when we get back." Oblivious to what's going on, Will happily agrees, "Yes mate whatever – where shall we stop for food?" Murray replies, "I don't give a fuck as long as I don't have to get out of the car."

They drive for a while, Murray not saying anything, the others equally quiet. They come across a drive thru, pull up and order a few things to eat. Murray stuffs his face with food but this is proving quite uncomfortable as his mouth is quite raw from where the gag had been fitted so tightly. He manages to have a drink and a few bites whilst mulling over how he might raise the money he owes the Russian. He decides to take the opportunity to discuss business with his new clients. Murray turns and faces the two lads sat in the back; they couldn't have been much more than eighteen years old, "So, what is it you want and how are you paying?" They both look at him and say, "Pills and we need laying on for a week." This disappoints Murray as he was half hoping they might have enough cash for him to pay the Russian off. Trying not to put off a new customer, Murray says, "Okay, leave it with me."

Now Murray knows he hasn't got the money, because he's spent it, the only way he can raise it is to juggle funds. Anyone that's been involved in drugs will understand that when the shit hits the fan if your credit is good you can juggle funds between a number of suppliers. This only works if you have a steady supply of what you need, but more importantly, a chain of reliable customers who either pay cash on delivery or are bang on time with payment. Juggling will only work with all of these things in place, and it takes a lot of prior planning associated with a series of calculated risks – if you drop the ball when juggling drug money, everything goes south very quickly. This presents another problem, Murray doesn't have any of the above, so he's already fucked.

He decides not to stress about it for now, it's Saturday and nothing is going to happen on a Saturday; he opts to just relax, get home, have a bath and then approach this with a fresh mind once he's sorted himself out. He just sits back, closes his eyes and drifts in and out of consciousness; he can't help wondering about his trip in the van earlier and the whole ordeal in the woods, dwelling on how close he might have been to death, or torture – strangely the worst thing that had happened was pissing his pants.

They arrive at Murray's house, he lives with his mum so he's hoping he can just sneak upstairs and straight into the bathroom; this is something he regularly does as bumping into one's mother whilst off your nut on coke, pills or both is always a difficult thing to explain, especially when it's the middle of the day. He tells Will he'll call him later. Will shoots off with the new customers still in tow. Murray heads in, thankfully his mother isn't in, and finally he can sort his life out. He spends the rest of the day mulling over his experience, but it's the sound of that gun he can't get out of his head.

Murray is half asleep in his room when he hears his mobile ring; he looks at it and it's a number he doesn't recognise, he chooses to ignore it, and it rings off after a few seconds. The phone beeps as it receives a text; he picks up the phone and reads the message. He doesn't have to read much before a massive feeling of anxiety hits him; it's the Russian, asking Murray to call him as soon as he gets this message. Murray just wishes they'd leave him alone but he knows this is one call he can't ignore. He just looks at the phone for a while, with his finger hovering over the call button, trying to delay the inevitable. He finally takes the plunge and calls the Russian.

The phone rings just once and the Russian answers. He asks, "How are you getting on?" Murray, trying to remain respectful and choosing to lie out of his arse says, "I've not been home that long, I need to get some calls made and see what's what—" The Russian butts in, "Stop fucking waffling, how much money do you have on you right now?" Murray's voice begins to falter slightly as he says "None." The Russian just calmly replies, "You have one week, make sure you answer your phone whenever I call – if you miss my call return it fucking quickly, and tell your useless fucking mate the same thing. I don't want to be put in the position where I'm having to chase you – you need to be chasing me." Murray agrees, the Russian puts the phone down.

Now here's the funny thing, the Russian and his associates don't need the money; they work on principle as do a lot of people in this industry. The money owed is actually quite a small amount in comparison to the amount that goes through people's hands who are involved in the supply of drugs, especially coke. Put it this way, it's less than ten grand – in the real world if someone tells you or a straight goer that you have one week to raise ten grand, this would usually mean bank loans, putting a charge against your house, maxing out the cards – stuff like that. But in the world of drugs this usually means sell off all of the useless shit you've recently bought to show off how much money you haven't really got, and you sell it cheap – things like cars, watches, clothes, games consoles – anything and everything goes up for sale, it can be replaced. You also get the rest of your firm, if they are committed to the cause, to do the same, so collectively you may get close to your goal.

Much to Will's disappointment this is the very action that Murray takes. He spends the Sunday advertising his and Will's worldly possessions; he's got the fucking lot up for grabs and what is more often the case is it's other drug dealers who buy it, usually the low-end dealers, they're like vultures hovering, waiting for someone's life to go tits-up. You can usually see the signs when someone is living a chaotic lifestyle and way beyond their means, it's only a matter of time before they need to raise money and down swoop the vultures waving their wads of dirty cash. This style of raising funds isn't ideal, you don't get offered that much as buyers can sense the desperation, so if you're lucky you might raise a third of the money back. There's nothing more frustrating than you being right up against it, eating humble pie and flogging everything you own, only to have some little shit bag calling the shots, but needs must.

Come Sunday night Murray has raised nearly half the money, he feels quite proud of his achievement as he still has about two grand worth of stuff left. Will however is fucking fuming, because it's most of his own stuff that's been sold; nevertheless they are getting somewhere. Murray does have a couple of people interested in what's left but that's not gonna happen until Monday, possibly Tuesday, so in a typical drug dealer's optimistic approach he adds this into the equation and calculates he's has to raise roughly another three grand. In order to do that he needs to lay on a few grand worth of drugs to begin his juggling act.

Come Wednesday, Murray has finally got rid of everything; they currently sit just shy of six grand, they had to dip into the pot to buy a cheap motor for running around. The car isn't ideal but it'll have to do. The new problem that Murray faces is who can he get his drugs from, he hasn't got the minerals to ask the Russian, the guy that referred him to the Russian is a definite no go, so this means he'll have to approach the people he wouldn't normally ask. This in itself presents a host of new problems. The kind of people left who'll be willing to give credit are going to overcharge him, much in the same way these payday lenders hit you with excessive interest rates, but at this stage of the game it's not about profit, it's about getting money and drugs moving in circles. Once you get the wheel spinning you can successfully juggle the money.

Murray starts calculating what he can realistically shift to pay the Russian; he has no choice other than to bang some of it out at near cost for cash, just to get it spun around in time for the Friday. This part of the plan is to arrange for two weeks' credit from whoever he gets the stuff from, this will give him a spare week to find them their money. He knows as soon as the Russian has been paid Murray will be into someone else for at least three grand. That doesn't concern Murray at this point, he needs to just focus on one stage at a time, he'll worry about next week, next week.

Murray looks at his phone for a while; he's feeling extremely apprehensive about contacting these people, they're not nice people. He's not worried about owing them the money, not at this stage anyway, he's more concerned that they will fuck him over or worse still have nothing in to give him. He's finding it very hard to push the call button, he's just got a bad feeling about these people. The last time he got anything off of them the quality was horrendous, it wasn't worth a wank and they refused to take it back so he ended up stuck with it. Desperate times require desperate measures, so he picks up the phone and makes the call.

"Hello mate, it's Murray," he says in an overly friendly way. The person on the other end of the phone humours him and asks what he wants. Murray takes a deep breath and asks, "Have you got anything in?" The person confirms that they do have some odds and ends and wanted to know what he was looking at. Again in a false and friendly tone he says, "I need a nine of coke and a thousand pills, I could do with credit for a couple of weeks." The phone goes silent for a while whilst someone makes an executive decision; Murray is literally holding his breath as this is his only real chance to raise the money.

"Murry, it's Si," says another voice on the end of the phone, Murray's arse twitches slightly. "If you want two weeks you'll have to take double because we're fucking off for a few days next week, so I'll load you up for the fortnight then you can pay it all when we get back," says Si in a slightly pushy manner. This news gives Murray a huge sense of relief, he's now got around twelve grand's worth of kit to start juggling with, he couldn't be happier. Si, now with a slightly more serious tone, says "Make sure it's all ready for when we get back, don't be late." Murray knows he's just leapt straight out of the frying pan and into the shit, but when you choose to live this lifestyle that's sometimes how it goes. Murray is given instructions which he passes on to Will of when and where to collect the drugs.

This would be a good time to tell you a little bit about Si – he's the sort of person that when you're on side he'll be very loyal and will prove to be a strong ally and business associate; but there is a ruthless element that flows through him, he will happily beat the living shit out of you in front of your mother just to prove a point. If you are late with money there's no second chance, if you're late you're fucked, simple. He will expect the money to be there, even if the goods provided at times may fall short of the expected standard. When you take on credit, you may not always get a say in the quality of what you will be buying. In this world, cash is king and those with money will always hold a commanding position.

It's Thursday, Murray is now loaded up with half a kilo of coke and a couple of thousand pills; what makes him even happier is that surprisingly the coke is pretty good, for repress anyway. He's negotiated with his new customers, if they can raise cash for their pills they can have them a bit cheaper. He then calls all of his other customers which at his level usually consist of quite a few low-end buyers, offering out the coke as a better deal than usual, bearing in mind he's going to need as many people on board to raise money to cover the new debt. He does get a fair bit of interest and based on this he begins planning the task of weighing and bagging it all up ready for Will to distribute it.

Weighing up coke and counting pills isn't particularly fun especially when you are living at your parent's address. Murray has to operate out of his bedroom, this isn't ideal but it does the job. First he has to ensure that his mother isn't in and if she is he needs to make sure that she won't be disturbing him whilst in the middle of such a compromising act. Once he knows he has piece of mind that he won't be disturbed, he can get set up; this will consist of a set of small digital scales accurate to nought point one of a gram – coke's expensive stuff and every point one makes a difference at this level. He'll need a selection of plastic snap bags, the ones that have a small plastic seal at the top; Murray has opted for bags that have the image of a cannabis leaf on them, very fucking clever. He'll also have a couple of containers to break the coke into, a spoon to measure it with and a twenty pound note. All basic stuff really, this should all be laid out in such a way that if the door does go, and trust me doors tend to go when you least expect it, he can quickly clean up and put everything out of sight. Murray's customers are small-end buyers, so they are looking at buying pills in bags of tens, twenties and maybe the odd hundred – his new customers want five hundred so that's fucking great news for him. The coke will be weighed into small measures, consisting of eighths, quarters, halves and ounces.

With a sense of trepidation, Murray is sitting there looking at the tools and materials of his trade he's got the lot laid out in front of him. His plan is to get the coke out first and whilst this is being delivered he can count out the pills. He grabs his first nine of coke, it's been repressed so it's far from pure, he's never even seen pure coke so he wouldn't know it from the stuff that's been stamped on anyway. It's shaped like a small book, no symbols or stamps to identify it – all he knows is it's white and it smells right. He begins to break it up into one of the containers, trying his best not to lose any of it on the carpet. He takes a look at his watch – he has an hour before Will arrives, plenty of time in his book. He thinks the best way to start this process is to have a big fat line; he dips the teaspoon into the bowl and scoops up some of the fine powder that has settled in the bottom of the bowl. Using a Tesco club card he racks one up on the table top, grabs the twenty pound note, rolls it up, shoves it up his bugle and takes a big long sniff. He can feel his heart pumping the Charlie round his body, and feels a lovely warm reassuring sense of confidence descend upon him – now he's ready.

He roughly estimates what an ounce looks like, zeros the scales and using the spoon places it on the shiny black surface of the scale– the measure reads twenty-five point three grams, not a bad guess only two point seven grams out. He then dips a teaspoon into the container and scoops out what he thinks could be the balance to bring it up to the ounce – this time it reads twenty-eight point two grams. Again with the spoon he removes an estimated point two of a gram, and this time the scale reads twenty-eight grams exactly. He fashions a makeshift funnel out of a piece of paper and shovels the contents into the little bag. Murray continues this delicate process, using the same method with all of his individual deals. Every now and then he gets the measurement bang on the first time and his choice of celebration is to have a line.

Murray is close to completing his task and funnily enough he's managed to get quite a few measurements correct first time, this means he's fucking hammered and mild paranoia has definitely set in. He knows this because he keeps thinking he can hear the front door go, which prompts him to stop what he's doing, freeze his position, cock his head slightly as if to try and aid his hearing in order to pick up a noise that isn't really there. He'll sit like this for a few moments and once he's positive he's imagining things he'll continue with the task of weighing up his coke. What doesn't help is the continuous ringing of his phone with impatient customers wanting their coke or pills; he has the same default answer for every single phone call, "I'm doing it now, I'll call you back in a bit." He continues this for the next ten or twenty minutes until he receives a text from Will "R U ready yet", Murray replies saying, "five minutes pop round now." With this in mind, and a certain sense of relief, Murray wraps up the last couple of deals and places the majority of it in a carrier bag ready for Will to go and deliver.

Murray is patiently waiting for Will to arrive, so he decides to start the ball ache of counting the pills. He starts counting them into piles of a hundred at a time; Murray knows that it's always worth counting them and to never presume that there will be exactly a thousand in the bag. Pills are manufactured and bagged up by weight so counting them will let him know if he's had a result, giving him extra pills or whether the bag is light, meaning he'll need to ring up Si and have a moan – that's a task he won't enjoy because he'll just be told to fuck off and wind his neck in. Murray's still waiting for Will to arrive; he's now fifteen minutes late. Murray texts him again "hurry up mate, people are screaming". No sooner than this message is sent his front door goes, he peers out from behind the curtains and looks down to see Will standing there. He pops downstairs and lets him in. Murray explains what's in the bag is straightforward stuff, but Will isn't exactly the sharpest tool in the box and he is more than capable of fucking everything up.

Will departs with the shoddy carrier bag full of coke. He gets into their newly acquired company car which, as usual, has a couple of idiots sat in the back coming along for a ride with the local drug dealer – dickheads. As Will departs, Murray feels a slight weight lifted from his shoulders, well it's more of a shift of responsibility as he's one step closer to the completion of his task. Murray, peering down the street, slowly backs into the house closing the door behind him. His mother is due back in a couple of hours, giving him more than enough time to get the pills counted, bagged and gone.

He's counting like a man possessed, he's got nine hundred counted out of the first bag and by the looks of it there's at least a hundred left along with a load of bits and a few grams of powder, all of which is worth something to someone. He counts out the last hundred, and as he had suspected there are roughly thirty pills' worth of bits and just less than four grams of powder. He then weighs all of this into one-gram bags and decides to sell these off as special deals; every penny counts because he very well knows in two weeks' time he's back in the shit. All the time his phone is ringing off the hook, this time he decides to ignore it as the coke has put his head in such a state he can't handle too much at once. Sniffing like he's caught the worst cold in the world and without delay Murray ploughs through the second bag, periodically having a sneaky line of coke worsening his cold-like symptoms. He's feeling drawn out now as the coke is no longer working, the only thing it's doing is increasing his paranoia, which when surrounded by Class A drugs in your mum's house could be a recipe for disaster.

Murray finally completes the task of counting the pills; he has a tidy up and disposes of the packaging that the pills and coke arrived in, so with a stroke of pure genius he decides to throw the rubbish in the kitchen bin. He can now start returning some of the calls he's been ignoring for the last twenty minutes. Firstly he texts Will "how R U getting on mate, I'm ready this end." Oddly enough he receives a fairly prompt reply from Will "with U in 5". Fucking bargain as Murray shoves another line up his nose, he can't wait to get this stuff offloaded as his mother is due any minute and he needs to be gone. He hears the car pull up outside and decides to run the bag out to

Will; to save time, he loads the bag of pills for Will's next part of the mission. Will departs without delay; Murray's part of the task is almost complete; all he needs to do is stash the excess ready to be warehoused when Will gets back.

Murray heads back into the house, grabs his phone, puts his jacket on, and discreetly puts a small bag of Persy and the rolled-up twenty into his jeans' pocket. He then stuffs the excess drugs in the inside pockets – he's got about four ounces of coke and six hundred pills left, which is quite convenient because this is worth about three grand to him. The way Murray sees it is even if he can't get any money back in time to pay his debt with the Russian, he may be able to offer this up as collateral along with the money he's managed to raise. So once again in Murray's world he's got this pretty much sorted and decides once he's stashed his gear he'll go on the piss.

Fortunately the stash place is on route to the pub. He lives in a suburban part of the city and with a jacket full of drugs, this also translates to about five years in jail. He always uses shortcuts, alleyways, fields – in fact he'll do anything possible to avoid any roads. This works well until you come face-to-face with the police, and with a pocket full of Class A drugs it's quite hard to not look dodgy. Murray takes the usual route from his house heading towards the pub; he's so strung out on the coke he really needs a few beers to balance himself. He turns into a lane which leads towards his drop-off. It's roughly a two-minute walk down this lane with residential garages on the left which back onto a row of houses and fields bordered by a large hedge on the right, so it's quite enclosed. As he slowly walks down the quiet lane he decides it would be a good time to have a bit of nose bag – he takes the damp coke-ridden twenty from his jeans' pocket along with the little bag of Charlie, dips the twenty into the bag and sniffs; it's pot luck how much he'll get as this method tends to deliver way too much, and you fucking know about it. Murray takes a big hit of the coke and much to his delight he's actually feeling it again, he looks at the bag and realises he's just done the lot. Completely unfazed by the fact that he has just done in the better part of half a gram, with the twenty still inserted he replaces the bag back into his pocket.

He closes in on his stash place which is under a bush opposite a garage with a red door, he knows this because the garage belongs to Will's parents which is where Will lives. Murray has a sneaky look around, takes the bag of pills out and pops them into a black bin liner which has been left out of sight under this bush. He then reaches for the bag of coke, and as he's putting it into the same bin liner he opts to take a small lump out of one of the deals he had prepared earlier – it's only a couple of grams so it won't be missed. This is safely put into the bag he has in his jeans' pocket for later on. Finally he stores the coke with the pills and puts it back under the bush. Will stores this into the garage when he returns from his task of delivering the pills.

After a relatively short walk from the drop-off point Murray, who is now completely off his tits, enters the pub – the same pub he was kidnapped from the previous Friday; he's so wasted this doesn't even register. He just strolls up to the bar and asks for a pint, the barman knows him well because he's one of Murray's coke customers, he pours Murray his pint, which he grabs and without paying heads off to his usual seat near the toilets and the side entrance that leads to the car park. Murray plots up in this area for a couple of reasons – the main one being is he can either go into the toilets or outside quickly to do any deals, but more importantly he's got somewhere he can have a sneaky line and the side door conveniently provides a quick exit if the need arises.

Murray sits down at the same table in the same seat – it's not that these seats are reserved, it's more like no one else wants to sit in them, the toilets stink and there's a constant draft coming from the side entrance. He takes his jacket off and puts his phones on the table, lining them up neatly next to each other – his personal phone on the left and his burner on the right. Holding the pint he surveys his empire, he tells himself, "I run this place, it's my fucking pub, I sit where I want, I do what I want, it's my place." In the real world it's a local pub, it's full of mature gentlemen who've just finished a day's graft talking and sipping pints of bitter, it's far from exclusive.

Whilst having his pint he sends a text to Will just to get any updates, "R we there yet". A short while passes, Murray takes a sip from his pint, in fact he's just considering having another line when his phone beeps – it's a message from Will "almost, just got 2 C 2 more people, I'll let U know when I'm there". Murray replies saying "thanx mate, don't forget to put the kids to bed before you get here". Murray takes another sip from his pint and decides to text the Russian with the good news, "hello mate all sorted this end can you let me know when you want to catch up". Almost instantly his phone rings and it's the Russian. This time Murray answers the phone in an almost arrogant manner, "Yes mate." He's soon brought back down to earth when the Russian speaks, "What the fuck did I tell you about blatant text messages?" To this Murray apologises, the Russian asks "How much have you got in your hand right fucking now?" Murray begins to break down what he has in storage, and what Will should have on him, and yet again the Russian feels the need to interject, "That's not what I asked, I said how much have you got in your hand right fucking now?" Murray slightly losing his cool snaps, "Well I've not got it on me have I, I'm just letting you know that it's all in." The Russian calmly replies, "Okay, firstly I suggest you get it all straightened out. I want that money to look like I've drawn it out of the bank – don't you fucking dare wrap it into hundred pound bundles, if you're too fucking dumb to count past a hundred then find someone who can. Secondly, I want to see you at half nine tomorrow morning – make sure you're available – and thirdly, if you ever raise your voice to me again I'll break your fucking arms." On that the Russian hangs up.

4. INTO THE FIRE

It's not easy sleeping when you're off your nut on coke, add a heavy dosage of stress, excessive amounts of alcohol with a mild hint of paranoia and you'll be lucky to get a couple of hours. The truth is your body hasn't got a clue what to do with itself, your brain is firing like fuck but your body is telling you it needs to rest. You almost go into a meditative state, relaxing, deeply relaxing, but the sleep just doesn't seem to come. What is strange though is how suddenly the morning creeps up on you, you can literally lose hours this way.

With an overwhelming feeling of anxiety Murray turns and looks at his phone – no missed calls, that's a result as his anxiety slightly subsides. He checks the time and it's just after eight in the morning. He gets up and wanders off to the toilet, then leans over the sink alternately blocking one nostril at a time and blows his nose successfully clearing out all the shit. He looks at the mess in the sink and sees a combination of snot, blood and what resembled bits of coke that didn't quite make it into his system. Part of him thinks he could have probably sold that. His anxiety is all but gone as he hits the shower, cleans his teeth and gets dressed; he's feeling pretty good that he has the Russian's money. This emotional roller coaster that he's been on has finally peeked and he's enjoying the fact that right now he feels fine, he's not thinking about next week or tomorrow, he daren't.

Murray quickly double checks the money; he ensures that it's exactly how the Russian wanted it – no mixed denominations, it's in thousand pound units and it's put into a couple of brown A4 envelopes, then safely tucked away in a small rucksack. He opts to take the initiative and calls the Russian – the dialling tone goes for a little while and the Russian answers "Are you ready?" to this Murray says "Yes mate, where do you want to catch up?" The Russian instructs Murray that he will pick him up from outside the local NatWest bank. He wants Murray to go into the bank for a few minutes and watch for his arrival; when he sees the Russian he then wants Murray to exit the bank and walk to the Russian's car where they will then go for a drive.

Slightly confused about all this cloak-and-dagger stuff, Murray agrees and gets ready for the half-nine meet. He climbs into his and Will's motor and heads off towards the bank – it's roughly a ten-minute journey there and as it's only ten past he takes his time. He's definitely feeling apprehensive about this meeting because he hasn't got a clue who's going to be with the Russian – and what the fuck is this going for a drive all about? The last time he went for a drive with the Russian he pissed his pants and dug his own grave. With that thought in mind he's now dwelling on the negative; once again his paranoia has kicked in and he's getting himself in a mess and now convincing himself that the Russian is gonna do something to him, but he has no choice, he has to get this over with.

Murray approaches the bank and parks nearby, he doesn't want the Russian to see his car for fear that he might want to take it as some kind of payment. He grabs the rucksack and gets out of the car, locking it as he walks away while looking up and down the road to see if there are any police around. Heading towards the bank, the Russian is nowhere to be seen, this doesn't settle Murray's nerves one bit. He enters the bank and takes a seat as if to be waiting for an appointment; he is able to see the parking spaces outside and as the bank has only just opened the spaces are mostly empty. He is approached by a member of staff asking if they can help; Murray, who doesn't realise how fucked he looks, just tells them he's waiting for his Mrs and they seem to buy it, so he just keeps an eye on the empty spaces, looking for the Russian.

Half-nine approaches and he sees a car he doesn't recognise pull up outside, but he does recognise the ominous figure sat in the driver's seat – it's the Russian. Murray, who's by now shitting himself, gets up and slowly walks out of the bank and towards the car. For some strange reason he's more worried now than he was when he was stood in his own shallow grave – maybe it's because back then he didn't have a choice, this time although he does have a choice there is a certain amount of duress involved as the choices are limited. Pay up and hope this all goes away or don't pay up and it definitely won't go away, some choice!

He walks up to the passenger door of the Russian's car and much to Murray's relief the Russian is alone, but this doesn't prevent Murray from feeling concerned as the Russian is more than capable of doing enough damage on his own. Murray gets into the car and closes the door, instantly reaching for the zip of his bag where the Russian grabs Murray's hand and says, "Keep your fucking hands where I can see them." Murray, trying not to provoke the Russian, innocently says, "I was only gonna grab the money for you." The Russian looks at him for a few moments and says, "I know, but I'm not doing this outside of the bank – we're gonna drive down the road. When I ask, you're going to show me what you've got, don't bother fucking counting it I just want to see what's there; once I'm happy I'll drop you back here." Murray, who is now feeling extremely relieved that this is going to be a straightforward transaction with no surprises, silently settles into his seat waiting for the Russian to give him the nod.

They drive for a few minutes and turn into a residential area where the Russian, without looking at Murray, says, "Right, slowly show me what you've got – if I see anything other than money you're fucked." As the Russian finishes speaking, Murray hears a tapping sound coming from down near the handbrake; he looks down to see the Russian holding a gun in his right hand which is partly resting on his left thigh, he's gently tapping the barrel on the trim surrounding the gearstick and it's pointing straight at Murray. Yet again Murray's arse twitches as he's instantly reminded of his traumatic ordeal the previous week. He slowly reaches into the bag and produces the two envelopes; he opens them enough for the Russian to see the contents inside. This seems to be enough to satisfy the Russian as he then says, "Okay, that'll do." The Russian starts heading back in the general direction of the bank and then goes on to say, "Right, well done for coming through, as far as I'm concerned this is over you've paid your debt in full. You know who I work for and he's happy to let you go now without any further action; however, he says if you breathe a word of this to the police we'll have you back in the woods and this time the bullets won't be hitting the ground – now fuck off." The Russian pulls up nowhere near the bank; Murray, with his head down, gets out and starts heading down the road in the general direction of his car – he doesn't look up at the Russian as he drives straight past.

Murray doesn't exactly know how he feels, relieved is the primary emotion but this is soon overridden by anger, now he knows that the Russian's organisation is out of the picture. He feels a strong hate towards them for the way he was treated. This feeling is then subdued when he starts thinking about how he's going to pay off Si. He gets back to his car, climbs in and heads home. During the relatively short journey his mind is in two states. In one state he's dwelling on everything and the other state is completely blank, but this is more linked to the come down from the previous day's cocaine use. He just feels very numb about the whole ordeal. What he wants to do is get back at the Russian and the person that he works for, but he knows that he's not in a position to do so. Even though Murray knows he's the one that was in the wrong he just feels that the methods were a bit excessive, plus he has to deal with Will's emotions after selling all of his stuff.

Murray chills out for a few hours mulling over his plans for the next few days and decides to do some calculating just to get an idea of what money he is owed and what he can sell in time to pay Si. He knows he cannot be late. A master plan is beginning to form in his mind; the aim is to have all the cash collected by the following Tuesday which still gives Murray at least a week before he has to pay Si on the following Wednesday. What Murray will aim to do is use Si's money to purchase drugs for cash from another supplier; he can then put this out on credit to be collected the following Monday and Tuesday, perfect!

Using other people's money is a high-risk strategy as you are effectively gambling with it; as it currently stands, and by Murray's calculations, he will have approximately nine grand in hand which includes any money made from the sale of the drugs he has in storage; however, this isn't going to be enough to pay Si so he has to risk it all in order to make up the shortfall. He'll be about three grand shy of his target but if everything goes to plan he'll be closer to thirteen grand, giving him a slight profit. What Murray has failed to take into consideration is the amount of coke he's stuck up his nose, he also hasn't considered the fact that Will has also been dipping into it – which is standard practice for a lot of drug runners – so Murray shouldn't be too shocked if his calculations are out by a few quid.

Murray spends the rest of the weekend making calls to potential customers and suppliers, trying to line everything up for the following week. He's working on the presumption that he will have about eight to nine grand in cash, and as cash is king he does have plenty of suppliers waiting to load him up the minute he has the money in his hand. Murray's next part of the plan is to start lining the customers up in order of priority; cash on delivery will be first, followed by the ones that can spin the stuff around in a day and what's left will be laid on till the following Monday. Will has shifted the rest of the coke and pills for the standard price; all of these sales would have made this a good week for Murray.

Murray always seems to begrudge having to give the money back. It's this attitude towards money that got him in the shit in the first place, and because the money goes through his hands he feels he has an entitlement to it. Not the fucking case, it's not his money and never was. His cut shouldn't even be considered until his bill is paid, that's how it works. This is a concept that just doesn't sit right with him; he makes the mistake of calculating what his profit might be and then spunks the fucking lot. This nearly always means him coming up short on payday, thus relying on other customers who carry the same approach as he does – it doesn't fucking work that way.

Monday is spent collecting up as much money as possible. Will and Murray are both on it; although payday with Si is still over a week away he is very conscious of the passage of time. Mondays can be a very sobering day for some drug dealers, it's the day that the partying has finally stopped, all the straight goers return to their nine-to-five lives and, believe it or not, it's the drug dealers who are left to pick up the pieces. It's their responsibility to run around, collect up all the money and get everything ready for the next weekend's partying. With that in mind, imagine how hard it is for Murray to get a hold of people who owe him money. A lot of small-time dealers aren't full-time dealers and most will have normal jobs, so the majority of cash will be collected after they finish work. Meaning Murray and Will running around quite late in order to meet their deadlines.

It's coming up for ten o'clock. Will has finished his part of the job but Murray is still running around collecting up money. He's got about seven grand put down at home and by his reckoning he'll have another fifteen hundred by the end of the night. He has to drive around fifteen miles out of town to meet two customers; he's quite enjoying the drive in his new company car. It has worked out quite well considering the money he paid for it. He's a few miles out from his pick-up so he makes a call, they answer and a meeting place is agreed. Operating at this time of the night is risky business but for some reason Murray fucking loves it, after all it's only money he's collecting up.

He pulls up next to a bus stop where a highly suspicious looking lad is standing, pretending to be waiting for a bus although the service has probably stopped hours before. In his mind it was a good form of cover. He gets in Murray's car; Murray says, "How did you get on?" The lad looks at him and replies, "Not great, I managed to shift half of them but I couldn't get rid of the rest."

"For fuck's sake, why didn't you tell me this earlier!" shouts Murray, who then says, "So what have you got?" The lad reaching into his jacket pulling out an envelope and an old tattered carrier bag says, "Six hundred quid and four hundred pills coming back." Murray grabs the envelope and says, "Okay, no stress." He drops the lad back off at the bus stop and continues on his way to his final pick-up.

Murray hadn't expected to be picking up any pills but on a positive note he has another six hundred quid. It's now just after eleven and Murray makes contact with his final pick-up, he's no longer enjoying the drive and just wants this done and out of the way. Murray is on the other side of town and the last pick-up location is near to where he lives. All he can think about is he now has four hundred pills on him. The best route he can take is the circular road which is a set of fairly fast-moving dual carriageways that have very little traffic on them at this time of night.

Murray's heading along the road, approaches a roundabout and slows down a bit. As he pulls onto it he sees a police car coming onto the roundabout from the previous exit. This is bad fucking news. Has he broken any traffic laws? He has four hundred pills, six hundred quid and it's past eleven at night so he's shitting himself. He becomes very conscious of his speed and road position as he exits the roundabout. He's anxiously looking into his rear view mirror, just hoping to see the police car pull off at a different exit. As the anxiety builds he sees the police car appear behind him, he's trying to think what to do; a million things are going around in his head but none of them seem to make any sense – what should he do, what can he do, nothing just keep calm and drive.

This is harder than you'd think when the new company car that has recently been purchased is a cloner; this is a big gamble because you won't know the history of the vehicle that it has been cloned from. Worse still and unbeknown to Murray is that the car that he'd bought had been cloned twice, this is rare but it can happen. The original car has a clean history as does the car that Murray has purchased; however the other version that's been floating around the south of England for a number of weeks does not. Murray's in trouble, he just doesn't know yet.

The police car follows Murray for a few minutes. All the time Murray is debating on what to do – does he put his foot down or try to style it out? He's definitely feeling torn. He knows the roads well but the car, although it's a good spec, won't be quick enough to outrun the police. He continues on his way and after a couple of minutes he approaches another roundabout, which he slowly drives onto. His anxiety is completely off the scale and he's constantly looking in his rear view mirror hoping that the police car has pulled over or turned off – no such luck! It's not close, in fact it looks like it's dropped back a fair bit but it's still in sight and this is making Murray feel extremely uncomfortable. He knows he's getting pulled, it's just a matter of when. Murray wants to chuck the drugs out of the window but he needs everything to cover his bill. It's dark, so in a futile effort to conceal everything Murray quickly stuffs the pills and money out of sight under the passenger seat so if he is pulled he hopes that they don't search the car; then as discreetly as possible he texts Will, "clean up".

A few moments pass and the police car is still there; it appears to have closed in on him and he then notices a dark-coloured car pass him, and as this happens he sees the sight he was dreading – the blue lights go on, simultaneously the dark car in front cuts into his lane blocking any escape route. Murray has no choice other than to stop; before he can do anything he has three police officers surrounding his car shouting all sorts of commands at him. He just remains still as one of the officers opens his door, grabs his hands and slaps a set of cuffs on. Murray's trying to understand why he's being pulled especially like this, but that's the gamble of driving a cloner.

He's firmly pulled out of the car, not aggressively but in a manner to indicate that his arresting officers are serious. Murray's asked if he has anything on him that he shouldn't or does he have anything in possession that can hurt them whilst they conduct a search. He is then asked if he has anything in the car that he shouldn't have. Murray just remains silent; he's in a state of shock, what a fucking week. He's ushered towards the rear seat of the police car that was following him and is told to sit in the back. He's anxiously watching the other police searching his car; he's hoping that they won't find the pills – this is pure denial as they will find the pills and the money, it's just a matter of time.

His arresting officer joins him sitting in the front of the car and starts asking a host of questions about the cloner. Murray has no answers so he just keeps silent. After a while, and what feels like an eternity, the officer who was searching the car returns and produces the envelope and the bag of pills. Murray looks at the two officers and one of them starts to read Murray his rights. Game over.

5. FULL OF SHIT

Eighteen months later.

It's been a turbulent time, my exit strategy for leaving the army didn't quite go to plan so the last ten years have been a constant battle of ups and downs, while the last year or so has been a fucking nightmare. I've always struggled to settle into a job. This isn't down to a lack of capability or motivation but more a lack of interest in the nature of work that's on offer – to sum it up, I find most jobs extremely boring. However I'm not afraid to try something new and self-employment has always been my preferred type of employment, because if you think I'm going to be in a position where some jumped up twat is gonna tell me what to do, you can think again! Please don't think me arrogant but the army has a way of making me feel like I'm worth more and this is where my problem lies.

    My latest venture has been up and running for about a year and is slowly beginning to bring in a small wage. I've got a Mrs and kids to feed. I've got a small plot on the edge of town where a daily market trades. It's not a big market and starts wrapping up after lunch but that suits me perfectly. My chosen product is car parts and accessories. I sell these out the back of my van but I also have a bit of frontage with a couple of display tables, it's not a great set-up but it does the job. If I am to be honest it's more like a glorified car boot sale and this is probably just a means to an end. On that my hours are pretty good – Monday to Friday, seven in the morning and I'm done by two, this gives me time to go and resupply stock for the next day and spend plenty of time with the family.

Today is your average spring midweek day. It's gone one and I'm just closing down for the day. Most of the other traders have long gone, leaving the market deserted. Packing up is a well-rehearsed routine and everything has its place. All that's left is to fold the tables up and stick them in the aisle that's left running along the centre of the van. As I look out of the van I can see a group of lads approaching my plot, this isn't anything out of the ordinary as I frequently have groups of people at my stand. As they approach I'm just standing in the back of the van, tidying up a few loose ends when I hear someone say, "Come here a second mate." I turn around to be greeted by a couple of familiar faces.

One of the lads is called Murray. I've not seen him for a while as he's been banged up in jail. I didn't know he was out and he must have been hitting the juice as there's no fucking way you can naturally pack on that much size in the time he's been there. He's looking big. Two of the other guys I've never seen before, but the fourth guy is someone I know very well, he's called Si.

What the fuck is going on?

I'm standing in the back of my van as Murray and the other guys walk towards me. My adrenaline spikes and the next thing I know all hell breaks loose. There's stuff going everywhere, car parts, tins of polish, magic trees, everything's being thrown at me. Murray's throwing punches, the folding tables somehow manage to fly over Murray's head and land on top of me, pinning me on the floor against a load of boxes at the back of my van.

Here's how I see it, when you are confronted by a group of people who obviously intend to beat the fuck out of you, you have to decide what to do and you have to decide quickly. Breaking it down, I'm trapped in an enclosed space with no room to manoeuvre or escape, I'm facing four attackers – the first one being Murray, he's not a fucking problem even with his new-found size he isn't an issue; the other two I'm not sure who they are, they seem to be there to make up the numbers so I'd have to take them as I see them. But Si I don't want to be up against him and this is for two reasons – the first one is I actually like him and feel that whatever reason has brought him to me must either be a very good one or utter bullshit;

the other reason is he's hard as fuck and very dangerous, the only way to stop him is to kill him and I don't fancy being lifed off for a twenty stretch. The only way to win this war is to lose this battle, which I did, quite easily.

So here I am wedged under a table, unable to get up. Murray is laying the boot into my body, but I'm fully conscious and very aware of what's happening. I can see the other two guys just standing there, I guess more as look-outs at this stage, but Si is hovering – I'm hoping he isn't going to get involved, it's unlikely, as Murray is having a whale of a time kicking me around. I can't help thinking about the size of Murray's head, it has grown considerably from our last encounter. I'm looking down at the deck and I can see blood dripping from somewhere, fuck knows where as I can't feel any pain, just the occasional impact from Murray as he sticks the boot in. I then get another thought which makes me feel quite positive about this encounter. Murray not only felt the need to bring down three other people but one of them is one of the hardest fuckers going. This in my eyes makes Murray a gutless fuck and no matter how many times he kicks or punches me it's only happening because I choose not to fight back.

After a while the kicking stops and Murray slowly backs out of the van. I can just make out the four of them standing there, the table is blocking most of my view so I can't see their heads just their lower halves, it seems that they're making some kind of plan and Murray for some reason seems to be calling the shots. After a bit of muttering Si says to me, "I'll call you later to sort things out." Now I'm a little confused, sort what out? I've just had a good kicking for no reason, so fuck – yeah there's some sorting to do and this will give me the chance to find out what the fuck Murray's problem is who incidentally seems to be getting rather anxious as he keeps saying "Come on, let's fuck off." Reading between the lines, as Murray's just been released from prison, he'll be on some kind of licences conditions and these will definitely mean not to go to a public market with a bunch of gangsters and give someone a kicking, but that's down to how he interprets the conditions. Either way if he gets caught he's straight back inside.

I'm looking down at my jeans which by now have a big blood stain from this constant drip that's coming from my face. I can still see the four sets of legs standing there, I wish they'd just hurry up and fuck off. No sooner than thinking this they all turned and walked off. I decide to sit tight for a while; I don't know why, I just am. As I'm sitting here I hear a noise outside – my first thought is, "shit they've come back." As I look out of the back of the van I see another set of legs and a voice says, "Can I help you, pal?" To that I reply, "I'm not sure." I stand up and throw the table aside. I walk towards the back doors of the van where a man is standing, he's one of the other traders who had partially witnessed what had happened. I don't know his name but he always seems to be pleasant enough. As I approach him his expression changes slightly, this time I ask him, "Are you okay?" To this he says, "Do you want me to call the police?" Not wanting to aggravate the situation I say, "No it's okay, they got the wrong person, something to do with me shagging his Mrs." The guy then says, "Do you want me to call you an ambulance?" I look at him in a confused way and say, "Why?" The man leans closer to me, "For your eye, it's quite bad." I slowly put my hand up to my face and gently feel around my left eye, it does feel quite spongy. I look at my hand and it's covered in blood. A trip to the hospital might be a good thing. I let the concerned man know that I'm actually okay and I'll drive myself there even though the van is a mess. Thanks to the help of Murray's friends everything is now in the back, all I have to do is shut the doors and fuck off.

I have a bit of a confession to make, I don't just sell car parts I'm also involved in the distribution of drugs. I know Si's involved in drugs and I know Murray was because he used to be one of my customers, well he was until he got banged up; but as to why they've come down here causing me fucking headaches is a mystery. It's a mystery I intend to figure out. The next problem I'm going to be faced with is what the hell do I tell the Mrs? She doesn't know about my other income; in fact no one knows – parents, in-laws, friends, it's a well-kept secret and that's how it will remain. Covering up how I got this injury is one thing, but any fallout or collateral damage linked to it could prove problematic. I'll just have to play it by ear and wait and see.

I jump into the front of the van, pop one phone in my pocket and throw the other on the passenger seat. I adjust the rear view mirror and take a look at the damage to my eye. My left eyebrow has been badly cut and is literally hanging down over my eye. It's worse than I thought but that's only because I still can't feel any pain. I start heading for A&E to get my eye sorted. It's a fifteen minute drive so I decide to make a call in order to get the feelers out, hopefully it'll give me an idea of what's going on.

I call a good friend, Han. He's been involved in this game almost as long as I have and he's always got his ear to the ground. If he doesn't know what's going on, then he's the best one to find out. I pick up my burner to make the call and notice several missed calls. By pure coincidence they are all from Han. Still looking at my eye in the mirror, I press recall and it doesn't ring for long. "Are you okay?" asks Han in an extremely concerned way. Putting him at ease I promptly reply, "Yes mate I am now, but it was a bit fucking hairy. I've had a bit of a thing with that dickhead Murray who brought down Si, and a couple of others for good measure." Han replies, "I was ringing like mad to give you the heads-up. I found out because one of the lads was asked if he wanted to join them but he wasn't interested. The first thing he did was to call me so I could let you know." I asked Han, "Mate, can you do some digging for me as I need to find out why Murray's got the hump?" Han replies, "Already on it." We say our goodbyes and I continue on my way to the hospital while periodically checking my eye. It has finally formed a nice clot and stopped bleeding.

My trip to the hospital is relatively painless; the hardest thing is the wait so while I'm sitting here I decide to make up some bollocks of how I ended up in A&E. This is easier said than done as so much of my life is a lie and as I daren't risk exposing that side of my life to my wife. I needed to think of something plausible so I came up with it was an attempted robbery involving a group of lads in hoodies. Fortunately she bought it, giving me one less thing to worry about. Three hours and three stitches later I'm on my way home. As I walk back to my van I'm hit with a shot of anxiety and jump into the driver's seat, pick up my burner and notice a couple of missed calls. One of them is from Han and the other is from a number that I don't recognise. This is a good news bad news scenario – what do I do first? I opt to go for the potential good news and call Han.

The phone rings just a couple of times and Han answers. "How did you get on at the hospital?" I replied, "All good, three stitches but better still I've managed to convince the Mrs it was an attempted robbery." Han chuckles saying, "You're full of shit, I don't know how you get away with it." He goes on to say, "I've spoken to the lad that refused to go down with Murray and he's told me the score and it's a fucking beauty." My anxiety elevates, "Go on then, what is it?" I say, whilst trying not to let on or give away my emotions.

The phone goes quiet for a short while then Han just blurts out, "Murray is telling everyone that you and the Russian kidnapped him, took him to some woods in the middle of fucking nowhere, made him dig his own grave, tried to shoot him twice, just because he was behind with his payments." I can hear Han pissing himself in the background, trying to contain his laughter but goes on to say, "Then Murray's blaming you and the Russian for his time inside because he was out running around trying to cover the debt." Han continues, "So he's told Si that you forced him to give the Russian Si's money and now Si wants to collect his debt, I think that's it." I have only one reply, "This is news to me mate, thanks, I'll call you when I get any updates."

So this trip to the woods with the Russian, Murray and I, didn't happen, the whole thing was a lie that Murray had dreamt up whilst in prison. The only part that is true is that Murray was behind with the money because he was fucking useless. It's highly probable that he was out late running around collecting dosh, juggling money to pay the debt he owed me. I can only assume the reasoning behind it was while he was in jail he had Si on his case for the money owed and that's the risk of juggling other people's money especially someone like Si. The added issue Murray had to contend with is his useless mate Will who didn't get the message from Murray asking him to "clean up". While Murray's life was falling apart Will was blissfully unaware, happily on the piss and didn't get the message till the next day, but by then it was too late. Murray's mother was woken by the police with a search warrant and a dog. The police found the seven grand under Murray's bed and the dog found the empty coke and pill packaging which had been innocently transferred by Murray's mum from the kitchen bin to the wheelie bin outside. I'm sure there's a lesson to be learnt there somewhere.

"How the hell do I get this sorted?" I ask myself. I need to speak to Si and get him to understand that Murray is full of shit and simply did what he does best and lied in order to try and cover his debt. I glance at my phone again and decide to call the other number as it's highly likely to be either Si or Murray; if it's Murray I'll fire some fucks into him but if it's Si I'll need to start negotiating. Again my anxiety levels rise as I call the number. Thankfully Si answers and in a casual but forceful way says, "Right, Murray's told me all about how you and the Russian treated him and although I don't entirely disagree with your methods, it did result in me being out of pocket to the tune of twelve grand – have you got it?" My answer is a straight, "No mate, I've been on my arse since all that shit last year. Look, Murray's full of shit, he's a pathological liar, let's not fuck around. Can we meet up over a coffee and have a proper chat about this?" Si happily agrees, "I'll give you a shout in a couple of days." This relaxes me already as Si knows me well enough that I am the sort of person that always keeps my word and would never fuck anyone around.

Feeling a lot more settled about this, I head for home. I've completely forgotten about my eye and how the wife and kids might react. As I approach home about a mile or so out I switch off my burner and remove the battery, I stick it all in the glove compartment of the van. I'm starting to get some mild pain in my eye as the anaesthetic begins to wear off; this reminds me of the day's activities and how full of shit Murray is, what a fucking liberty trying to land the blame for his own fuck-ups and shortfalls onto me, I don't need this, not now. I can just picture him sat in his cell, fucking stewing about money and how everyone has let him down. Honestly, he thinks that highly of himself and talks so much crap that he actually believes his own lies, but do you know what the worse thing is, if he dropped the act and was just himself he'd do well because all things aside he's actually a decent guy. As I turn into my road my thoughts turn to how my family will react to my injury, and then my extended family; sometimes I'm so sick of lying to the people I love, sometimes I wish I could just turn the clock back ten years and be back in the army where life seemed so much simpler – harder, but simpler.

I get home to a warm welcome and for a short while all my problems just ebb away. I spend the rest of the day being pampered and trying to relax but when involved in drugs it's impossible to completely relax. The door can go at any time but the police are the least of my problems, I don't carry any hardware in the house. The most that's around is a baseball bat and the standard set of kitchen knives. I'm not a gun-toting gangster – my days of playing with guns have long gone. To live like a gangster or a villain I need to commit to the cause involving everyone around me; this makes them liable, vulnerable and partially responsible for my actions and I'm not prepared to do this to the people I care about, so keeping my address secret is an absolute priority, but this doesn't help me to sleep any sounder.

* * *

Six in the morning comes around way too quickly and as I wake I notice that my left eye is swollen and is partially closed over, plus my ribs are killing me. I wander into the bathroom standing with my back to the mirror. I look over my shoulder trying to have a look at my back. I can just about make out two or three large bruises. I'm sure I can make out an image of the tread from one of Murray's trainers. All this bullshit has fucked my routine right up. I really don't feel like going into work but I have to and besides I have to use the time to make a load of calls to keep my drugs business going, because that's certainly not happening while I'm at home. I also have to consider the possibility that Si might still want his twelve grand. It's twelve grand that I don't have and I'm not in the habit of paying out money that I don't owe.

Everyone in the house is still asleep so I quietly get myself sorted and head out, gently closing the front door behind me ensuring that I lock it. As I approach my van I can feel my stress levels increase. This is an all too common feeling for me lately. I hate it as the anxiety just takes over and it makes my normal logical thought process quite difficult because I'm too busy worrying about all of this stress rather than concentrating on the things that matter, but I just have to soldier on and push through. I jump in the front, start the van up and set off for work. I'm already feeling stressed out so I reassemble my phone that's been stashed in the glove compartment. I'm almost guaranteed to have a couple of my regulars texting things like "call me please". These aren't the problem, the barrage of messages linked to yesterday's events are what I'm dreading. There has to be some kind of fallout, there always is. I continue driving and I switch my phone on. As it powers up I've got one ear listening eagerly waiting for a load of random beeps, but they don't come; the relief that I feel is immense, making the rest of my journey to work quite pleasurable. I'm now feeling relieved, almost euphoric.

As I approach the market the sun is just coming up and the whole place is coming to life with all the traders getting set up for the day. I'm becoming conscious of what they might say. It can be like an old wives' club with rumours so you can almost guarantee that the guy that offered me assistance yesterday would have told every fucker that I've been given a slap for hanging on the back of someone's Mrs, but better that than the truth. I drive up to my plot and can't help feeling a bit deflated about the whole ordeal. I've been trying desperately to find an income that can support my family so I can get out of this shitty way of life, then from nowhere some fucking dickhead appears with an axe to grind for no other reason than to make himself feel better. I reverse my van up to its usual spot, switch off and get out. I casually walk round to the back of the van, still very conscious that the other traders are staring at me. None of this is a problem, I just have to ensure I have enough bullshit loaded so I can get my lies and excuses spot on.

I stand by the van doors, briefly look around the market and funnily enough no one has batted an eyelid. I pull the doors open to be instantly hit with a stark reminder of yesterday's chaos – oh my god, what a fucking disaster zone! I'd almost forgotten the level of violence but to be fair I didn't really care at the time. I've got my work cut out now, setting up takes me half an hour on a good day let alone dealing with this mess. As I plough through everything I soon realise that it's mostly cosmetic, once I've yanked the tables out and set up the stall, the van is actually in pretty good order. A few bits on the floor and a couple of broken bottles that don't take long to sort out. It's just after half seven and I'm good to go, all set up and plotted up in my chair. I just need to go get myself a brew from the coffee van two plots down.

I casually walk back to my plot with a hot brew in hand and still no one has said a word. Maybe the guy didn't tell anyone after all, but I find this very hard to believe – if it were me I would have told every fucker going. This almost feels like a normal day and I'm trying to get my head around what might happen over the coming days. I'm hoping this might just all go away but that's just wishful thinking. When it comes to money with the added involvement of someone like Si, debts always get paid or people get hurt, seriously hurt.

I spend the better part of the morning tending to customers, whilst periodically enjoying the odd brew. I use the term 'enjoy' very loosely as any form of pleasure will be tainted by the mere thought of what might be. There's no point in making any calls on my burner as it's highly unlikely anyone will be awake to take the calls. I generally wait until about eleven then send a brief text asking them to call me. I need to start preparing myself for the worst case scenario. The thought of paying a debt that I don't owe doesn't sit right with me. If I'm put in a position where I'm not given much choice I'll have to box clever.

My first message is sent to Alfie, a very close business associate who I have recently teamed up with. He brought me on board and offered a number of services in exchange for some better prices for his drugs. This was and still is a mutual agreement that works well for the both of us. The problem I am faced with is Alfie is quite sporadic and is sometimes up until the early hours of the morning either getting smashed or at a fetish party of some kind, more often than not he's usually doing both. As usual I send him a message just simply saying "can you call me when you get 5". I receive an alert from my phone indicating that the message has been sent but nothing else, so I expect his phone isn't on yet.

I'm just sitting, people watching, and the sun is warm so I angle my chair to soak up some rays. The time is just approaching twelve and my phone rings. It's Si. Now I don't know why but my heart skips a beat and as per usual my stress and anxiety hits the fucking roof. I just can't put my finger on it and I don't know why but I've got a bad feeling, the sort of feeling that makes me want to curl up into a little ball and die. I look at my phone, briefly mulling over what the content of this call might bring. "Alright mate, how's things?" I say, trying not to show any signs of the stress that I'm under. Si responds, "This meeting tomorrow, you can fuck off, I'm not interested in talking, you owe me twelve grand and I want it sorting out – when will you have it?" My heart sinks as the gravity of what I'm facing begins to hit home. I reply, "Si, I didn't take your money, Murray owed—" Si interrupts, "I don't give a fuck about Murray, what he owed or how you treated him, he gave you my fucking doe, he's sold the debt to me. I want that fucking money, if you don't pay I'm gonna go and see your brother and get it from him." This puts me in a very difficult position, I've tried my hardest to keep this side of my life away from all the people I care about, if Si goes to my brothers, that's it I'm finished, I have to buy some time to get Si on side so he can see the truth.

One thing I can do is negotiate, and that's what I start doing quickly. I change my tone slightly, "Okay Si, if I'm to consider paying I need you to understand something – are you willing to listen?" Si in a much calmer manner says, "I'm listening." I go on to say, "Bottom line, Murray has fucked up, juggled your money to pay a debt to me, and that we can both agree on." Si acknowledges this with a simple, "hmm". I carry on, "What we need to do is work together to recover this debt – now you know my business has taken a serious knock and I've been trying to recover ever since, this means I don't have any spare money lying around." Si again just replies with a bit of a grunt. "The only way I'm going to get this paid is in instalments – is this something we can work on?" I put it across in a confident way without sounding too cocky. Si replies, "Yep okay mate, what can you pay?" Now I'm fucking shocked because I wasn't really expecting this. I was hoping, but not expecting, so I reply, "I'm not sure, I'll need to make a few calls to see what's what and maybe look into getting some goods off of a couple of people who owe me a favour." Si gives the impression he's happy with my offer. He's not stupid, as he knows I don't owe the money and what I know is he'd rather work with me than try to chase that idiot Murray. This gives me an in to another source.

I have to look at this as an opportunity; Si can be a very useful ally in this world of organised crime. The way I'll play this is, if it costs me a couple of grand to get Si to know me and realise that I'm worth working with then it's money well spent. I have no intention of paying the whole lot. I just need to buy some time to find out a way to discredit what Murray is saying. It's a straightforward plan. The only problem is that I will be tapping into an old source that I have done my utmost to avoid working with; this guy is on top, hot as fuck, but he gives plenty of credit with a variety of goods at a low cost. I know this sounds like some kind of advert from your local supermarket, but why wouldn't it? Drugs are a commodity, they are treated by us as stock and are advertised in the same way, just not publicly.

Cliff is a greedy, selfish and self-centred individual, but then again the majority of drug dealers are. It's a common trait in this game and if you're not then it's probable that someone will take advantage of your good nature. This is a problem that I have had to manage in a number of ways. I can't stand working with these kinds of people but there are times when I have to break my rules. This is one of them. I scroll through my phone, looking for a number that I haven't used in ages – there it is, Cliff is saved as, "Cliff DO NOT USE". This is a reminder that he is hard work, but I don't have any choice. The funny thing is my anxiety has completely gone. When I go into work mode I switch my mentality so my stress doesn't bother me, in fact I need the stress to function, to operate. It's the same feeling I used to get when on operational duties back in the army. I used to love it and I still do, I almost thrive on it.

I call Cliff, I know he wants to work with me, he owes me a favour after I took on that halfwit Murray a few years ago. Cliff owed me some cash and he said he had a good customer. I could take Murray off of his hands and make the money back in a couple of weeks, fat lot of good that did me. Cliff brought Murray into my life, what a pair of fucking pricks.

The phone rings for a while and it's eventually answered, "Alright mate, it's been a while," says Cliff. Between gritted teeth I respond, "I'm all good, how's it going?" This polite bullshit goes on for a few minutes whilst we catch up on how things have been. It's all bollocks. He doesn't give a fuck about me because he's a selfish prick. I have no time for him, but business like this requires mutual respect in order for it to function. Once all the pleasantries have finished I get down to the point, "Do you have any cars for sale or rent and what kind of power are they putting out?" Cliff replies, "When did you get back in the game?" I reluctantly say, "Today, I'm starting up again so I need reliable motors running high power; I've had a few old contacts get back in touch so I'm rebuilding the business."

Cliff rambles on for a while about how well he's done and how much money he's made, he goes on to bore me about his nice house in South America and where he's set up direct links with the cartels – most of this is bullshit but I have to entertain it in order to secure some kind of deal. What I want him to say is, "Here's a couple keys of coke and you can have it at cost, pay me when it's gone," that would be ideal, but it'll never fucking happen, not with Cliff because he's a greedy bastard.

Finally the bullshit finishes and Cliff gets to the point, "I've got a few motors due in over the next few days – are you looking at parts or the whole car?" I respond, "Initially I'll take one car at a time on a sale or return basis but I do have the market to move a few motors at a time. As I'm just starting, what sort of flexibility is there for the return of the money?" Cliff reluctantly says, "I'm flexible to a point and I can cover a certain amount of the money. How long are you looking at?" I say, "Between one and two weeks." He doesn't seem too bothered about the length of time. I've got him. He wants to give me the goods on tick and plenty of time as well. This will give me enough time to figure out a plan to sort this mess with Si. Whilst I'm silently celebrating this news, Cliff goes on to say, "The cars that I'm trading with at the minute are modified and you're looking at about twenty per car," I immediately ask him, "What kind of power are they running at?" Cliff, who understands my language and knows not to bullshit me, replies, "They're slightly down on power and they're putting out approximately forty percent of their original output." I'm happy with this and I know I can work with it, especially with the potential for extended credit. I ask Cliff to give me a heads-up when he has an idea of some timings.

6. ALFIE

My phone beeps and I look down to see that Alfie has switched his phone on; finally now I can get to work. A few moments pass and as expected my phone rings. It's Alfie so I answer the phone, "Hello mate, late one was it?" Alfie replies in his usual rough hungover voice, "Yeah, I spent all night running around someone's house dosed up on pills and Viagra." He then asks, "What's the plan?" My answer is brief, "A lot has happened over the last day or so, we need to catch up for a chat," to this Alfie says, "Yep, pop over when you're done, I'm not going anywhere." I knock the call on the head and start thinking about packing up my stand. I could do with getting over to see Alfie sooner rather than later.

As I'm packing up I'm still semi-conscious of anyone that may be aware of what went on this time yesterday. As usual the market is quiet and the other vendors have all packed up and gone home or hit the local pub. For me packing up is a bit of a ball ache. I could really do with Murray's mates popping down again to give me a hand; they got it all done in a few seconds! Lastly I stick the tables in the back; one of them is slightly damaged from its unscheduled flight it took yesterday but nothing to write home about. As I close the back doors I feel slightly uneasy, I still can't put my finger on it but the feeling is there niggling away, I think it's linked to a combination of things – Murray, Si, Alfie and Cliff, all of these characters and the people they associate with that are in my life are very different to the people that I am used to. Back in the army the people I lived and worked with I knew well, we all did, it was a case of having to, we could rely on each other. It's the brotherhood that I miss, the feeling of complete and utter belonging that has gone, I'm now putting my life in the hands of people that only care for themselves. Alfie is slightly different. He does care, he's just so fucking wild it's almost impossible to be able to rely on him, but his heart and morals are in the right place. He's someone I call an honorary squaddie, I meet them all the time. They are cut from the right cloth, they just didn't join up, but I can see the qualities in them.

I jump in the van and go through my usual routine of putting certain phones in the right place; I don't need to worry about resupplying any stock so I head straight for Alfie's place. It's not too far so the journey will take me about twenty minutes. He lives in the city centre, in a shitty area, the truth is I fucking hate where he lives as it's hot with the old bill and the main reason is that the area is flooded with prostitutes. I'm quite sure that's why he moved there; why else would you move into a shithole located in the rough part of the city. Alfie doesn't really care about these sorts of things. His life at times can be so chaotic that he doesn't always see the wider picture. Alfie's train of thought is he finds living in a central location makes it easier for his work. If he has the added bonus of a prostitute on tap that he can take advantage of when smashed out of his skull on drugs, then that suits him just fine.

I always become hyper vigilant when entering the area. It's just the way I am; whether I'm loaded up or not I always treat these meetings in the same way. It's the way I would have done as if I was still serving as the thought process is exactly the same, and I mean identical, that's why it feels so natural. Alfie's road is a tight residential area with parking on both sides, I always recce it first by driving along the complete road; I'm on the lookout for anyone or anything that looks suspicious, not just the police but individuals or gangs that might be potentially casing the place and people coming and going. In the case of it being the police, the outcome is obvious but if it's gang related then I'll be looking at being robbed, kidnapped or worse, especially in this area. The only backlash of conducting a recce in this area is that I look like a kerb crawler and I don't fancy getting nicked for that. My drive-by is complete and apart from a couple of the usual rough-looking crack whores; there doesn't appear to be anything out of the ordinary. I park up a bit further down the road, the further away the better. The walk towards Alfie's place is no different to the drive into the area. My head is telling me to remain cautious. I had a bad experience not a stone's throw away from this place a few years back; trust me, it really is a fucking shithole.

Alfie's flat is one of several. I need to push an intercom button to gain access via a communal door; ultimately I may be hanging around for a while and this is where I feel most vulnerable. I push the button. Fortunately Alfie promptly answers it in exactly the same way he answers his phone; roughly and with a voice that sounds hungover. I identify myself and he pushes the button that unlocks the door. I quickly go through, locking it behind me. I just need to get into his flat now; it's on the ground floor and to be fair it isn't that bad from the outside. I quietly knock on the door trying not to alert any of his neighbours of my presence; however this is highly unlikely, I've seen them and they're worse than Alfie, but still the less people that see me coming and going the better.

The door opens and I am immediately confronted by Alfie wearing nothing but his underpants – this doesn't shock me, he's always in his underpants but it can become off-putting when I'm trying to be serious. He just half smiles and ushers me in. As I walk into his flat I never know what I might be confronted with – half naked women, men or animals, honestly sometimes it's a fucking lottery. This time however it's just Alfie and the remnants of last night's drugs scattered across a large wooden coffee table that is situated in the middle of the lounge.

Before I take a seat I scan the sofa ensuring that there's nothing left on it that may cause me a problem or embarrassment, things like slices of pizza, vomit or an old pair of Alfie's skiddies. Alfie's sofa should be a registered disaster zone; when I first started working with him I blindly sat on his sofa, only to leave with a dirty, wet, half eaten dog chew stuck to my leg. He hasn't even got a fucking dog. That being said, the sofa does look relatively safe to sit on so I take a seat. Alfie sits next to me, takes a deep breath and proceeds to cough his guts up; this coughing fit goes on for some time while I just sit here, pondering on where my life has ended up. Alfie's coughing fit gets so bad he vacates the room and heads for the bathroom where the coughing is now amplified as he coughs up any and everything into the sink. Several minutes pass and Alfie re-enters the room still wearing nothing but his pants. He plonks himself down next to me, leans forward and grabs a half smoked joint from one of several ashtrays that are randomly placed on the coffee table. He lights up, takes a massive pull on it and says, "Right, what's the crack?" I look at Alfie who is now sat in a cloud of heavy smoke and looking somewhat relaxed, considering the state he was in just a few minutes ago.

I spend the next ten or twenty minutes getting Alfie up to speed, most of which would have gone right over his head because he's not only hung over but he's now stoned. Either way Alfie is Alfie; what you see is what you get and when he's on form he's spot on, plus he'll do anything for you, he's committed and selfless and this is one of those military qualities that I see in him. This mutual agreement that we share gives me access to Alfie's safe house and runners. This is much needed since the Russian and I parted ways a while back. The only backlash to this is that Alfie's runners and safe house staff are equally unreliable, which proves to be extremely frustrating but I have to accept this help otherwise I'll be doing everything myself. That doesn't bother me, it's the lack of time that's the problem.

Alfie trawls through the ashtrays looking for another half smoked joint but struggles to find anything worth smoking. He reaches for a small tin container hidden amongst the rubble on the table, and he pops it open revealing a small bag of skunk, a packet of rizla, and a lighter. Alfie reaches for a magazine which is covered in bits of broken-up fags, ripped up rizlas and a couple of whole cigarettes. As he begins to build a fresh joint he seems to have a moment of clarity and says, "Shall we go and kidnap Murray for real this time?" I look at him thinking he's completely missed the point and say, "No I don't think that'll work, what I need is to get everyone to pull together and run things smoothly in order to get this mess sorted out." Alfie looks at me as he starts pulling bits of skunk out of the bag and dropping them into a roll-up, and says "Or we could do that.

I'll have a chat with the lads and make sure they know the score." As Alfie finishes speaking he lifts the joint, licks the seal and rolls it up.

Alfie sits back looking at his joint in admiration. He hasn't done a bad job considering the state he's in. In a confident manner he says, "Don't worry mate, we'll sort it." I look at him sat in his pants just staring at this joint, trying not to laugh at the state he's in and say, "Cheers mate, I'm gonna get off for now, don't get up I'll see myself out." We shake hands and I get up and double check that nothing from the sofa has attached itself to my clothes. As I let myself out I look back to see Alfie lighting up the joint that he spent so long admiring, "Speak to you later," I say as I close the door. I can just hear him reply, "Yep, laters." I exit the flat and head back to my van still remaining vigilant, but nothing seems to have changed over the last hour, even the prossies are still hanging around in the same place, that's a good sign because they soon disappear if the police arrive. I climb in the van, pick up my phone and take a quick look at the time, it's getting on for half two so I decide to head home.

Things are slowly coming together, none of this is out of the ordinary. All of the planning and coordination that I'm about to undertake is perfectly normal. I just have the added pressure of working with the likes of Cliff in order to pay Si; relying on a firm run by Alfie, this should prove interesting.

Whilst on route home I call my customers and start preparing them for a delivery. This usually occurs on a Thursday and it's always prudent to advise them of what may be happening. One thing they don't need to know is that I'm up against it – if they smell blood they may go for the jugular; on saying that, I've spent a long time building this client base. They are extremely loyal and most of them are good with their money, if they don't pay cash they pay on time, unless they encounter a problem. Despite all of this loyalty it's not good practice to show any weakness. When the Russian and I parted ways we divided the customers up; unfortunately for the Russian he underestimated how difficult it is to manage a business like this and his skills in debt collecting weren't enough to hold on to anyone. He struggled to maintain strong relationships with the people he worked with and this resulted in his customers coming back to me. This was because I was able to provide a consistent supply of coke and pills. The only reason for this is down to years of building bridges with people cementing a very good reputation.

Next thing I know I'm closing in on my home, I didn't even notice the journey. All my calls have been made and as far as I can tell everyone is on board, so long as Alfie's lot can do their job without fucking up, this week should end well. What I should have done is called Si to update him but I'm sure he'll be okay until tomorrow, besides he hasn't called me in the last few hours so he can't be that desperate. He knows what I'm all about – if I make a deal to do something I'll see it through even if I don't agree with it. All I have to do is wait for Cliff to get in touch, I won't call him as that will make me look desperate and he's the kind of person that will pick up on that and take the piss. I'll just switch off, go home and relax for the night. I'm getting a strong feeling that I won't be doing much of that for the next few days.

* * *

Thursday comes and goes with no real interaction from anyone, Cliff hasn't called. I've spoken to Si and he's happy with how things are looking although we haven't agreed on any prices; he knows I'm on it. Alfie's lads are primed and ready; Alfie's keeping them busy so it's not as if they're sat around twiddling their thumbs. What I'm finding more frustrating is the market stall was quiet, too quiet; in fact after the attack my heart's not in it, I'm just not feeling it at the moment. I'm beginning to seriously consider knocking it on the head or finding someone to run it for me, but this will mean paying out a wage, a wage that I don't think I can afford. The problem that I am faced with is simple. I can sit on my stall barely earning a wage and then spend the afternoon running around like a blue-arsed fly doing drug shit, or I can employ someone to do the market, paying them a part-time wage allowing me to go full-time working with Alfie. This would allow me to spin the drugs around a lot more efficiently, getting Si off my case and blowing Murray out of the water.

Friday morning, I get up and go through the same tedious routine; it's taking every ounce of my will power to not just fuck it off, but for my family's benefit I need to keep the charade going, at least for a little while longer. As I'm heading out of the area, I have no emotion, no anxiety, and no happiness, I'm just numb. My head has taken a bit of an emotional battering over the last year or so. I just wish things could be normal. But what the fuck is normal? I've never had normal, normal for me is watching someone get filled in at the NAAFI bar whilst someone else drinks a pint of piss. Normal for me is at the age of twenty walking around with a loaded weapon whilst people are actively trying to kill me. So where the fuck do I fit into 'normal'?

On route to work I reassemble my burner, this time hoping for some messages and as much as it pains me I'm hoping to get one from Cliff. Just a few short moments pass as the phone powers itself up and there's the noise I was hoping for, a selection of beeps. I take a look at the display and see a text from Cliff; I open the text "the cars have been valeted and serviced, they are ready for collection". Happy fucking days, at last I feel a bit of a positive emotion, all for the wrong reasons but I still feel good. This positive emotion helps put a better spin on everything else, making the rigmarole of sitting on my stall that much easier. I approach the market and set up for the day, still no one has said anything about the attack, but that seems ages ago.

Once again I'm sitting there with a coffee, tending to the odd customer. I'm having a good think about whom I could offer a part-time job to in order for me to do my thing. There is someone who springs to mind. I have a good friend, Lance, a straight goer who knows the score but doesn't get involved in anything. He has a pal Carl who is always with him and is always looking for work. These two often pop down to my stall just to chill out, they know what I do and they find it all very interesting, especially recent events. I know it's a bad idea getting someone else to run my stall but I don't feel that I have a lot of choice; the reality is I'm just looking for an excuse to get out and once my mind is made up, there's no going back.

I strike while the iron is hot and call Lance on my straight phone, the phone rings for a while he then answers, "How's it going – you down the market?" I reply, "Yes, are you with Carl?" A few seconds pass and Lance says, "Yes mate, he's sat next to me, shall I put him on?" I hesitate for a second... "No, come down, I've got a job offer for him." Lance says, "We're only round the corner, see you in a bit." Speaking to Lance on the phone is fraught with danger, because he's a straight goer and finds this all so terribly exciting he's likely to say things which could be potentially compromising so we say our goodbyes. It's never straightforward saying goodbye to Lance because he continues saying bye until the phone goes down so what you get is a constant stream of "byes" getting quieter and quieter until he finally presses the red button.

Eleven o'clock I text Alfie the standard message "call me when you get 5" and as to be expected his phone is off. I don't even want to guess what sort of a mess he was in last night, I just hope he's changed his underwear. While I'm trying not to imagine such a sight of Alfie in his pants smoking a joint it's hard not to, he's such a strong character he imprints an image in my mind that just doesn't go, I wish it would, it's fucking traumatising.

I hear a familiar voice as Lance arrives with Carl in tow. Lance looks at me and says, "Your eye's not that bad is it, Murray must hit like a girl." I chuckle saying, "I think the cut came from something that was thrown, possibly the table." Lance just smiles in disbelief, I know what he's thinking – he's wondering why I would want to be involved in all this bullshit. He doesn't understand my journey and probably never will. I spend the next hour talking to Carl trying to convince him that it's safe to work here and it's a job that will suit him down to the ground. He's definitely keen. What does help is Lance has offered to help out as well. Lance does have a job but he only does a few bits and pieces when he can be arsed. They both have a good understanding of my business. I can let them use my van and Carl will lend me his car, so I don't foresee any problems. We agree that they can start Monday next week. We arrange to link up over the weekend to swap vehicles and go over any last minute details. Seemingly happy with the arrangement, Lance and Carl head off.

This is really good news. I'm back in the game, full-time with a front business to boot. I can tell the Mrs that Carl and Lance are helping out for a while, this is fucking perfect. My phone beeps. It's Alfie; I can't wait to hear what he's got to say. It's never straightforward stuff but always highly entertaining. The phone rings, it's Alfie; "Hello mate, how are you?" I ask. Alfie's reply is short, "Fucked." Now Alfie's fucked and my fucked could be two different things. It's a word that means so much. I ask him, "What's happened? Is everything okay?" Alfie tries to speak but is hit with one of his coughing fits. This could take a while and I'm thinking 'I'm glad it isn't my credit that's being used up.' In between coughs he says, "I was arrested last night," he then continues coughing. I'm thinking 'shit what for', and being completely selfish 'how will this affect me?' Alfie, still coughing, tries to speak, "Drink driving." 'Thank fuck,' I think, at least it wasn't drug related. I ask him, "What now?" Alfie doing his best not to puke says, "Nothing changes. I just don't get caught driving." This is a typical answer for Alfie and to be fair there's not much I can say. He'll do what he wants, how he wants, when he wants and the only way he'll change is when he dies. I tell Alfie, "I'll pop down after work, so I'll see you in an hour or so." Alfie gives his usual generic response, "Yep laters, I'm not going anywhere."

As I pack up my stall for the last time I can't help feeling like I'm making a bad decision, but I need to commit to this in order to get myself out of the shit. Emotionally I'm right up there and as it stands it'll take a lot to faze me; I just hope that the coke Cliff is supplying is as good as he says. I also need to invest in some pills. This is relatively straightforward as my pill supplier can access as many as I need at almost any time. I normally grab ten thousand at a time and I'm always given a couple of weeks to get rid of them. The money made on the pills is marginal. I supply some of my customers pills purely because they have coke as well, this keeps them on board; the last thing I need is for someone to venture elsewhere looking for pills only to be offered coke from another supplier, it makes good business sense to offer them everything. I stand at the back of the van looking at everything stored in the back feeling quite relieved that I don't have to worry about going through the same tedious process of unpacking it for work on the Monday. I give the doors a good push closing them for the last time, feeling quite elated I walk round to the driver's door and get in.

Driving away from the market prompts me to make some calls. I mentally list the names of the people I need to call and put them into sequential order. I don't need to be calling people more times than I have to. Alfie knows I'll be on route so no need to call him. I'll call Cliff first, then Terry for my pills and finally Si. I can arrange all the logistics once I'm at Alfie's. Looking at Cliff's name with "DO NOT USE" next to it still makes me second guess what I'm doing; but for all of his faults and there are a lot, he can have his uses. The phone rings just once, "Yes mate, when are you gonna get this car?" I reply, "I'm just sorting the logistics; definitely today, can you send me a contact number?" Cliff acknowledges this, "Yes, I'll send you Flash's number." Whilst I'm thinking what an arrogant prick he is, my phone beeps as I receive a text from Cliff. I open the message and it's a number for his runner Flash – who the fuck is Flash? Cliff's runners are usually the same kind of breed as Murray. I'm glad it's not me meeting them. This whole circle of people are all the same, plastic fucking gangsters, noisy dickheads who just bring it on top.

As I make the call to Terry, my pill supplier, I can't help thinking he's the complete opposite to the likes of Cliff; he's calm and professional. The phone rings just twice, it always does. He asks, "How's things, I heard Murray's been throwing his weight around with Si?" I say, "I'm all good, yes I had a bit of a moment but nothing that can't be put right in time. Are you working this week?" Terry replies, "Yes." I say, "Okay, you'll get a call a bit later," and on that we finish the call. Terry and I are singing from the same sheet and it makes him a pleasure to work with. We don't feel the need to talk shit, we just say enough to let each other know what we're dealing with.

Looking at the phone I still feel the odd burst of anxiety as I press the call button for Si. I never know quite what will happen. One minute he's my best mate the next he's planning my death. This is the reality of what I have to deal with on a day-to-day basis. Si answers, "Got my doe yet?" Unsure how to take this I say, "Not yet but I've got a busy weekend planned, so long as nothing goes tits-up I'll be able to sort something out." Si immediately replies in an extremely positive manner, "Okay brother, call me next week." For fuck's sake, all this anxiety for nothing. That was painless enough so long as he remains positive I'll be fine but Si's mood will be dictated by what happens in his life not mine. If he has a bad weekend or takes a loss, he'll have to apply pressure elsewhere, and that pressure will roll downhill to everyone in his debt and unfortunately this means me.

Approaching Alfie's place again puts me on alert. I do the usual recce, notice a few lads knocking around but not a problem, well not yet anyway. They are plotted up at the other end of the road which prompts me to park away from them and nearer to Alfie's. I prefer not to do this but I have to choose the safer of the two, and parking nearer to Alfie's carries less risks than having to deal with a bunch of lads whose intentions are not clear. I ring the bell, feeling quite conscious of these lads who I can see just a short distance away. I don't need to look at them; I can see them in my peripheral vision, it's enough to let me know if they move. Sounding quite pissed up Alfie answers the intercom "Who is it?" I answer, "It's me." I hear the buzzer go as Alfie unlocks the door.

As I walk into the communal area near Alfie's door I can smell the unmistakable sweet pungent smell of skunk coming from Alfie's flat, well I think it's coming from Alfie's, it could be his neighbours. I gently tap on his door, Alfie opens it holding a bottle of white wine in one hand and one of the fattest joints I've ever seen in the other. Fortunately this time he's given me the courtesy of wearing a vest as well as his underpants, but all of this is eclipsed by him being completely covered in blood which would appear to have come from a big fuck-off cut running across his forehead – it's deep, any deeper and his face would drop. Alfie looks at me and says, "Yes I know." I can't help saying, "What the fuck mate?" I'm so busy thinking about this cut on his head I haven't even noticed the state of the flat – it's fucking wrecked, I don't mean messy, it's been totally trashed. There doesn't appear to be anywhere to sit because the sofa has been stripped of its cushions and is upside down in the middle of the floor next to the coffee table so I just lean against a wall. Alfie standing next to me does the same, not saying anything he just slumps down onto the floor; looking down I see a relatively clean spot beneath me so I do the same, we just sit here in silence, Alfie's not in a good place.

What I want to do is treat this cut on his head, but I haven't got a clue where Alfie's been, what he's taken or if he has any kind of first aid kit; after all this is Alfie, the only drugs he'll have will be controlled or illegal and he seems quite content puffing away on his joint sipping wine from a bloodstained bottle. Either way I have to do something, I walk into the kitchen to look for some kitchen towel; I'm pretty sure Alfie doesn't use this room as a kitchen it's more of a bar, it's rammed with bottles of beer, three-litre boxes and bottles of wine plus a selection of spirits and liqueurs. He's definitely never used the cooker. I think he used the grill once to warm up a nine bar of solids to make it easier to cut but that's about it. There is nothing here of any use, only a scabby old tea towel which looks like it's never been washed. I grab what looks like a clean cup off of the side.

I now have to consider the thought of venturing into Alfie's bathroom. I did go in there once, and I told myself never again. I precariously walk across Alfie's lounge avoiding bits of ashtray, broken beer bottles, cushions from the sofa; surprisingly the coffee table has survived. As I pass Alfie who is still slumped against the wall I say, "Sit tight mate, I'm just looking for something for your head." Alfie doesn't even flinch, he attempts to take another drag from his joint, he doesn't notice that it's gone out, but this doesn't stop him trying.

It would be an understatement to say Alfie's bathroom is in a hell of a state, it doesn't smell, it's just well used. I slowly venture in and notice a toilet roll on the side and immediately notice Alfie's bathroom mirror has been smashed and all the glass has fallen into the sink. There's a lot of blood in the sink and as I look around I begin to notice blood. How could I not have seen this straightaway? It's fucking everywhere – walls, floor, ceiling, in the bath and all over the sink. It doesn't take much to work out what's happened. Alfie's stuck the nut on the mirror. What the hell has happened? I need to know, because as reckless as he is, I like Alfie, I need to know if he's on the verge of a breakdown and if so I need to consider my own operation and what to change in order to support the both of us. At the end of the day Alfie has put himself out for me and if he's having a shitty time I need to be there for him. I fill the cup with water, grab the bog roll and head back to Alfie.

What a fucking mess! I kneel in front of Alfie, place the cup of water on the floor and take a good look at this cut on his head. He mutters, "Thanks for this." I just smile as I unravel some toilet roll and dip it into the water, I start to clean this cut, Alfie doesn't flinch – he's either tough as fuck or so wasted he can't feel anything. Alfie's not making this very easy, he's fidgeting around in his pants. I ask "What are you doing, keep still." He replies, "I'm looking for my lighter." In disbelief I say, "What in your fucking pants?" Alfie starts laughing "yeah" as he produces a lighter from his pants. Alfie leans forward, looks at the joint, flicks the lighter and starts lighting the joint; he slowly rolls it back and forth in order to get the flame to take on all sides avoiding any side burns. The end of the joint begins to glow bright orange. Alfie smiles. I hear the joint's contents incinerated as Alfie takes a big puff. He's inhaled with such intensity I can feel the heat radiating from it. I continue dabbing this wound with wet toilet roll until it's clean enough to get a good look; all the while Alfie's not saying a word he just continues to drink and smoke.

This wound is too serious for me to manage. I look at Alfie and say, "Look mate, I need to get you to hospital – this needs stitching. I can give you a lift. Are you feeling up to it?" Alfie just looks at me as he takes the last swig of wine and says, "Fuck it, go on then." I stand up and pull him to his feet. I take a long length of toilet roll and fold it into a makeshift bandage. Alfie's not bleeding so I just want to cover the cut. I place the bandage on his head saying, "Put your hand on there and don't move." Alfie in an almost childlike way complies, dropping the empty wine bottle on the floor then placing his left hand on his forehead. He's keeping the other hand free to finish off his joint. "Where are your trousers?" I ask. He gestures towards the bedroom.

I leave Alfie standing there not moving and venture into his bedroom. It's a stark contrast to the rest of his flat, it's extremely clean and tidy. I look in Alfie's wardrobe and see that all of his clothes are neatly ironed and hung up. Alfie doesn't possess any jeans and very few T-shirts as he's always dressed in a pair of trousers and shirt. He's well-dressed considering how unhinged he is. I grab a set of clothes and head back to Alfie who hasn't moved. He's still holding the makeshift bandage on his head, and puffing from the joint which is almost gone. I look at Alfie and say, "I'm not fucking dressing you mate," as I hold the clothes out to him. He takes one final puff on his joint, stubs it out on the wall behind him and just drops it onto the floor. Alfie pulls off the blood-soaked vest and puts his shirt on; without buttoning it he grabs his trousers and slips them on. While he looks around the devastation surrounding us he slowly buttons up his shirt and walks back towards his bedroom and emerges with a pair of brown shoes, his phone and a set of keys. He puts the phone and keys in his pocket and it appears that he is beginning to come round from whatever state he was in when I first arrived.

Alfie starts chuckling to himself as he tries to balance on one foot whilst putting his first shoe on, I would help but this sudden sign of independence is a good thing. I might actually get some sense out of him in the next hour or so, I need to because these drugs aren't gonna deliver themselves. Alfie succeeds in putting both of his shoes on, without falling over; the bandage has begun to unravel and drop from his forehead, and it's just stuck on by a thin strand attached to a blood clot. Alfie stands up straight, looks at me with this toilet roll hanging down in front of his face and body. He gathers it up and holds it against his forehead and says, "Come on then." I lead the way out of his flat looking back, ensuring that Alfie has closed the door behind him. He looks a bit unsteady on his feet but apart from that and the cut he seems okay. We both emerge onto the street from the communal door; I look up and down the street – nothing to worry about. We head for the van. I get in, lean across and let Alfie into the passenger side, he gets in and sits down.

I start up, pull away and ask Alfie, "What's happened then?" Alfie takes a deep breath and says, "Yesterday I had to attend a doctor's appointment." I look at him and acknowledge saying, "Okay." "Basically I'm dying. The doc had my test results back for this cough I've had for the last eighteen months and it's confirmed that I have the early stages of pulmonary lung disease. He said if I stop smoking I'll last maybe ten years, if I don't I'll be lucky to last five years." I look at Alfie in disbelief and say, "Shit mate, that's bad news I guess you're gonna stop smoking now." Alfie just looks at me and says "Am I fuck, I'll just have to make these next five years good ones." This doesn't surprise me one bit. Alfie then says, "So when I got home I got on the piss went out of town to drop some stuff off, on the way back I got done for drunk driving, they arrested me and seized my car. I got released this morning, so when I got back to the flat I just fucking lost it and smashed the place up. I'm kind of regretting it a bit now." I can't help feeling sorry for him, but he doesn't want sympathy; he needs help.

As we arrive at the hospital I find somewhere to park up. We both exit the van as I've decided to go in with Alfie; one to make sure he actually gets treated and secondly to see if we can start making plans to get my shit sorted out, the clock's ticking here. As we wander into A&E, Alfie goes straight up to the reception desk and checks in. He's definitely getting his faculties back. He checked in, in what I would describe as a coherent manner. Alfie returns and sits next to me. Producing his phone from his pocket he says, "What do you need doing?" Thank fuck he's back in the room; conscious of anyone overhearing us I quietly say, "I've got a key of coke needs collecting and ten thousand gurners." Alfie smiles saying, "Good news I'm out of pills – how many can I have?" "Half of them at the usual price." Alfie nods and says, "Cheers." Part of our agreement is that Alfie can have his drugs at cost, especially the pills; he's got a good market for pills and pot at the universities so he bangs out a fair few. Alfie says, "I'll get The Boy onto it."

For all of Alfie's nightmarish faults, when he goes into work mode he just gets things done. All I need to do is give him an idea of who has what, which is usually a standard list – week in week out.

As we sit here conspiring to arrange the movement of the drugs, I don't ever switch off to my surroundings. I am constantly looking at the doorways and people. A healthy level of paranoia can help, and this is not to be confused with the type of paranoia induced by excessive drug use; they're very different. I finish casing the place and look at Alfie who is now looking less sorry for himself. He says, "I'll call The Boy in a bit to go and collect the coke and I'll contact Spice to get the pills. I'll get Jeff ready to do the counting and weighing." Staring at his crusty-looking cut I say, "Thank you, do you need anything else from me?" Alfie says, "No you're okay, I can sort it from here. I'll get Kate to pick me up, you can shoot off if you need to get back." I take another look at Alfie who now seems to be okay, apart from the obvious problems he has to deal with. I hold my hand out and we shake hands, he smiles and says, "Thanks, I owe you one," still holding his hand I say, "No you don't, let me know if you need anything."

Walking back to my van I'm racking my brains to see if there's anything I can do to lighten Alfie's load but I know he's got a handle on it, and his Mrs Kate will take good care of him because she's a fucking diamond. I wouldn't have put them together not in a million years, but they make a good couple. They're poles apart and I guess she keeps him from completely self-destructing. He's going to need her more now than ever, and she's definitely got her work cut out with Alfie. I get in my van and head home. I don't need to call anyone as the baton has been handed to Alfie who will have contacted his lads and got them primed to work.

7. REBUILDING THE BUSINESS 1

Alfie's lads are an assorted mix of characters and our warehouseman Jeff is one of the main guys; his role is pivotal as he is responsible for checking, counting, weighing and storing the drugs, he has his own house and it's situated in an okay part of town, so the likelihood of being robbed or burgled is low, not impossible but low and that's good enough for me. Jeff's only problem is he does like a drink, who doesn't, but he likes his when he gets up. Despite this, Jeff functions at a very high level, he is very meticulous and extremely reliable, when he does a job he does it properly and that's all I can ask for. He and Alfie go back a long way, they're both from out of town; they've lived here for a while now, but definitely not local; if I'm to guess, looking at the way they dress and conduct themselves, I think they may have been skinheads in a previous life.

Alfie does his best to restrict the activity in and around Jeff's place especially when he's busy. The last thing Jeff needs is people knocking on the door disturbing him whilst he's working. The only people that Alfie will allow to the house are the runners and that's only when Jeff has given the nod. This is because when Jeff drinks he uses speed to balance the books, this works well to prevent him from getting completely shitfaced but on the flipside Jeff suffers from some serious paranoia, and it's serious enough to go into a complete meltdown. Put it this way – if you knock on Jeff's door when he's not expecting you and he happens to be on a para, you'll be greeted with a fucking axe, and that's enough to spoil anyone's day.

Putting aside any paranoia, the drugs have been collected and successfully offloaded to Jeff's who is now beavering away, counting and weighing everything. Alfie's not interested in coke, he has no market for it, plus he knows that coke carries a lot of baggage, if he gets asked for some he just refers them to me. I reciprocate the deal with anyone who asks me for pot. I used to sell pot but when I moved into the class A's I didn't really feel the benefit of having it around. Naturally this is another arrangement that works well for both of us. So at any one time Jeff can have coke, pills, speed and all types of cannabis in storage, all weighed, counted and ready to go. This is a heavy burden for any warehouseman, especially one suffering from paranoia and alcoholism.

Leaving my fate in the hands of Alfie's firm is a concern. I don't know them that well and I have very little interaction with them. I know they work well for Alfie and that should be good enough for me but it doesn't stop me stressing. They tend to do things a lot later than I would. I like to get things done during the working day, allowing me to operate within a normal time frame with plenty of traffic and people to blend into. Working at night vastly increases the chances of being pulled. It also means I need to have my burner switched on at home and that's not happening, so I have to start taking drug-related calls on my straight phone. I can handle this so long as the Mrs doesn't clock on and the calls that I'm taking are suitably coded from another straight phone. But that's in the ideal world and that's not the world I live in. The world I live in is full of risks and danger just waiting to go wrong, so having to use my straight phone to take drug-related calls is a calculated risk I have to accept.

These problems make sitting at home stressing about something that hasn't happened a common feeling that I have to deal with. The stress can be that intense. I would rather be out doing the running around myself, at least then everything is happening in real time and I know what my capabilities are. Put it this way, if I get caught it will be for a very good reason and not because I've fucked up. If a runner from someone else's firm gets caught with my stuff on board as a result of problems in their life or for being a complete fucking halfwit, then that's a very bitter pill to have to swallow. Consequently there's nothing worse than waiting for the runners to check in with the all clear, so trying to act normal with all of this going on takes its toll. When I know I'm in for the night I nearly always start drinking, not heavily but enough to take the edge off of the anxiety. I used to smoke pot but that's out of the question the way things are at the moment.

It's gone ten and I'm as relaxed as can be when I finally get a call from Alfie. I answer the phone mindful that this is my straight phone and hoping that Alfie doesn't forget and calls me from his burner, I say, "How's things, did you get your head sorted out?" Alfie replies, "Yes mate I'm much better now, Kate picked me up, we went for something to eat and the lads did some running around for us as I was stuck at the hospital for quite a while, they said to pass on their regards." This is the news I was waiting for. I say, "That's great, I'm glad they've pulled together to help you out, I'll give you a shout Monday next week." Alfie replies, "Yes, I'll be around, thanks for your help today." "Not a problem, speak to you later," I say and finish the call; at last I can finally relax and enjoy my drink, trying my best to switch off to any issues that may be about to rear their ugly heads.

* * *

The weekends come and go so quickly. I try to spend as much quality time with my family as possible, doing my best not to spend too much cash as I'm mindful that next week I'm gonna be busy collecting money. This makes it almost impossible to completely switch off to the possibility that I also have to raise some money for Si, with a complete dickhead like Cliff potentially breathing down my neck. I haven't agreed on a figure with Si yet. I don't want to aim too high as this will set a benchmark that he will expect each time, plus I don't want to be paying any more back than I really need to. On the other hand if I aim too low this could upset Si and that's not a good idea. The aim is to get him on side, costing me as little as possible. All the coke has been dished out, plus around nine thousand pills half of which went to Alfie; so putting any problems aside my profit should be around two and a half grand. I'm going to offer Si about seven hundred and fifty, this should keep him sweet and if it doesn't I have some left to bump it up to a grand. I guess I'll just have to wait and see.

Saturday was spent doing the better part of fuck all. I tried to contact Lance so we could meet up and arrange for Carl to start working on the stall and get our vehicles swapped over. Much to my frustration he wasn't answering his fucking phone. I had more success on Sunday. Lance called me apologising for missing my calls on the Saturday. We all met up and went over all the finer details of running the stall. Carl seemed to be excited about his new position, I can't think why, I found it pretty boring, but then again my version of excitement is very different to most.

Monday arrives so soon and even though I don't have to get up at sparrow's fart in the morning, I still wake early. It would be nice to have just a little bit of a lie-in, but with the amount of shit going on in my life a lie-in is a rare luxury. Even back in my days of getting hammered, after an all-nighter, if I went to bed at seven in the morning I would still get up a couple of hours later and that's just the way I am. It must have something to do with basic training and having some fullscrew screaming at me, "Get out of your fucking bed you useless piece of shit." At the age of eighteen, experiences like that tend to bed in and never go away. In fact basic training for me back in the eighties seemed a lot more brutal. The PC brigade hadn't got involved so the whole time was total madness. So when I'm up I get ready and get on my way, what's the point in sitting around doing nothing when I can be out and about rallying around getting things sorted or prepped for when the late risers finally surface.

So sitting in the house is achieving nothing, I'm going to take a drive down to the stall and see how the lads are getting on. It won't do any harm showing my face, it'll kill a bit of time, allow me to start making some calls and for my wife's benefit it'll look a lot better if I'm not sat at home doing fuck all. I don't think she'll be too bothered, I would just prefer for her to think I'm busy, she's far from stupid and will soon wonder where the money's coming from. She knows how much the stall earns, so if she does get suspicious I just tell her any extra cash has come from the odd security job that I do. This is the perfect cover as I just explain to her that due to the nature of the work carried out the details are confidential. This has worked well over the years and I use this cover for all of my friends and family.

On route to the stall I send the usual text to Alfie, quite aware that he won't be available for at least a couple of hours. I just hope the weekend has passed without incident; generally speaking I would have heard by now if there were any problems. Driving into the market was a bit weird as I'm now conscious of what the other traders will be thinking about me not being on the stall. If they have any sense they'll put two and two together and figure it out. I can't access the stall by car so I park up in the public car park and walk. The market is surprisingly busy so the walk through to my stall goes without any issues and nobody bats an eyelid, not a thing, but then again it's old news now. I'm the only one who cares enough for it to be a problem.

As I close in on my stand I can see Carl stood there with a coffee and Lance sat in the back of the van, which is a fucking relief because they've turned up and would appear to have set up without any problems. I can't help thinking that people are going to let me down. It's happened so many times in the past, simple fucking tasks that I can do in my sleep and some dickhead fails to do it. I wouldn't mind but when they don't even have the balls to let me know they've fucked up, that really gets me. I'm used to people communicating clearly; doing exactly as agreed and if a problem does arise it's dealt with, promptly. Carl notices me approaching and gives Lance a nudge, who looks straight at me, gets up and smiles. We all engage in some random conversation about how the stall is running and how much have they taken. The truth is the way things are right now I couldn't really give a fuck, so long as the stall makes enough to keep Carl in a wage that's all that matters. I reiterate to him that I don't have any other money available to pay him if the stall takes a loss, it's down to him to make it work and if it doesn't I'll just fold it and bin it. I'm not gonna get roped into paying a wage for someone who's just happy to coast.

Hanging around the stall engaging in conversation isn't helping my situation. I keep thinking that not having my own firm is beginning to frustrate me. More so now than ever before I need my independence back. I've got a feeling that at some point I'm going to be under a lot of pressure from Si, which will put me in a difficult position with Alfie as I'll have to be on his case for his lads to do their job properly. I don't want to do this because I'm grateful for Alfie's support but his lads' methods and timings don't fit in with how I like to run things. I could do with having a chat with Alfie to see if he'll let me have direct interaction with his lads, seeing if I can push them a little bit harder, getting them up at a respectable hour and not having them running around carrying all sorts of shit in the middle of the night. The way I see things is surely with his recent encounter with the police and his pending ban from driving, along with the fact that he's now on borrowed time, allowing me to take a little control of his lads will give him time to sort his life out – but this is Alfie and as I've said before, he does things in his own way.

Fuck this waiting around, it's time to make some calls. If I can get an idea of how people have managed over the last few days this will potentially alleviate the stress that is slowly building, and the stress does build because I haven't got a clue what's happened over the weekend. Put it this way, I could try to call my most reliable customer who always has cash ready, only to find out he's been arrested, kidnapped – anything can happen, there's no rule book when you are on the wrong side of the law, you only have to get it wrong once and you're fucked. I don't have too many customers to worry about. The way I see it is if the stuff I'm selling is good enough quality and the prices are fair it gives my customers enough room to build their client base, saving me all the running around. I'm not being a twatt, I've been there. I started at the bottom and built what I have from nothing; these are standard business models used if I want to get to the wholesale stage. Someone told me once "the less numbers you have in your phone, the better you'll be" – this is advice that I took on board as it makes perfect sense.

Most of my stuff goes out of the city to the surrounding towns, which in turn supply the smaller villages; the irony is that the majority of the people who are supplied will venture back into the city to hit the club scene to get off their tits, and when they inevitably run out they will more than likely be topped up by the local dealers who I may be a supplier of, so either way they're probably indirectly buying from a part of my supply network. All of my customers are very different and are from most walks of life – they change from time to time; some I've met and taken on board myself, others have been inherited by default, this usually happens if someone gets busted owing money, the logical thing to do is take on board their customers, then even if they don't have enough money to cover any outstanding debts it can be recovered over time, plus the inherited customer is normally quite happy to have moved up another link in the chain.

Mick was a good customer when I used to supply him with pot. He would easily do one or two kilos a week and the money would always be there waiting on the Monday; however his ability to manage the money in the world of Class A's, particularly coke, has diminished as it's a very different world. Once a pothead is stoned, worst case they'll get the munchies and go and spend a few quid on food but that's about it. Cokeheads on the other hand will keep sniffing until they've exhausted all supplies, but it doesn't stop there, they will require a huge amount of alcohol to drink whilst coked up. Worse still, any up-and-coming coke dealers especially the ones who supply the low-end deals will be trying to impress everyone by drinking champagne – even the cheap shit adds up. And this whole thing about sniffing coke off of a bird's tits or arse doesn't work that well. You try racking up a line of the good stuff on the cleavage of a hot female, she could be the best looking girl you've ever met, she still sweats like the rest of us so the coke just disappears into her sweaty body with nothing left to sniff. Still it's good fun trying and I would never try to deter anyone from giving it a go. Consequently you take one reliable pot dealer, introduce cocaine into their life and things usually go tits-up.

My stress levels rise once again as I look up Mick in my phone and make the call. It starts ringing which is a good sign. "Hello," Mick says. "How's things, are you good to catch up a bit later?" I reply. "Yes, I'm all good," Mick says in a confident manner. "Good stuff, do you need to work again this week because I still have some car parts left to sale?" I ask as my stress levels once again return to normal, the aim is if Mick needs any pills I can have those dropped to him when the money is collected a bit later. The phone is quiet for a second or so while Mick is contemplating. "I don't need to work with the expensive parts but I could do with a couple of boxes of nuts and bolts?" Mick asks. I replied, "Yes mate, two boxes. I'll get them to you a bit later." That's a bit of a relief as Mick is the most unreliable of customers, the rest are good.

Jay is next on my hit list. He lives in the same area as Mick, in fact Mick introduced me to Jay some years back. Jay is a very good customer, in fact one of my best. He always pays cash. The only downside is he is extremely fussy and scatty as fuck plus he's recently been released from jail. I can cope with his fussiness as he pays cash on delivery, but his scatty behaviour is a risk in itself. Jay can become so preoccupied with the job in hand he ends up completely oblivious to everything else around him. This makes meeting up with him a fucking nightmare, because you can guarantee things will not go smoothly, there will always be some kind of problem. It might be something as simple as him being five minutes late but it could be something as frustrating as finding somewhere safe enough for him to test the coke, and his definition of safe and test and mine are two very different things. Jay's a coke head so he won't even entertain the shit that I have in stock. He'll accept nothing less than the high-end stuff, minimum of seventy percent and the price needs to reflect the quality, if it isn't what he's asked for it's coming back with a load of fucking headaches.

Calling Jay brings little stress or anxiety, it's generally a straightforward transaction. I know he doesn't want the coke I have, I'm just going to try and throw the rest of these pills at him. I would like to get shot of them as soon as possible so I can pay the bills, plus I don't want too much stuff sitting around at Jeff's. The phone starts ringing and it goes on for a short while before Jay answers, "Alright bud?" I say, "Yes all good. I've got some parts left on the shelf if you're interested." I can hear Jay banging away at something in the background. He's a builder by trade so he's generally on site somewhere. Jay says, "Yes I could do with something – what have you got?" One of the other problems with Jay is he tends to stray from whatever code we use. I always use the car parts and car sales code because that's what I do. Jay will be inclined to use his own code that fits his lifestyle and this is where we have to find a way to compromise. Jay says, "I'm putting up a wall next week and I need some bricks." Now this has thrown me because this is the code that we used when I used to sell pot. I ask Jay, "Mate what kind of bricks are you looking at, the bigger ones from a while back or these new smaller designer ones I've been getting?" I fucking hope he clocks on, the last thing I want is to be sending someone down with eight hundred pills when he's expecting eight kilos of pot. Jay responds in an equally confused way, "For fuck's sake, I don't know." I start chuckling and slowly say, "These bricks are designer, they are small, round and have a pretty picture on the front." At last Jay has clocked on and says, "Oh fuck, yeah sorry mate, yes how many do you have?" I say, "Eight pallets approx eight hundred." "Yes mate, send them down," he says. This is good news because I've got rid of everything, all I need to do is round up the dosh. I say to Jay, "No problem mate, you'll get a call a bit later after work." We say our goodbyes.

Miles is my last customer from this area, he's a bit on and off, this isn't down to a lack of ability it's because he's new in the game. Sometimes he pays cash but usually he needs credit, this depends on what he's having; Miles is another one slowly moving into the coke market. His market isn't big, maybe a few hundred pills and a bit of coke, however because he's a decent straight-up guy he has the ability to expand his business into the surrounding area, an area that I don't yet cover. This won't be a rapid aggressive expansion. It'll take time, I just need to ensure he's given an endless supply of good quality coke and pills and this will be enough to do the job. The phone starts ringing and Miles answers, "How's it going?" he asks. I reply, "I'm well, how was the weekend for you, any problems?" Miles says

"Nope, all went well but I could do with seeing you again before the end of the week." This puts me on a high so I say, "Yes that's no stress; someone will be passing your neck of the woods later – are you about?" Miles says, "Yes I'm ready when you are." Feeling pretty relieved that things are going to plan, I say, "Good stuff, they'll call you later." As I switch the phone off I get that all too common sense of wellbeing that comes when things are going to plan.

The order I'm working in isn't random. I'm visualising the route that may be taken in order to see these people with as little fuss and driving around as possible. Billy lives on the edge of the city and he's someone I can visit myself. Now, he prefers not to have runners coming to see him. What he does respect is that when it comes to dropping off drugs it won't be me that he sees, but he does insist that it should be the same person and not a barrage of different people every week. In turn I respect this as it shows a good understanding of personal security and awareness. This is how I operate and it's this very style of working that I'm trying to introduce into Alfie's workforce. Billy is regular, consistent and he can pay cash if need be but I'm always happy to collect the cash myself after the drop off. This saves Alfie's boys running around with cash and drugs on them at the same time, and then there's the matter of trust. I do trust Alfie's boys. It's just that coke money is so much more than pill, speed or pot money. For example, let's say Alfie's firm is used to dropping off a nine of whatever Alfie is supplying. Any money collected will be in the multiple hundreds, where a nine of coke will be thousands, and they just aren't used to operating at this level – it's a different kettle of fish.

Billy's been in the game for a long time and he's a career criminal, calling him is simple. He answers the phone, "You popping round later?" I say, "Yes mate." He responds, "Okay, see you then," and puts the phone down. He's not being rude, that's all that needs to be said, he knows that I know he has the dosh, why bother talking on the phone when we can have a natter when I see him later.

AC on the other hand is operating on the other end of the scale. He's a middle man and doesn't actually have any direct customers. He's literally a go-between, this makes trading with him random at best. I wouldn't normally work with people like AC but he was referred to me by a friend who I owed a favour. AC is asked for all sorts of stuff and this makes him quite hard work. He doesn't mean to be, he just has a huge amount of leg work to do in order to dish out the drugs and collect up any money that is owed. I can only assume his profit is minimal, so he's more than likely skimming off the top of each deal. He lives in the same area as Billy and they do know each other; however, AC isn't a threat to Billy's business, trust me there's enough customers for everyone in their area. I try calling him but the phone just rings off, this isn't usually an issue, and he's good at calling back, I'll just try calling the next person on my list.

I always get quite a disconcerting feeling when contacting Boe. He's one of Alfie's customers. He's a lot younger and a bit of a lump. He buys a lot of pills and pot from Alfie and again like some of the others he's gradually venturing into the coke market. This is where a conflict of interest kicks in between Alfie and myself. Boe will have one pool of money to pay his bill, so if both Alfie and myself are in need of money he needs to figure out who he should pay first. The beauty of mine and Alfie's agreement includes who should have what share of money from any mutual customers. It's worked well so far, and where Boe lacks experience he's good at having the money ready because he's a heavy hitter and none of his customers will fuck with him. Boe's very much like Alfie in the sense that he won't be up yet so I just send him a text "call me when you get this message, cheers"; the message goes through and a note indicates it has been received, job done.

I'm feeling pretty relaxed, actually it's more a sense of relief; as far as I can tell by the close of play tonight most of the money should be in. I'll be able to make a sensible offer to Si, and pay Cliff for the coke. The intention is to open the door to a few more customers who I've held off from contacting, for no other reason than I wanted to gauge the feedback and quality of Cliff's coke before I take on some bigger numbers. I just need to speak to Alfie, Boe and AC. Alfie owes for half of the pills but that won't be a problem, besides I'm not interested in getting any more pills yet, there's fuck all money in them and I don't want them hanging around at Jeff's.

I look at Lance and Carl happily tending to a couple of customers. I say, "I'm off, got some running around to get on with," they both look over at me Lance responds, "Okay mate, see you later." I take a look around the market thinking how mad it is that things can change so dramatically in such a short space of time. None of these people who are innocently going about their business have got a fucking clue about the world that I live in, and why should they – as far as they're concerned the sort of stuff that I have to do on a daily basis doesn't enter their minds.

I say goodbye to the lads, and as I walk away I begin to get the feeling that I probably won't be back down for a while. I need to let them get on with it if I keep turning up – what's the point in handing over to Carl. As I slowly walk through the market towards the car, I keep thinking about what direction my life is going in. This isn't what I planned when I left the army, a fucking drug dealer with a shitty market stall as a business fronting my illegal income. If my old man really knew what I was doing, I think he'd disown me. I have such a huge respect for my dad and to end up in a life like this I can't help thinking I've turned out as a bit of a disappointment. I get in the car and shake off all of these emotions. I decided to give AC another go, it would be nice to have a full house as far as getting the drugs out and all the money back in.

The phone rings and AC answers, "Sorry I missed your call, I ran out of credit and couldn't call you back." I say, "That's okay, are you ready to catch up later?" AC says, "Yes, should be – I just got to see a couple of guys when they finish work – is seven okay?" I pause, now when someone says "they should be" it usually means "no" and this sets my alarm bells ringing, so I ask, "How much have you got in at the moment?" AC quickly responds, "A couple of grand." Actually that's not too bad, he only needs to raise a few hundred quid. I say, "Okay, so you'll be good for all of it later though?" AC replies, "Can't see it being a problem but you know what it's like." I have to agree, I do know what it's like, there's no point giving someone a hard time for no reason. I'll just have to wait and see. "Okay, I'll see you later, bye." AC says "bye" and I finish the call.

Aside from Alfie and Boe that's the planning done. It's just coming up for twelve and Alfie needs to be getting his arse out of bed. I'm going to head in his general direction, just hoping that he switches his phone on before one. I'm not going to cold call on him. If need be I'll park up and get some lunch. That's the beauty of this lifestyle. I can do whatever I want, more or less anyway. Driving into town I'm totting up the numbers in my head. I've calculated what will definitely be in and what is potentially going to be in and the two figures are close. I don't like arranging things prematurely but when I have to make a negotiation as delicate as the one I'm about to undertake with Si then I need to be making the first move. I look through my phone and select Si's number and the feelings of anxiety build again.

The phone rings for a while, longer than usual, it's not like Si to leave it that long, I cut it off, knowing that Si will see a missed call from me. If the shoe was on the other foot and it has been in the past and no doubt will be again, it's quite reassuring to see that someone who's made an arrangement with you is actually on the ball. It's pointless sending a text to Si, the missed call will be enough to prompt him to call me when he's ready. No sooner than placing the phone down onto the passenger seat it rings, I pick it up and it's Boe. "Hello mate," I say. Boe, sounding like he's just got up says, "I'm okay, what did you want?" Well that's a stupid fucking question but this is what I have to deal with sometimes. I respond, "How did you get on over the weekend? Someone will be popping down to you a bit later." I can hear Boe fiddling around with something in the background. I can just make out the sound of him counting; after a few seconds Boe says, "Yes all good. I'm a little bit light at the moment but that's getting dropped off to me in an hour or so." I'm pretty happy with that. "Nice one. You'll get a call later," I say. The phones go down and I continue on my way.

The drive to Alfie's isn't half bad. The spring weather is becoming warmer as the summer approaches. I'm certainly not going to rush, for this short and brief moment in time the biggest decision I'm faced with is where shall I go for lunch and in the grand scheme of things that's not a bad place to be. I've done everything I can to get things prepped in order to lighten the load for the lads, so I may as well do my best to try and relax. Driving through town looking for somewhere to buy my lunch brings a feeling of calm; every now and then I get these moments of serenity where I'm quite happy living in the moment, nothing else matters – whatever happens now will be out of my control so it's pointless even worrying about it. However, no matter how relaxed and in order I have my life, this feeling of temporary tranquillity is quickly shattered if the phone rings. It doesn't matter who's calling, when faced with the kind of problems that I have to deal with, just the phone ringing is enough to do my head in. Even my straight phone brings its own problems and usually means I have to lie or be evasive about what's going on in my life. And that can be even worse because I risk being exposed for what I have become and that's worse than all the shit that Si, Cliff and the like can dish out to me in one go.

Fortunately I remained in the moment of serenity long enough to purchase and eat my lunch without the phone ringing and bringing me a shit load of stress. Unfortunately now that I've finished my lunch I've departed this brief moment of tranquillity; this is the time that I want the phone to ring and I'm stressing because it hasn't. I can't fucking win as now I have to get on Alfie's case. I still won't cold call on him but I will slowly head in his direction. If only to recce the street for any problems. It's gone one so he should have switched on by now and with Alfie's life taking a severe downward turn I wouldn't blame him for losing his mind. It's only been a few days since his arrest and he smashed his place up, so he might not even be there, he could have stayed at Kate's. So out of all the possibilities, staying at Kate's would be the preferred one. Without any doubt Kate will ensure that he behaves; she knows exactly what he does so that isn't a problem, I just wish he'd switch his phone on. It feels like the hours in the day are slowly ebbing away and as the day shortens the workload will obviously intensify, not for me but for Alfie's lads, and this means they will be running around later with a fair bit of cash on them.

Fuck it, change of plan – I'll head up to see Billy, and while I'm in the area I'll try and catch up with AC. It's a good thirty-minute drive with daytime traffic, so a quick call to AC on route won't do any harm. The phone rings a couple of times and AC picks up, "Hello." I ask, "I'm heading your way as I've had to reshuffle the day a bit. How likely is it that you'll be ready?" AC replies, "I'm pretty much there, I can make a quick call to chase this last person up." I'm not overly bothered if he does or not as it sounds like he has the majority of the money, but a little pressure won't do any harm so I say, "Yes please. I could do with it all being in. I'll ring you when I'm five minutes out." AC acknowledges and puts the phone down.

This area is a typical large council estate, the sort developed back in the sixties and seventies. Street after street of redbrick houses and small terraced flats with a couple of high-rise flats thrown in for good measure. The estate is on the outskirts of town, surrounded by fields on one side and the inner edge is quite open. This area is rife with crime; and as a result of this you do get police operations going on in and around the area which presents a very real danger for anyone moving into or out of the area carrying drugs or money. It's extremely difficult for any police operation to set up in the area as they will more than likely be compromised by the locals. Every fucker knows someone who's at it and if the filth are on plot the word spreads very quickly. If there is any kind of police sting it's going to be on the edge of the area on the main roads leading in, so if any cars have been pinged by ANPR then they'll likely pounce when the time is right.

This is when a recce is needed, not just for my sake, but everyone else's. If I see anything that looks even the slightest bit off then I'll be making some calls. The good thing with being dry is that if I do get pulled there's fuck all to do me for. Driving into the area I have a good clear line of sight. I can see all the way to the end of the road. There are a couple of side roads on my right whose entrances are well exposed by a good few car lengths, which can provide an optional escape route if the road ahead looks a bit dodgy. But this in itself will bring attention to me, sometimes I just have to roll the dice – if I'm on a road and I feel that I'm committed, deciding to keep going is sometimes the better decision. This whole thought process is no different to the way of thinking if I was on a patrol in Northern

Ireland, fucking identical. I have to weigh up the options on the move – if a street or crossing point of a field in the bandit country looks a bit suspect, I have to approach with caution and assess the route as I close in, constantly planning alternative routes. This mindset comes in very handy when operating on the wrong side of the law.

I take a steady drive around the main road that runs along the perimeter of the estate. Once I've driven past all the roads that lead into the estate and I'm happy that there's nothing out of place I then call AC. "I'm ready when you are, are you here yet?" asks AC. I quickly reply, "Yes mate just a few minutes, where shall I see you?" AC confirms the location and an approximate time. AC's usually on foot; there's a fairly quiet side road that leads onto a residential street. I park up and just sit tight, he shouldn't be too long, and this is where I start to get a bit sketchy. I know what this area is like, and with my military background, I look more like a copper than a criminal and in this neck of the woods this is a bad thing. That's the thing about these kinds of estates, once I've breached the perimeter the police are no longer the problem. I'm in and I'm reasonably safe. It's when I park up and hang around waiting for someone, especially someone like AC as he can be late, this in turn means I stick out like a sore thumb, that's when the natives get restless.

Looking in my driver's wing mirror I see AC emerge from what must be a small cut through between houses, I drop down my window and discreetly stick my arm out, he won't recognise the car so he'll more than likely wander straight past. As he approaches he just clocks me and moves round to get in the passenger side. I'm busy scanning my mirrors for anyone that may have followed him. This might sound excessive but it's an old habit that I've happily maintained. AC sits down, looks over and says, "Alright mate?" As I pull out and start driving down the road I reply, "Yes good, how's things?" AC reaches into his jacket pocket and removes an A5-sized envelope, which looks pretty stuffed and says, "All here." It's too early to feel any sense of relief as the job isn't done yet but I say in a relaxed and grateful way, "Nice one, do you need to go again this week?" AC immediately says, "Yes but I'm unsure of numbers yet."

This is quite standard for a Monday. It's way too early to start loading folk up; fuck me, most people are still coming down from the previous weekend so the thought of getting on it again for some isn't worth thinking about. I pull up and drop off AC, and as he gets out I say, "Give me a shout in a day or so with your numbers. I hope to be good for Thursday." AC turns and as he leans into the car he says, "No problem. I'll be in touch tomorrow, see ya." He closes the door and just seems to vanish into the estate.

I place the envelope into the glove compartment as there's no point stashing it. If I get searched the police will find it anyway and it looks more suspect if it's stashed. That in itself will raise questions. Fuck me it's only a couple of grand, as long as the money is out of sight that's enough.

I start heading towards Billy's which is literally a couple of minutes away. The drive there is all residential streets and it's the middle of the day; that makes no difference in this area, hardly any fucker works so the day and night are almost the same when it comes to people's movement. There will be people hanging around regardless of the time of day or the weather. Closing in on Billy's place is no different to any other meeting. I still recce the route and park up in a way that means I can pull off in any direction without bringing attention to myself. Years ago one of my instructors said to me, "Be consistently inconsistent." I've always tried to maintain that ethos and it has worked well so far. I can tell Billy's in as his car is on the drive. This is the one place I'm happy to park outside of someone's house. One, because he's well known by locals and nobody will cause any problems, and secondly with an envelope full of dosh in the car it's the best place to park to reduce the risk of the car being broken into.

I knock on the door and it's opened by Clive. Clive is Billy's close pal, and he may as well live there because as far as I can tell he's always there. He welcomes me in and says, "Good to see you." I reply, "You too," as I walk through the hallway and into the lounge. Billy is sitting at a large dining room table covered in clutter, with a cup of tea on the go; he smiles and says, "Fancy a brew?" as I sit down and relax I say, "Yeah please, coffee, white with one, cheers."

Doing deals at Billy's is done in a certain way. If he welcomes someone into his house they will be treated as a guest and in return you will be expected to act like a guest. This means a conversation over a brew and not to drop off drugs or pick up money and fuck off out of the door straight away – that's the rules, like them or lump them. It just means that whatever plans have been put in place an extra thirty minutes or so needs to be dialled in. Moments later Clive appears with a cup of coffee in hand, he places it down on the table next to me; I immediately pick it up and take a sip. Billy says, "That coke was okay for the price, do you have any more?" This is music to my ears. I reply, "Not yet but I'm sure I'll be okay, I just need to get this bill paid." No sooner than I finish my sentence and Billy produces another envelope to add to my small collection and places it on the table in front of me. He says, "It's all there." I don't even need to check or question this as it's never been short. The denominations might be a bit mixed but I can live with that. I say "Nice one, Bill." We spend the next forty minutes or so just chatting shit. I'm happy to do this as I like Billy, but I do find it hard to relax as I still need to get this money out of the area; plus I still need to speak to Alfie and Si, and this is tainting any positive experience that I might have.

Having put plans in place for Billy's next load of coke, I walk out of the house feeling fairly confident about how the day has panned out so far. Billy lives in a corner house so I can discreetly look up and down the roads leading to and from his house. I do this in such a manner so not to look obvious and draw any attention to myself. I get in the car and put the money in the glove compartment with the money collected earlier from AC. I've now got nearly ten grand in the car. If I get caught with this it'll take some explaining and no matter what reason I come up with it won't be enough and the police are gonna be seizing it straight away. It will be held until they launch some kind of financial investigation, so every move I make, every time I do a recce or take my time assessing something, it's so I can do my utmost to prevent being caught.

Driving out through the area and heading towards the main road that leads out of the estate puts me on high alert and for good reason.

If there is some kind of operation going on this is where I'm most likely to be picked by the police; I can only hope for a bit of traffic to provide some sort of cover giving safety in numbers. So far so good, there is a fair bit of traffic flowing out of the area. I've got a bus, a couple of vans and some random cars creating a steady flow out of the area and onto the dual carriageway that flows past the estate. I'm positioned smack bang in the middle which gives me good cover in both directions. As I move with this body of traffic I look down the road and it looks clear. There's no sign of any police cars or any unmarked cars that could be undercover. I emerge from the estate and onto the dual carriageway heading back towards the city centre and Alfie's.

 I grab my burner and have a quick look. I've got missed calls from Si and Alfie. I should feel happy but I don't. The day has gone well so far and it's bound to go tits-up at some stage. The nature of both of these calls is likely to be very different so I'm having a bit of a personal debate on who to call first. Calling Alfie would make more sense, at least after talking to Alfie I'll have an idea of the complete picture therefore putting me in a much stronger position to negotiate with Si.

 I dial Alfie's number and he picks up pretty quickly. "Yes mate, are you popping down?" asks Alfie. "Yeah, I'm not a million miles away – are you at home?" I say, kind of hoping he is because Kate lives quite a way out of town. Alfie replies, "I am, I'm going nowhere." I say, "Nice one, I'll see you in a bit." Quite shocking stuff really, that's the best Alfie's sounded in months, I can only hope that his positive attitude on the phone is also reflected by way of a productive weekend.

 Without any delays I call Si. He answers, "Sorry I missed your call, you okay?" Fuck me, Si's apologising to me. I don't know if that's a good thing or not. I say, "No probs. I was just gonna give you some updates on how the weekend went, maybe look at getting some money to you either tonight or tomorrow." Si goes on to say "Look, don't stress about it too much, there have been some developments over the weekend and it looks like I backed the wrong horse." I instantly feel like a weight is being lifted from my shoulders.

I ask, "What's happened mate?" Si then says the words that I was hoping to hear. "I've been doing some digging over the weekend, you know Murray's mate Will?" I answer "Yes." Si then says, "Well, me and the boys were out on Saturday night and we bumped into him in town. We all went back to his place to get smashed and the conversation came up about you and the Russian kidnapping Murray. Well, Will let the cat out of the bag that he and Murray had fallen out because Murray blamed him for losing all the dosh and drugs on the night of Murray's arrest. And how Will had to flog all of his stuff to pay you. Basically cutting a long story short, you're right, Murray is full of shit and he lost most of my money to the police and not you. This does leave a small amount of my money that he gave you but it's just shy of three grand."

What a fucking relief, finally Si sees Murray for the bullshitter that he really is and to be landed with a three grand debt I can live with that. I don't agree with it so while I'm feeling confident I'm gonna make an offer to Si. "Mate, that's good news, so as it stands I owe you three grand. Will you take a couple of bags now and call it quits?" Si says, "Yeah fuck it, go on, as I feel a bit of a twatt for wrecking your stall." I have a bit of a laugh and say, "Don't worry about that, it saved me putting it away. When do you want to catch up?" Si says, "Whenever mate, I'm in no rush, give me a shout when you're ready." "No problem, I'll be in touch in a day or so, let me know if you need it sooner and I'll get one of the lads to drop it off." The call ends on a high.

Two grand, I can live with that. It's money well spent because I know that Si can be good to work with, and I'll be paying that bill tomorrow before Si changes his mind, which he has been known to do from time to time. I'm in a good place right now. In fact for the first time in quite some time I'm on the up. This is a feeling of empowerment that I rarely get to enjoy, but fuck me I'm going to enjoy this.

I'm nearly at Alfie's and as long as his weekend hasn't gone completely Pete Tong then I think this week will turn out just fine. I drive into Alfie's road and do the usual recce; I can see the standard crack whores stood at the top of the road that means the filth aren't on plot, so I park up and stuff all the money into the pockets of my cargo shorts. I exit the car and head for Alfie's. As I push the bell for Alfie's place I'm very conscious that I've got the better part of ten grand on me, and that's a perfectly healthy level of paranoia for what I'm doing. What I cannot do is let how I feel affect how I operate, so employing a bit of common sense I remind myself it is the middle of the day and I'm not exhibiting myself to be an easy person to rob so the chances of any fucker trying it on are quite remote.

Alfie answers the intercom, "Who is it?" I reply, "It's me you nob." He laughs and pushes the buzzer letting me through the outside door. Strange I can't smell skunk as I enter the communal hallway, this is a first – so either Alfie has run out or he's knocked it on the head. I walk in and Alfie is standing at the door, and for a change he's got some clothes on, well the bottom half anyway. He smiles and says, "Come in mate." This is a very different greeting to what I've been used to over the last few weeks. I walk into Alfie's lounge and it's been straightened up quite well. No signs of damage anywhere, if I am to be really picky I'd say it did smell a bit like a brewery but apart from that it looks like a normal dwelling. Even the settee looks safe to sit on without the need to double check for foreign bodies.

Alfie takes a seat next to me and the first thing that comes to mind is Frankenstein's monster. There's a set of staples running along the width of his forehead, but apart from that he looks well. "Thanks again for everything last week, and those pills were spot on," Alfie says. I reply, "No problem. I was a bit concerned about you but it looks like you've got yourself sorted." Alfie smiles and says "Yeah, Kate got right on my case and said she was gonna bin me if I carried on the way I was." I sit back and say, "To be fair mate, you look better now than you have for months – have you stopped smoking?" Alfie shrugs his shoulders and says, "Sort of. Kate made me sell the car to stop me from driving." This doesn't really answer the question but it's a good start.

Alfie and I chat for a good hour about recent events and I ask how he got on over the weekend. It appears to be good news all round. It turns out that Jeff sold Alfie's car to one of Jeff's mates giving him a few grand to pay for his pills. And Alfie has promised Kate that he'd cut down on his smoking and drinking, so he's quit smoking cigarettes, however he still likes a puff every now and again. This became evident when he started skinning up during mid conversation, and he wasn't holding back on the green stuff either. For my own peace of mind I just need to know that he's strong enough to carry on doing what he's doing. In light of Alfie's apparent turn around and my debt with Si being sorted, a lot of pressure has been released. It hardly seems necessary for me to attain more control over Alfie's lads; why should I interfere when I don't need to. I drop off the money that I've already collected with Alfie. This is to be added to whatever gets collected tonight. And by my calculations everything will be in, bar a few hundred quid. I leave Alfie feeling confident that he has all the instructions needed to round everything up and get the bills paid.

Walking back to the car I still can't believe how well today has gone. It's been several months, possibly over a year, since I last felt this comfortable. As I sit in the driver's seat once again the car is clean and dry so I don't need to stress about anything. Now would be the best time to call Cliff and give him the heads-up. The phone rings and Cliff picks up, "How did you get on?" he asks. I replied "Good, someone will be ready to see you later or first thing tomorrow – do you have any more cars left on the lot?" Cliff says, "Yes and the transporter is due to arrive again later to drop off some more." What do I do, shall I load up or not? One kilo isn't enough but two might be a tad over at this stage; fuck it, I know how greedy Cliff is and if there's a chance he can earn some more dosh then he'll go for it. He knows how I work and he has a good idea of my capacity to shift some decent numbers. I say, "If I take two motors there's no guarantee that they will be sold in time – is this okay?" Cliff happily replies, "Yes that's fine just let me know, give Flash a call to arrange the finances." I respond by saying, "It's already in hand, he'll get a call later but it may be in the morning if it gets too late." "Okay, bye," Cliff says and he puts the phone down. This is the start of a strange working relationship. There's no love lost but it's all about the money, so we just have to tolerate each other's differences.

Well I may as well head home, what I need to do now is start to concoct some sort of plausible bullshit for the Mrs. I don't like having to lie to her but if there's going to be some money coming back into the house I have no choice. And for a level of deception this bullshit needs to be laid on a foundation based on basic fact. I'll just say I've picked up some more confidential security work, simple, why complicate it. The feeling of stress slowly disappearing is such a nice experience. I've been suffering with high levels of stress since the Russian and I parted ways. The stress wasn't brought on by the split but more around the circumstances I was facing at the time. So for the first time in fucking ages I feel good. There will always be a slight level of apprehension about things that could potentially go wrong and as a result of this I will always be half cocked, but the day-to-day running of the business is much easier when there are no unnecessary headaches. I can think a lot clearer and focus on what's important, and that's spending quality time with my family and living every day like it's my last.

8. DARK TIMES ON THE HORIZON

Three months later.

I've been busy rebuilding my life; I've managed to get most of my clientele back on board for the coke and some for the pills. The positive thing is there have been no dramas whatsoever, which is almost unheard of in this game. This doesn't mean I haven't had the standard work-related stress waiting for the runners to check in but apart from that it's been sweet. Si was paid off ages ago, and although we haven't worked together I've kept a close link with him. Alfie has stayed out of trouble; he's still smoking pot and enjoys a drink. He's been given a year's driving ban and as a result of this he's stayed off the road and managed to stick to lifts or public transport, trains being his preferred choice. Alfie's boys are doing well. It's surprising how well they work when there isn't any pressure on getting the money in. Carl has kept his head above water, he's barely earning himself a wage, but the stall is ticking over so it'll do for now and like I said if it fails I'll just bin it. Cliff's been a bit of a twatt as he gets a bit gangster every now and again, but his coke has remained quite consistent in supply and quality. I'm shifting about four keys a week. He's at the point where he thinks I need his services more than he needs me, and the annoying thing is, he's right.

I've managed to fabricate my income so it doesn't look too suspicious. I just ploughed any extra cash into my car which is my true passion and where I now spend most of my spare time; don't get me wrong the Mrs and kids are enjoying life as well but I have to keep it relative to my visible lifestyle. Every opportunity that I get I'm in my car. I daren't think how much money I've thrown at it. I must have put twenty bags under the bonnet alone, but that was done a couple of years back when I first got bitten by the bug for tuning cars. Don't think of me as some idiot street racer because that's not the case. I genuinely love driving and it's the only outlet that I have found apart from selling drugs that gives me a proper buzz.

I was out for a late drive last night so I'm just surfacing from a good night's sleep and without these high stress levels I'm sleeping so much better. It's quite a liberating feeling to just get up and enjoy myself. It's a bit like being back on leave from my old army days. It's midweek and yesterday evening I took on a fresh batch of coke, another four keys were dropped off to Jeff's by Red Gee. Red Gee works all day so he has to do his running around during the evening. He doesn't appear to be particularly motivated and goes about his business with no real sense of urgency, but still he gets the job done. I'm okay for pills as I still have a couple of thousand left and they can go out tomorrow or Friday. I've even got a little bit of green in. Alfie was struggling so I grabbed some for him; only a key but it's all he needed. So all in all I'm ready for another prosperous weekend.

I've been looking forward to today as I'm taking Lance out for a spin in the car. He hasn't been out in it for a while and his friends are having a break out in the sticks, so we thought it would be good to take the morning off. Fuck off out for a drive and meet his friends for a late breakfast. It's about an hour away and we haven't set any times but I'm guessing Lance will be at his garage. He has a bit of space that he rents out for storage and I keep the car there. I don't have any room at mine and there's no fucking way it's being parked on the street. I get my shit together, say my goodbyes to my Mrs and get into the car.

Driving to Lance's is just a short trip, literally five minutes, and as much as I appreciate being able to use Carl's car while he uses my van, I feel that a slight upgrade might not be a bad idea. I have to maintain this cover, so any upgrade will have to be carefully selected, but I'll worry about that another day. It's almost nine and the weather is okay. It could be hotter for July. I'm happy as long as it doesn't rain. I get to Lance's lockup and as I pull into the drive I can see

Lance has the door open and it looks like he's warmed the car up and given it a bit of a clean. I pull up just away from the doors giving us enough room to manoeuvre out and not block any entrances.

I get out of the car, lock it up and say, "Morning, how's it going?" Lance replies, "All clean and fuelled up." I smile and say, "Cheers, shall we head off?" Lance closes the doors to the garage and says "Yep, they're expecting us to be there for about ten." I look at my watch and get into the car. Lance climbs into the passenger side. I start the car up and I'm instantly hit with an overwhelming feeling of anxiety – a level that I haven't felt for a good few months. Lance looks at me, he can tell somethings not right and says, "Are you okay?" I reply, "I'm not sure, let me just call the Mrs." I ring home and ask the wife if everything is okay, to which the answer is "yes", no problems. I decide to shake it off as an emotional glitch which can happen from time to time. I start up, slowly pull out and start heading for our destination. Lance and I are just chatting about random things like the stall and how Carl is getting on, and for the better part of the journey we just laugh and joke. Ordinarily I would be enjoying the simple pleasure of driving but it all feels tainted by this anxiety which is gradually building in the back of my mind, something is wrong. I don't know what but there is definitely something going on. I text Jeff and Alfie, "Can you call me please." The message doesn't go through to either of them but that's not surprising because Jeff is the same as Alfie when it comes to switching his phone on.

After a fairly pleasant drive we pull into the campsite and slowly drive along the central path looking for the plot where Lance's friends are camping. After a short while we came across them sat at a plastic picnic table outside of a couple of small caravans. They look over at us and wave as we approach. It's hard to make a discreet entrance in a car like mine on a campsite as quiet as this but I do my best and tentatively reverse into a space next to one of the caravans. I shut the car down. Lance exits the vehicle and heads toward his friends who are just chatting amongst themselves. I have another look at my phone and still nothing. I don't know why but I just can't shake this feeling that something is wrong. I get out of the car, walk over to Lance and take a seat. We've all met before and courtesy of Lance they are also fully aware of my secret income so I don't need to be on my guard. This doesn't settle these negative feelings that are beginning to manifest.

Another half hour passes and the weather closes in, it's not raining but the temperature has dropped enough for us to all want to retire into one of the caravans to continue our food and drink. I'm sitting here drinking coffee, eating a Mr Kipling's Country Slice and for some bizarre reason I am not in the room, my head has left the building, and it's saying "it's time to go". I need to make my excuses and get the fuck out of here. Lance can do whatever he likes, but I have got to go, right now. I look at Lance and say, "I'm really sorry mate but I need to get on, something's not right – do you want to come?" Lance, looking a bit concerned, says, "I'll come with you, what's wrong?" I look at everyone just sitting there staring at me and say, "I'm sorry guys but I forgot to sort something yesterday and I need to be around to get it done before a certain time." They just nod as if to say "yep no problem". Lance joins me as I head back towards the car.

I'm sitting in the car staring at the phone. Seeing a lack of activity is seriously bothering me. I do feel a bit of a twatt as I know Lance was looking forward to today. He'll struggle to understand what's happening with me emotionally, I know this because he's still laughing and joking when he gets into the car. He's barely closed the car door and I'm pulling away. Driving home is sending me nuts. I need to do something and even though I have no delivery report from Alfie or Jeff this doesn't stop me from calling them, and that's when my heart begins to sink. When I call a phone that is switched off I'll get a certain response, but when the phone is deactivated it'll be unavailable, and that's what I get from both Alfie and Jeff's. What the fuck is happening? I opt to break protocol and call Red Gee. I know he's at work but this is important. The phone rings a few times and Red Gee answers "hello" trying not to install any form of panic. I say, "Hello mate, just a quick one, have you heard from any of the lads today?" It sounds like Red Gee is heading somewhere quiet to talk and says, "No but I wouldn't have any reason to." I respond by saying, "Okay no worries. Did you manage to drop those cars off last night?" Red Gee says, "Yes, four motors," this would normally be good news but right now it's not. I say, "Okay, I'll call you later."

The next one of Alfie's firm I'm going to try is Spice. We've spoken on a number of occasions but never met. He seems keen and as far as I can tell he's quite reliable. The dialling tone for his phone rings a few times before he answers but the way my head is slowly frazzling even that feels like it's taken forever. He answers, "Alright? I don't normally get a call from anyone at this time." I say, "I know but I was trying to get hold of the lads, got any ideas?" There's a bit of a pause before Spice responds, "No, but I can call Milly if you want." Milly is Jeff's girlfriend, she's quite a character and originates from the Manchester area. I don't know her that well but what I do know is it's not worth bothering her just yet, not until I have some answers.

I say to Spice, "Leave it for now, but something isn't right, both of their phones are saying disconnected and that seems a bit weird. When did you last speak to them?" Spice who now sounds a bit concerned says, "I was there last night when Red Gee popped over. Alfie was there briefly and Jeff had a couple of friends around where we all stopped for a bit of a drink and stuff." I replied, "So what time did you leave and who was left there?" Spice says, "I bailed out at about half ten and left Jeff there with his two mates." I responded, "Okay mate, so all was good when you left – do you know where Alfie was?" Spice has a bit of a think and then says, "He left Jeff's at about eight, he needed to go out of town for the night. He was dropped off at the train station and that's the last we heard, so he might not have a signal." I'm slowly building up a picture of everyone's movements and so far I'm not seeing anything out of the ordinary. I ask Spice, "Are you local to Jeff's?" Spice says, "Not really mate, I'm busy at the minute." I say, "Okay, no problem I'll call you in a bit. Try to be ready if need be." "For what?" Spice asks. I reply, "Anything," and I end the call.

On the face of it everything seems normal, but the phones being disconnected aren't making a great deal of sense. I have one more person to call. He can be quite hard to get hold of plus he doesn't live locally, but he might just have the answers that I need. The Boy's phone is switched off but that's no surprise so I send a text "call me ASAP". In my mind I'm trying to justify why both of their phones are showing as disconnected, and no matter what reason I come up with it doesn't make any sense.

Topper or Tops, as he's sometimes called, lives fairly local to Jeff, and he used to do some running for me a few months back. He's good as gold and he introduced me to Billy and AC. Tops has been to Jeff's before but not for a while. I think the best thing to do now is see if Tops can do a recce for me. I give him a call. "Long time mate," Tops says. "Yes it's been a while, how's family?" I ask, trying to be polite as I'm about to throw him into the lion's den. Tops says, "They're all good, what can I do for you my friend?" I suck it up and just throw it out there. "I need a big favour." Tops being the kind of person he is, says, "Yes mate, what can I do for you?" How do I put this across in a way that it won't put him off, but then again he does owe me a bit of a favour as I took on AC as a customer. "Do you remember where Jeff lives?" I ask. Tops says, "Yes mate, unless he's moved." I give Tops a set of instructions, "No he's still in the same place. I need you to go and have a look and see if all is okay. Don't drive onto his road just park up and walk past and have a look at the house. Whatever you do, don't go in or hang around. If you see anything that looks out of place fuck off out of the area and give me a shout." Tops willingly agrees and says, "No danger, I'll be in touch."

I look across at Lance and it fucking amazes me that he can't comprehend what is going on in my life right now. He can't do because if he did he'd wipe his stupid fucking grin off of his face, but I shouldn't be annoyed with him it's not his fault, I chose this life not him. Lance is happily fiddling with the car stereo. It's nothing special but this doesn't stop him changing the tunes or retuning the radio; to be fair he can do what he wants because none of it fucking matters, not the way I'm feeling. I just need to get back, drop him and the car off and get to the bottom of things. I've still got about half hour's drive and I'm not in the mood for thrashing the car so the journey does feel as if it's dragging a bit and there is an uncomfortable level of quiet in the car. Most normal people would attempt to make some kind of sensible suggestion in order to alleviate any stress, but Lance remains oblivious and I don't think that's a bad thing because right now there's very little that Lance can bring to the table to make me feel any better.

Another twenty minutes pass and I'm finally closing in on Lance's garage. The phone goes and it's Tops; if I thought my anxiety was high before then this is something else. It's off the chart. "Hello mate," I say with bated breath. Tops answers, "Bad news, he's been nicked." Fuck, fuck, fuck that's all I can think, nothing else comes to mind. Okay I need to think – fuck, shit, for fuck's sake, is this really fucking happening? I need to get some sort of confirmation. I say to Tops, "So what did you see mate?" Tops replies, "I parked up at the end of the road and straight away I could see a couple of police cars parked outside. I was gonna bin it but because I brought the dog I thought it wouldn't look out of place walking past his towards the park. Besides I was curious and needed to see whose place they were in. I walked towards his gaff and slowed down as I passed his place. I could see into his front room. I saw Jeff next to a couple of coppers. He looked straight at me and slowly shook his head; at that point I fucking shot off."

Now at this point I'm still trying to think of another reason why the police are at Jeff's. Has he killed someone? Has he had a domestic? It might not be what I'm thinking, this is plain and simple denial, I'm fucked. I say to Tops, "Mate, I really appreciate you doing this, I'll be in touch." Tops says, "No problem, let me know if you need anything." I can't help thinking I'm going to need all sorts of help now.

I can't be bothered to tell Lance the score; not yet anyway, to be fair. I still don't know exactly what's happened, so until I do I'll just get rid of him, swap cars and figure out what the fuck I'm going to do. Dropping off Lance and the car is easy enough. He's happy to stick it back in the garage for me and seeing as he's still completely oblivious to what's happened we say our goodbyes and I get on my way. Right it's time to commit. I need to get over there myself and have a bit of a look. I call Spice; almost instantly he answers the phone and asks, "Any news yet?" I reply, "Jeff's definitely been nicked and the police were still there a little while ago. I don't know why yet – can you contact Milly and see if she knows the score? I'm gonna head over and plot up in the area. Are you in a position to meet me over there?" Spice says, "Yes mate, I'll give her a call now and head your way."

I start the drive across town. My mind is completely numb to whatever future I may face. There's so much I need to get my head around but right now there's very little I can do about any of it. I can't even think of anyone to call either. The text to The Boy hasn't gone through yet, so fuck knows what's going on there. I just hope he gets the text in time. This will be about damage limitation; and there will come a point that I have to assume that Alfie and Jeff have also both been nicked. Now if that is the case, and I pray that it isn't, there will be certain protocols that I may have to put in place but none of this can happen yet. First I need to get eyes on and no matter how much I don't want to do this, I need to verify that the stash of coke has been taken. For all I know Jeff has simply twatted someone and put them in hospital, and at the risk of sounding selfish, I fucking hope this is the case.

My burner rings. I look at it hoping to see Alfie's number but it's not, it's Spice. I take the call, "You okay mate?" Spice answers, "I've got Milly with me and this is all news to her. She hasn't got a clue what's happened. She spoke to Kate and she can't get hold of Alfie, so something's definitely up." It's beginning to add up and it's not looking particularly good. I say to Spice, "Look, I'm in the area and I need to have a look around first, so don't go to the house just yet. I'll meet you on the main road in about fifteen." Spice says, "Okay, see you in a bit."

Believe it or not, conducting a recce at Jeff's is fairly straightforward. The area lends itself perfectly; first things first I take a steady drive past the entrance to Jeff's street. It's a heavily residential area situated in an old part of the city with cars parked on both sides of the road, so for a car to slowly crawl along doesn't look out of the ordinary. As I approach the end of Jeff's road I slow right down, slow enough to see if there are any police cars still on site, and as far as I can see there aren't. Okay, next I need to get eyes on the back of the house. This is going to require a degree of maths and good guess work. The area that Jeff lives in is extremely hilly and the back of Jeff's street is facing downhill. It's so fucking hilly I can drive into an adjacent street, park up and see the back of the whole terrace of houses where Jeff lives. I just need to figure out which set of windows is Jeff's. I need to count along from the end house, identify the correct set of blinds or curtains and surmise which might be Jeff's kitchen window. I'm not particularly close to the house, and don't ask me why but I always carry certain items with me. I have a really handy-sized monocular with enough zoom to get a better view of Jeff's place. Doing this is all well and good, I just need to be sure someone doesn't see me, call the police, and get me arrested for being a fucking perv. It's really hard to see; I can definitely make out Jeff's place, but I'm not seeing any movement. It looks like his bedroom curtains are drawn and the kitchen is empty. Fuck it, that will have to do. I do a return journey and have another look down his street and there doesn't appear to be any changes, it looks as if the police have fucked off.

I pull back out onto the main road, where I instantly clock Spice; he's standing next to his car smoking and talking to a woman sitting in the car who I presume must be Milly. I drive past them and continue up the road for a hundred metres or so. I then do a U-turn and head back down the road passing them again. Spice hasn't moved and he still hasn't clocked me. I need to be completely sure in my mind that this area is clear of police and so far that would appear to be the case. If there are any around then fair play to them they've dug in well and they deserve the catch of the day. I park a bit further down the hill and on the opposite side of the road to Spice; I remove the battery out of my burner and leave it in the car, lock it and start walking back up the hill and towards Spice. I'm still on the other side of the road, he still hasn't clocked me but it is the middle of the day and it's a main A road out of the city, so there's a lot of traffic moving in both directions. I cautiously approach Spice and ask, "How's it going, any news at your end?" Spice says, "Nope," as he looks down at Milly who is still sitting in the passenger side of the car. Milly at this point gets out of the car and introduces herself in a strong Manchester accent. She's not what I was expecting. I remember Alfie telling me about her in the past, and in retrospect looking back at his description of her I felt that maybe he'd added a bit of dairy to it, but this is not the case, she's a fucking unit.

Together we take a walk around towards the far end of the street. It's a dead end and leads straight onto a park. We walk through the park and towards the entrance to Jeff's road, it's quite open from this end and as far as I can tell there are no police cars there, marked or unmarked. My nerves are jangling now as we approach Jeff's house. We all slow right down and none of us are talking, in hindsight we should have agreed on a plausible reason to be there. I guess Milly being his Mrs should be good enough and we are just giving her a lift. I'm not carrying anything and Spice shouldn't be either but if he is, he's fucking stupid. Jeff's front door is quite discreet. It's tucked behind a small tree and a neighbour's fence so you can't see his door from the street; you have to physically walk around the tree to even see his door. All three of us briefly stop at the gate, before we commit and head for the door. I go first and as I walk around the tree I look at the door. Fuck I've seen the first bad sign. Two round indentations on the door right next to the handle and lock. I know what they are and they're definitely new as I can still see flakes of paint hanging off of the edges.

What the hell do I do now? I'm here, so fuck it. In for a penny, in for a pound, I'll knock on the door. I gently tap it three times and take a couple of steps back. I don't know why but I'm politely waiting. Without warning Milly walks up to the door, looks at me, and with one swift kick she takes the door off its fucking hinges. Fucking hell, I wasn't expecting that, I know she's a unit but that was fucking nuts. We all make our way into the house; my idea of having a quiet discreet poke around has been slightly bungled by Milly taking the door off. Too late now I just need to do one thing. I know where Jeff would have stored the coke. He's worked with a lot of Bass which he always stores in the fridge, because coke is a white powder and in Jeff's mind they are the same, they're not but anyway I'm not splitting hairs, I know for a fact he would have stored it in the fridge.

There's nowhere else in his house that it can be. I head straight for the kitchen. Milly goes upstairs and Spice hangs around by the door. Either he's on the lookout or his arse is going. It's becoming quite clear that the house has been searched as there's stuff everywhere. Jeff's messy but not this bad. I walk into the kitchen and first thing I notice is the blinds on the window and realise that I was looking at the right house earlier, not that that matters now. The kitchen looks fairly undisturbed. I look at the fridge and momentarily I just hope that when I open the door it's still got my coke in it. I pull the door open – it's empty, completely empty, no food, drink, nothing. I am officially fucked. It's just a case of how fucked. I head out of the house as I pass Spice I say, "I'll see you back at the car," he just nods.

I walk back onto the street, and head back towards the park, emotionally my mind is still totally numb. I don't know what to feel. I know that I'll need to start putting things in place. I've never had anything like this happen before so I need to find a way to process what's happening. Cutting through the park I'm really on edge. The police could still be watching the area, after all they've just had a successful drugs bust and as yet I don't know who's been lifted. I know Jeff's gone, and all the signs are indicating that Alfie has also been nicked, so potentially two down. I opt not to go straight back to my car and I plot up a little way up the road where I can keep an eye out for Milly and Spice, who I hope will be out of the house soon. I guess I have this ridiculous notion that maybe Jeff had stashed the drugs somewhere else and Milly's going to find them and solve some of my problems. I say some, because coke or no coke Jeff's been nicked and I just won't know how far the collateral damage will spread, and if there is an aftershock it'll be soon.

Several minutes pass and I've been constantly scanning the main road for anything that may look out of place. I'm looking down the road towards my car. I see Spice and Milly emerge from the side road that leads from Jeff's place and they don't have anything in their hands, so it's confirmed I'm in trouble. Not only with the police but Cliff, and I don't know what's worse – the thought of being nicked or owing eighty grand to Cliff. I cautiously approach them. I already know what to say; this is where I have to take control, because this has now become about damage limitation and without someone taking control we're all fucked. I look at them both and ask, "Did you find anything helpful?" Milly replies, "No, I looked in the place where Jeff keeps the money, but there's fuck all there." I look at Spice, who is just looking a bit bewildered by it all and says, "Right, I need all of the numbers for Alfie's customers who may owe him money. I need the names of the people who he owes money to, and I need any back-up numbers for you. The Boy, Red and anyone else he works with. I also need someone to contact Kate, she may be able to confirm what's happened to Alfie." Spice says, "Yep no problem mate, I'll get on it." I quickly say, "Don't text me any numbers, write them down and we'll do this face-to-face. Milly can you speak to Kate?" Milly looks and responds saying, "Yes lad, I'll get myself home and call her from the landline."

Even though the shit has hit the fan, I'm feeling relatively calm. I finally say to the both of them, "I'm going to get rid of my burner. Spice, you do the same and do it now. Milly, have you got your contract phone on you?" She taps her pockets and says "yes". I look at her and say, "Put this in your phone." I give her my contract mobile phone number. I then say to the both of them, "This is not to be called from any burners. Can you pass it on to Kate? Spice, call me from your contract mobile and we'll sort the numbers out later." He replies, "No need mate, I have them all in this phone here." That's a bit of a result. I spend the next few minutes taking down any useful numbers, what good it will do I don't know, but I have to try. "Okay, let's see what happens over the next few days. I've got a lot of shit to deal with so bear with me, in fact fuck it. Spice, let's shoot down to Tesco's and get ourselves a new phone so we can start to clean up now." Spice nods in agreement.

On that, we get into our respective cars and head off to the local supermarket. I can pick up a cheap burner for thirty quid, and the type of phone that I buy allows me to Bluetooth my numbers straight across from phone to phone. Still feeling extremely cautious, I head into the shop and make my purchase. I exit the store still on full alert and look across to my car, half expecting to see it mobbed by the filth, but it's not so I go back to the car. Still being mindful of my surroundings, carrying out a simple task such as a number transfer can look dodgy in itself. I set up the phone and transfer all of my numbers across from my old phone to my new burner. As soon as this is done I dismantle my old one and discard it into a bin. I look over at Spice who is parked just a few cars away. He would appear to be doing the same. He looks over at me and nods. I walk across and tell him my new number, which he inputs straight into his new burner, he then drop calls my new phone and I save the missed call under his name. One down a few to go. This process is a pain in the arse but I can't risk contaminating phones that may have been compromised by the police. This process will require some face-to-face meetings with any customers that might be potentially caught up in the collateral damage of what's just happened. Any others I can simply text my new number.

    I'm achieving fuck all by being here. We say our goodbye. I've arranged for Milly to call me a bit later with any updates on Alfie or Jeff. It's quite likely that someone will be getting a call from one of them once they are allowed to make their one phone call from the police station. I get in my car and get the fuck out of dodge. The sooner I'm out of this area the happier I'll be, but happy that's a bit of a fucking joke. I'm gonna be up against it now. Happiness is no longer an emotion that is available. I leave the car park again. I'm scanning my arcs as I leave and pull onto the road. I'm looking for any cars that may be following me; fortunately the layout of roads in this area are in such a way that I can pull off into a residential street with little or no notice – this will force any cars that might be tailing me to take a turn onto a quiet road and risk being compromised. And this is exactly what I do. I take a series of turns onto quiet roads, still heading out of the area. I don't know where I'm going yet, I just need to be happy that I'm not being followed.

    After several minutes of counter surveillance, I'm satisfied that I'm not being followed. I head for an area of town which is reasonably close to home. I'm not going home yet, I simply need to start making calls to everyone I know and figure out a plan. This is a plan that I have yet to formulate. Fuck, I'm in so much shit I don't know where to start. I'm looking at three main areas of concern. The first one is am I going to be arrested, secondly is the Mrs going to find out, and finally how the fuck am I going to pay Cliff. No doubt there will be other things to contend with but these are the primary concerns. If I'm arrested then the Mrs will find out and Cliff will be more concerned about his own freedom than any money that may be owed. I know this because it's how I'm feeling now and the debt is secondary. If I am in the clear I'll need to lay down a huge smoke screen to disguise what's happening from my family and that's not going to be easy. It will require so much bullshit I don't even know where to start. So presuming that I don't get nicked and my family remain oblivious to my plight, then I can solely concentrate on getting this debt sorted, which by my calculation sits at eighty grand.

First things first. I send a bulk text out to all of my customers and suppliers, saying "this is my new number call me ASAP" – any responses from this text will filter through slowly and I need to be selective on what I say. If I'm honest and tell them it's on top, and we're all potentially fucked, then they will be forced to drop me out and I'll struggle to get them back on the books once it's safe to start trading. This will be one of those times where I'll just have to play it by ear. Once I've got Cliff's firm up to speed on what's happened I'll make a start on the list of Alfie's contacts provided by Spice. Now I know Alfie owes me money but I'm sure he doesn't owe any other suppliers. Any money that can be rounded up from his customers will be thrown into the pot with any funds that I can gather up from my end. This will be used to start taking lumps out of the debt I now have with Cliff.

I need to speak to Cliff and gauge how he reacts; depending on how he reacts will give me an indication of how hard my life is going to be over the coming months. Fuck it, this needs to be done face-to-face. I'm going to have to meet Cliff and tell him the score. My stress levels have more or less peaked, so making the call has zero effect on my state of mind. I look at his name in my phone and it still says "Cliff DO NOT USE". I'm starting to think why the fuck didn't I drop him out when the going was good, but it's too late for that now, plus who knows – maybe he'll be okay about it and exercise some flexibility. Fuck, who am I kidding, he's going to be a fucking prick and I'm dreading it. I make the call, I instantly notice that the dialling tone is indicating he's not in the country, I hang up straight away. This could be a bit of a blessing in disguise; I did hear that he was intending to fuck off for the summer so maybe he'll be away for a while.

I decide to call Flash instead, the phone rings a couple of times and Flash picks up, "Hello," he says. I reply, "We've got a serious problem. We need a face-to-face ASAP." Flash sounding a bit worried says, "What's up?" Again I respond, "Mate, we need to meet up now. I'll tell you then." Flash reluctantly agrees and says, "Okay, I'll see you at big Tesco, how long will you be?" Perfect I'm not far from there and say, "I'm local, ten minutes tops." I put the phone down.

Big Tesco's that'll do. While I'm driving there I'm thinking of the best way to break the news. How do I tell him that it's on top and we could all be fucked. Oh and by the way, I owe you eighty bags. So how I manage this meeting will dictate Flash, or more importantly Cliff's, next move.

What might happen is all of their arses might fall out and self-preservation might kick in and they may say, "Fuck the money, we're shutting down." But if I know Cliff he'll not give a toss as he's not the one running around taking the risks, he'll happily allow other people to take a fall for him as long as he gets his dosh. I'll just have to maintain an open mind and see what's what. If I can make it look as if we really are in trouble and the money will have to wait, it may give me enough wiggle room to come up with some kind of workable plan. At the end of the day, the most important thing is we all stay out of jail – if we're in jail there is no money, simple.

Considering the amount of shit that I'm in I'm not feeling too bad, although this is more than likely going to be down to shock rather than not caring, because I do care, I care about a great deal of things and one of my pet fucking hates is letting people down, even a jumped-up prick like Cliff. I've spent a long time building a good name for myself and I'm highly trusted with a good reputation. Put it this way, I've never been refused credit from anyone, ever and that's good, I always pay my bills. I can't always guarantee that it will be bang on time but I will always pay my debts.

Pulling into the so-called big Tesco is one of those places that I don't mind going into. It's usually very busy so that works well for both me and the police. I've got safety in numbers, and the police if they are on my case will have plenty of cover provided to hide behind, but seeing as I'm not carrying anything I'm not overly bothered. Fuck me, I haven't got anything left to carry, the filth already have it. I park up smack bang in the middle of the car park. I make a call to Flash, it rings for a while before he answers, "Sorry mate, I was driving, are you there?" he asks. I reply saying, "Yes mate, I'm going to be on foot near the cash points." Flash acknowledges this saying, "Okay, two minutes, I'll see you there." On that I exit the car leaving all my phones in the car and head for the area near the cash points.

I purposely park a little way from the meeting point. I'm constantly trying to draw anyone who might be following me out of the shadows, not just the police, any fucker could be following me. Drug dealing always leaves me open to robbery and kidnap and I will not let any fucker get the jump on me. I can see the cash points situated near the main door. It's a busy area next to a selection of disabled parking bays. There are a couple of benches there, and it's mid-afternoon so sitting here I won't look out of place. Fortunately as I arrive I see Flash pull up straight into a disabled bay, fucking typical behaviour of one of Cliff's boys. They have a total disregard for anyone. Little actions like this will increase the chances of problems, and these problems don't have to be illegal, they just piss people off. Pissed-off people are more than likely to cause problems when you don't fucking need them.

Flash exits the car and he's brought Skimmer with him. I like Skimmer, he's one of the good ones. He brings a sense of calm to the otherwise chaotic approach that Cliff seems to install into his runners. They both walk over to me. Skimmer holds out his hand and we shake hands. Flash just stands around looking dodgy. Skimmer asks, "What's up, mate?" I look at him and think to myself, 'how the fuck is this going to pan out?' I take a deep breath and say,

"The warehouse has been busted and my pal that looks after the stuff has been nicked. I've lost the fucking lot and then some." I need to add some dairy onto this as I have to make it sound much worse than it is. I'm not lying, I'm just being open with the truth. Flash just looks at me. Skimmer says, "Fuck, that's bad when did it happen?" Trying not to give any false hope I respond by saying, "Either late last night or early this morning. I don't know how it came on top or how many have been busted. I know that Jeff's definitely been lifted and potentially one other. What I do know is the house was searched and coke has been taken."

Flash and Skimmer look at each other. This is way beyond their pay grade. Skimmer says, "We'll have to let Cliff know the score; he's out of the country for a couple of months so I'll give him a shout later." So far so good, they haven't tried to bundle me into the boot and they aren't displaying any signs of stress. This is telling me that they probably have the debt covered, and as a result of this they won't have anyone breathing down their necks for the cash; however, on the flip side this means that it'll be Cliff I'm going to have to answer to. This in itself doesn't concern me, Cliff doesn't bother me, what bothers me is that I know what I'm like, and if I'm in debt I will do whatever it takes to pay the debt off, and a character like Cliff will take full advantage of this.

I look at Skimmer and say, "Give me a few days to see what I can do. First I need to find out who's been lifted and why or how it came about. Secondly, if I am in the clear, and I won't be sure for a week or so, I'll start looking into working this debt off. In the meantime I'll get the lads to round up what's available so I can take the edge off of it. The last thing I want to do is dive in head first and get us all fucking nicked." Skimmer again looks at Flash, who is now looking suitably concerned and says, "Yes mate, that sounds good to me but I will have to check with Cliff." It's very hard to gauge how this is really going to pan out. I just have to deal with one problem at a time, regarding any backlash from the initial arrests. I'm far from being clear and this is my biggest concern. Again I look at the lads and say, "I suggest you change your numbers ASAP, Skimmer nods in agreement and instructs Flash to go into the shop and purchase two new phones.

Flash wanders off into the shop and as he disappears out of sight Skimmer asks, "Are you okay mate?" What a breath of fresh air, someone else in this game that has a fucking heart. I put on a brave face and say, "I don't know mate, this is going to be a hard fucking slog. I just need to know if it's on top." Skimmer looks up and around, I can tell he has a sense of empathy, and at a time like this I could do with someone on my side. Flash is a foot soldier and he'll do as instructed. He doesn't have the capability to think outside of his role. Skimmer on the other hand has a mind of his own and will exercise as much discretion and flexibility as possible. He'll identify if I'm struggling or bullshitting. I look him in the eye and say, "My biggest problem is hiding this from my family. If my Mrs finds out I'd be better off in jail." Skimmer half smiles and says, "Let's see how this pans out. I'll put it across as best as possible to Cliff, but you know what he's like." I smirk and say, "Yeah he's a prick." Skimmer doesn't respond but he's not stupid. I say, "Look mate, I need to get off. I need to figure out a few things and round up what money is available. I don't think it would be wise for me to work just yet so bear with me." I hold my hand out and we shake hands. Skimmer says, "I'll send you my new one later." I reply, "No problem, speak to you later – if I have any updates I'll see you face to face. I would prefer to keep the phone calls down to a minimum for now." Skimmer agrees and I head off back to my car.

I casually walk back to my car. I'm still having a good look around for any police but to be honest this is more out of habit than necessity. So that's that, it's just a case of waiting for a response from Cliff, and no matter how well the lads have taken the news, I can almost guarantee that Cliff will overreact and he'll immediately start applying pressure for the money to be paid back. This is what pisses me off. I don't need to be pressured for the cash. If I have it I'll fucking pay it. Too many people judge me by their own standards. Cliff is the sort of person that will spend someone else's money and not give a toss about the debt. So he'll naturally assume that everyone is the same, and this is why I hate working with Cliff and people like him, fucking idiots. I get into my car and head out of the car park. It's fairly busy and I do my usual routine of deploying counter surveillance drills as I head out onto the main road. Everything looks good to me so it's time to put on a brave face and head home.

It's approaching four in the afternoon. As I drive home I slowly slip into a period of reflection. I was really looking forward to a nice relaxing summer, maybe a holiday with the family. We've not been away for ages and I was going to surprise them with a holiday in the sun. Our youngest has only just turned one so it would have been a chance to just get the fuck out of town for a couple of weeks; that's certainly not happening now, good job it was going to be a surprise.

Eighty grand that's a lot of doe to find. For some it may seem impossible and others may think that's fuck all, but it may as well be eight million, and that concerns me. I take a brief look at my phone. I have no missed calls or texts. I pull over and send a text to Spice. "Any news at your end?" I'm shutting down for now, call me on the other if need be." I pull back out onto the road and continue towards home, moments later I'm back in my area and I reverse into my parking space. I still feel emotionally numb. There's still way too much unfinished business to get my head around before I can think straight, that's just the way it's going to be for a while. I have to accept that my life is no longer my own and will be in the hands of the likes of Cliff until the debt is repaid in full.

9. THE BUTTERFLY EFFECT

It's extremely difficult trying to maintain any kind of normality in the family home when waiting for a potential barrage of bad news. The hours slowly pass by and I do my best to engage with my children but I'm struggling because my head isn't in the game. How can I be a proper father to my children when I'm knowingly going to drag them through this mountain of shit that stands before me. I can't, and it makes me feel terrible.

It's just after seven and my phone goes. I nervously look at it and it's Spice. Fuck this could be the news I've been waiting for or not, depending on what he says. I know I don't want to hear what Spice is about to say so I head out of the room for some privacy. I answer the phone and ask, "How's things?" Spice responds, "Am I okay to talk on this one?" By the sounds of it he's got some news. I really don't know what to think so I just say, "Yes, but just be careful what you say." Spice says, "Right, updates and it's more or less what we thought. I've just got off the phone to Kate, she's had a call from Alfie, he has been arrested along with Jeff. They also nicked another lad that was at Jeff's at the time. I don't know who it was but he has nothing to do with us. I think he's one of Jeff's mates who just got caught up in the net. Alfie was arrested first and this led to Jeff's place being done." For fuck's sake, I ask, "Okay, anything else?" Spice then says, "Jeff's pal was released on bail but Jeff and Alfie are both being remanded. I guess the girls will have to book a visit to go and see them and hopefully we can get a fuller picture." I shouldn't stress because this is the news I knew I'd be hearing, knowing they've been nicked is one thing, I just don't know how it happened and that's quite a bitter pill to swallow. I say to Spice, "Thanks mate, keep your ears open, maybe we can catch up tomorrow for a chat. Can you get Red to be around as well?" Spice responds by saying, "Will do mate, see you tomorrow," on that we end the call.

Twenty four hours earlier.

Alfie's plotted up at Jeff's with Spice having a smoke; he's just finishing off prepping himself for an out-of-town excursion to visit friends down south. There's a reasonably good market for a few odds and ends in the area, and Alfie seems to have it pretty well boxed off so he's going to be loaded up with a few hundred pills. So rather than rushing around and getting late trains, he's going to stay for the night and this will more than likely result in Alfie getting smashed out of his skull, and this is fine because he isn't driving and won't have to worry about getting hassled by the police. On the flipside, because Alfie doesn't need to drive, there's very little to prevent him from getting pissed or stoned from the off.

There's a light knock at Jeff's door, Jeff heads out of the kitchen. He knows who's at the door as he's just received a heads-up phone call. He opens the door and Red walks in loaded up with four keys of coke. Red greets everyone as he walks into the kitchen and places a heavy duty carrier bag full of coke on the kitchen table. This is where Alfie gets uncomfortable; although he's doing me a favour by offering his services, he really doesn't like the coke industry as it carries way too many problems. So when there are four keys of it plonked on the kitchen table right next to him, his primary feeling is he would rather not be here. The fact that there's also a kilo of bass, a couple of thousand pills and key of green in the room all being prepared for delivery doesn't seem to matter. Red grabs a beer from the side, walks out of the kitchen and sits in the lounge with a couple of Jeff's pals who have popped round for the evening.

Jeff is busy weighing up some bass for Spice to go and deliver to Alfie's customers. He's also sorting out some of the green. Alfie's phone rings once and it's The Boy. This is Alfie's que to leave, he stands up, grabs his bag of pills, and an ounce of green for The Boy, sticks the pills in his overnight bag, the green in his pocket and he checks his pockets for his wallet and phone, confirmed. Alfie is one of the few people I know in this game who only uses the one phone. That's not a bad thing, it just means that he doesn't have to live a lie and therefore is reasonably open about his lifestyle to everyone he knows. He looks at Jeff who is just staring at the pile of coke on his kitchen table, which is parked next to the rest of the drugs. Not wanting to keep The Boy waiting, Alfie walks straight out of Jeff's saying bye to everyone as he passes. He doesn't want to be in the house so the quicker he can go, the happier he'll be.

Closing the door behind him, Alfie walks towards The Boy who is parked directly outside of Jeff's with the engine running. Alfie gets into the car and as The Boy starts to slowly manoeuvre out of the parking space Alfie says, "Alright mate?" The Boy who is more intent on not hitting anything just nods. Alfie deposits the ounce of green into the glove compartment. Alfie indicates towards the glove compartment and says, "I've put that in there for you." Again the boy seems preoccupied with driving and says "cheers". Alfie looks down at the ash tray and sees a joint smouldering away. He picks it up and takes a big puff. The Boy winds down his window and slowly says, "Careful mate, I've loaded that one right up. That green you have is spot on." This would explain the lack of communication from The Boy, he's stoned; he can barely talk let alone drive. Driving stoned or pissed doesn't bother Alfie. He's an expert and is well accomplished at both, but even he has his limits and if he gets pulled again he will be going down. So he's just glad to have people available to give him a lift in his time of need.

The train station is literally five minutes down the road, but when your driver's under the influence of a strain of skunk strong enough to put an elephant on its arse this journey can take two or even three times that. It's just one road, one straight A road from Jeff's to the station. It's approaching eight on a pleasant summer's evening, there's fuck all traffic around yet The Boy is driving like an old woman, fifteen maybe twenty miles an hour in a thirty, and of course Alfie is completely oblivious to this as he's also smashed. He's just looking out of the car window taking in the scenery. Finally after a good ten minutes they arrive at the station. The Boy leisurely drives up to the main entrance and pulls over, as he does so he looks across to his right and amongst the waiting traffic sees a couple of police cars parked up. He's unfazed by their presence as they're only transport police and in The Boy's mind they aren't real police. Alfie gets out of the car, leans back in through the open door and says "thanks" to The Boy who is busy staring at the two police cars. Alfie closes the door, joins a steady flow of commuters, and heads into the station. The Boy pulls off and very slowly heads back out of the station.

The station foyer is fairly busy with people purchasing tickets and going about their business. In a brief moment of clarity Alfie wonders how many of these people are loaded up with drugs. This moment soon passes as Alfie becomes aware that he is more than likely the only one. Ordinarily these thoughts are enough to bring on a sense of paranoia, but not Alfie. He remains calm and undeterred. It's taking the majority of what's left of Alfie's normal thought process to figure out what train to catch. He did have it all figured out earlier but that smoke hasn't helped. He walks towards the counter and joins a small queue. It's only two people deep and there are four tills in operation so he needs to think fast, but fuck all is happening. What Alfie doesn't realise is where he's trying so hard to figure his shit out he's actually talking to himself and pulling some ridiculous faces to rival his level of confusion. He is extremely confused. Add this to what looks like he has put his face into a wood chipper and you've got someone who is looking and acting like a fucking nutter.

The next counter is made available by an automated speaker saying, "can the next person please proceed to counter number 3". The man at the front of the que walks up to the counter. The person in front of Alfie shuffles forward a space and immediately the speaker system delivers another announcement "can the next person please proceed to counter number 7". The person in front of Alfie heads off and Alfie is still none the wiser. He's completely forgotten his script – too late the announcement goes off again, this time it's Alfie's turn and he wanders off towards counter number 4. He stands in front of the glass panel and places his bag at his feet; he reaches into his pocket and takes out his wallet. The ticket attendant looks up and says, "Yes sir?" Alfie just stares at him vacantly, this goes on for long enough to make the attendant visibly agitated. Alfie rifles through his wallet. It's so full of crap, a combination of money, old sales receipts, savers cards and old train tickets, even this simple action is a drain on Alfie's mental resources. The attendant is still patiently waiting for Alfie to sort his shit out, finally Alfie remembers his script and asks for his ticket. The attendant processes the ticket and says, "Twenty-eight pounds please." Trying not to drop any of the junk stored in his wallet Alfie takes thirty pounds out and pays the attendant. He grabs his change along with his train ticket, picks up his bag and ambles off.

Alfie walks towards the platforms where there is a large screen displaying all of the trains' departures. Alfie stands amongst a small crowd and looks up to discover that the train he intended to catch departed ten minutes ago. 'Bollocks,' he thinks to himself – now he's got an hour to kill. He proceeds directly to the bar. Alfie walks into the bar where a few late evening commuters are enjoying after-work drinks. He walks up to the bar and says, "A large glass of red please." The bartender walks off and starts to prepare a glass of red wine for Alfie. Alfie again digs into his wallet and pulls out a tenner. The barman returns and places a very large and full glass of red wine on the bar and says, "Two seventy-five please." Alfie hands the barman the tenner thinking it would be cheaper to buy a bottle. The barman returns with a handful of change and hands it to Alfie.

Alfie takes a large sip from the glass of wine, walks over to a table. He places his wallet on the table, his bag on a chair and takes a seat looking out of the bar and towards the train platform. Alfie's faculties slowly return as he gradually gets over the smoke he's just had, and as normality returns so does Alfie's frustration of missing his train, but there's fuck all he can do about that now. It's not the boy's fault, he's one of the few people around who's happy to oblige with a lift, even though most of the time he is off of his trolley. Alfie gazes out of the large windows that provide a view of the old Victorian-style train station. He can't help thinking that although a life in crime has its problems, it also provides moments that allow him to sit back and enjoy the simple things in life, like a large glass of wine.

Alfie polishes off the glass of wine within a few minutes. He looks at his watch and sees that he still has a while before his train arrives; on that he opts to go back to the bar for another drink. He grabs his wallet and walks back up to the bar. The barman looks at him and says, "Same again?" Alfie nods and says, "Please." The barman walks off while Alfie pulls a fiver from his wallet. On the barman's return Alfie asks, "How much for a bottle?" The barman says, "Sorry sir we don't sell by the bottle." Alfie, feeling slightly hard done by says "okay" and pays for his second glass of wine. He returns to his seat and continues to stare out of the window. His train is due in about forty minutes and it's on another platform, so while Alfie enjoys his drink he mentally calculates how long it will take him to get to the platform. He doesn't want to be running last minute as he can't afford to be missing the train.

Alfie's head has now returned to normal and for most people this is a good thing, but Alfie prefers to feel like he's under the influence of something. He knows he's getting on it when he finally gets to his destination, so he necks the glass of wine. By his calculations he can do a few more glasses before he needs to head off for the train. So yet again Alfie heads to the bar; the barman has already poured Alfie's wine. Alfie rifles through his change, pays the money and returns to his seat. He's definitely feeling a bit fluffy around the edges and this brings a warm yet false sense of security for Alfie. This is where Alfie likes his head to be. Well it is for now, he is mindful that he is carrying so he wants to maintain an element of control and not be too pissed up.

Three, four, five glasses later and not only is Alfie half cut but he's ready to head off for his train. He gathers his belongings ensuring he has his wallet, phone and bag in possession. He gets up, bids the barman good evening and exits the bar which is now fairly empty. He wanders off towards the large display screen and has a look to confirm his train time and departure location – fucking cancelled. Still undeterred, Alfie just looks at the information to see if there are any other options. He doesn't want to take certain routes as he knows that police activity on some trains can be heavier than others, this is why he gets this particular train. He looks down the display to see that the next and last train is at ten forty-five, that's a bit fucking late for Alfie but he has no choice.

Alfie starts heading back to the bar but stops short and has a think; he's got nearly two hours to kill so thinking sensibly he decides to save some money and fuck off down to the offy to purchase his drinks instead. He knows there's a corner shop just a few minutes' walk from the station, it's a nice night and he has plenty of time. Alfie heads out of the station and casually walks down the road towards the exit; as he approaches the main road he looks across the road and can see the shop he's aiming for and it appears to be open. Alfie quickens his pace slightly, he has this niggling thought that it might close at nine and, as it's just after five to, in a state of panic he breaks into a run. Alfie legs it across the main road and beelines straight for the shop. Although Alfie's health is fucked he's in relatively good shape, so a burst of energy lasting for a few seconds isn't really a problem especially for something important like booze, it just means he'll be coughing up lumps for a while, and as far as Alfie is concerned that's a small price to pay for salvation.

Alfie gets to the shop entrance and is relieved to find it's open. Trying his best not to cough his guts up he walks in and heads straight for the alcohol section. He looks at the selection on show, he knows exactly what he wants – he always buys these three-litre boxes of cheap plonk, the ones where you punch a hole in the box and remove a tap that is attached to a foil bag filled with wine. Alfie loves this shit, because these boxes used to fit perfectly on the dashboard of his car while he was driving and the weight, shape and low centre of gravity of the box would still allow Alfie to drive carefree without the risk of spilling cheap red all over his fine upholstery – and he wonders why he got banned. After a few moments he finds the one he's looking for and grabs two boxes off of the shelf. He heads to the cashier, places them on the counter and takes out his wallet; the Asian gentleman behind the counter rings them through the till, while Alfie pulls a twenty from his wallet. The cashier says, "Eighteen pounds please." Alfie smiling at himself hands the man his money, the cashier gives Alfie his change and says "Thank you sir." Alfie just nods and walks out of the shop.

With six litres of wine and several hundred pills in possession, Alfie now feels ready for a night out, that's if he ever gets there. This time he steadily crosses the road and heads back up towards the station entrance. It's just after nine and there are still quite a few people knocking around. Alfie decides to head back to the bar, not so much for a drink but for a glass, he isn't in the habit of drinking straight from the tap, although if push comes to shove he will. He enters the bar which is still fairly empty, walks up to the bar and notices that the previous barman isn't here, this is a bit of a knock – Alfie was hoping to ask him for a glass to drink his wine from, so he reluctantly decides to purchase yet another glass of red, just to secure a glass. The new barman returns with a large glass of red, Alfie pays the bill and heads off towards a quiet table in the corner of the bar, somewhere where he can drink his own wine without being caught.

He sits back, digs in and readies himself for a moderate session. He places his wallet and phone on the table, and his bag on the chair next to him in a position where he can discreetly top up his wine, Alfie has a quick scan around the bar, it's more or less empty apart from a couple of late night commuters. He enjoys the wine he's just purchased as it's considerably better quality than the shite he has in his bag. He looks at his phone and sees zero activity, this is quite normal for Alfie. He's well established in the game and the traffic on his phone is minimal. It probably won't ring at all, if he makes an arrangement it just looks after itself, plus Alfie gives his runners strict instructions not to bother him when he's running.

Alfie has successfully made a dent in the first box of wine, the only way he can tell if it's running low is when the pressure drops off and he has to start tipping the box forward in order to access the wine that remains in the corner, but thankfully he's not at that point yet. He's sat here people watching, and as the time passes he sees the station gradually empty out. An hour passes and he's still going strong, his train is due in about forty-five minutes so he's just doing his best to not plough through all of his wine as he would prefer to have a box left for his journey out of town.

Ten o'clock strikes and Alfie hears the barman say, "Time please." This comes as no surprise to Alfie but it doesn't stop him feeling a tad put out that he has to leave the relative comfort of the bar and head out onto the platform to continue his party. He looks across the bar. It's empty apart from this one chap sat by the door who's just finishing off his drink, so aside from him and the barman the bar is empty. Alfie gathers up his possessions and, discreetly placing the glass into his bag, gets up, slowly walks out of the bar and onto the platform. As Alfie exits the bar he looks around and apart from a few stragglers roaming around and the standard complement of staff, the station looks deserted.

Once again Alfie walks up to the display screen to confirm if there are any last minute changes to his departure and thankfully this time there aren't. His train is due in around forty minutes on platform eight; with this info in mind, Alfie heads for the overpass which will take him towards the various platform gates. He's not in a rush so he just casually strolls up the stairs and onto the overpass, which is also devoid of any people. Alfie looks out across the multitude of rails converging on the station and he can just about see the sun starting to drop down behind the buildings that line the urban horizon. It'll soon be dark o'clock and for most running drugs at night takes on a whole new set of characteristics, but not Alfie he just soldiers on.

As Alfie drops down the stairs and onto platform eight he notices a couple sat on a bench on the opposite platform, but apart from them the place is more or less deserted. He walks along the platform to find a bench that is out of sight and isn't covered in pigeon shit which is easier said than done. Alfie still has a forty-minute wait and a fair bit of wine to get through. He spots a fairly quiet bench at the top end of the platform, away from prying eyes but still close enough to look like he's not hiding from anything or anyone and therefore not drawing any unnecessary attention to himself.

Alfie takes a pew and places his bag next to him; he unzips it slightly and removes the glass. He then reaches and grabs the lighter of the two boxes of wine and also removes it from his bag, and this is also placed on the bench between his bag and his legs, so it's not hidden but out of sight. Alfie pours himself a large glass and sits back to take in his new scenery. As he looks around he sees that the couple on the opposite platform haven't moved, but the man that was in the bar is now sitting a couple of benches down from Alfie. He's not doing anything so Alfie just cracks on with his wine.

Another ten minutes pass but to Alfie the time seems to be dragging, he refills his glass and decides to put the wine back in his bag. As he shifts the contents around to fit the wine in neatly he notices a small tin; fucking bargain, it's his pot tin. Alfie's over the moon, he can now have a smoke before he gets on the train. Alfie's pot tin is one of these old original style tins that people used to have for putting their rolling tobacco, papers and rolling machine into, it's got a hinged lid which when opened all the way doubles up as a perfect tray for rolling joints.

Alfie places the tin on his thigh and opens the lid all the way; he glances at the contents and as far as he can see it's fully equipped. Alfie takes another sneaky look down the platform, just to double check for the filth; no changes and all he can see is this couple and that guy from the bar. Alfie proceeds to build a joint, and seeing as he's an expert he can complete this task in a fairly short time. Another five minutes pass and Alfie has completed two things – the joint and he's drunk his wine – this is working out quite well. He places the pot tin and the empty glass back into his bag. Again he has a sneaky look up and down the platforms before he sparks up his joint, no changes all round.

Alfie leans forward and holds the joint down between his thighs where he can give it a brief inspection prior to ignition, everything looks good, no holes, wet patches or bits of wood poking through the paper. He rips off the twist at the end and flicks it away in the direction of the track. He leans back, looks up slightly, puts the joint in his mouth and lights the fucker up, he pulls on it, hard; this is pure pleasure, he knows it's killing him so why not make the most of it cherishing every moment of this experience. Alfie exhales a huge cloud of dense smoke and smiles as his lungs start to burn, this mild discomfort means he's on his way to utopia.

Alfie gently slips into a world of his own as he gradually works his way through his joint; ideally he would like it gone before the train arrives, but seeing as he still has about twenty minutes to kill he just sits back and enjoys the sensation of being stoned. Time does tend to drift when in this state and Alfie is fully aware of this, fuck me he used to drive in this state, always making his destination so the simple task of getting on a train is well within his capabilities. Puff after puff the smoke slowly disperses, across the quiet platform, which is still populated by the four of them – the couple across the way, the man from the bar and Alfie.

Alfie looks at his joint, which is almost done; he then looks at the time and it's approaching ten forty-two. He takes one last pull on his joint, gets up and strolls towards the platform edge where he drops the joint onto the track below and returns to his seat. He hears an announcement confirming the arrival of his train in two minutes, about time he thinks, this has been a right fucking mission – he's been on the road since half seven, and has only travelled a couple of miles. He gathers his possessions and stands by the platform edge eagerly waiting for the train to arrive. Concentrating like fuck, he can hear the familiar sound of a train approaching as the running gear crosses the points where the tracks are joined. He looks out into what is now darkness and sees a set of lights approaching the platform, Alfie is trying to gauge which door to line himself up with as the train slowly pulls onto the platform and stops.

Alfie starts walking towards the nearest door, as does the man from the bar, Alfie gestures to the man to go first but the man reciprocates the gesture to which Alfie accepts and opens the door to the train. As the door opens he sees two men standing there. Alfie is thinking, 'fuck, I don't like the look of this, why are they just standing there?' From nowhere Alfie feels someone grab his left arm and say, "Excuse me sir, British transport police, would you like to come with us, everything will be explained in the office." Alfie's first thought is to start fighting, but he knows this probably isn't the best course of action. He's got pills on board so he needs to remain calm, for now at least. The two men disembark the train, one of them takes the bag from Alfie while the other assists the man from the bar to handcuff Alfie.

Being arrested isn't a new experience for Alfie, but being arrested for drugs is. The three police officers escort Alfie from the platforms to the cop shop which is situated at the end of the main building. He is led into the building and towards a small custody desk, not as grand as the ones you might find in a regular police station but nonetheless still fit for purpose. The police officer that was in the bar says, "You are now being detained for the purpose of a drugs search." On that they remove Alfie's cuffs, one of the officers turns Alfie to face him and he says, "Do you have anything on you that you shouldn't have or anything that may harm me?" Alfie just looks at him and shakes his head, he's saying fuck all. The officer completes the search and apart from Alfie's wallet, some loose change and his phone, nothing is found.

Placing these items on the custody desk, the officer then looks at Alfie's bag. Alfie tries not to show any signs of distress because he knows he's fucked and in Alfie's usual twisted way he's half looking forward to the reaction that will follow with the discovery of the pills. The officer kneels down, unzips the holdall and opens it up as wide as possible in an attempt to reveal its contents. The officer looks into the bag and carefully removing the first item he says, "One large unopened box of what appears to be wine." Alfie looks at the copper thinking, 'you anal fucking twatt.' The officer continues to remove the bag's items one at a time, commentating as he does: "One opened container of what appears to be wine, approximately a quarter of a box remaining; one large stolen wine glass; one, two, three, four pairs of underpants; two pairs of socks; two shirts." Alfie's thinking, any fucking minute, when he gets to my shoes. The officer delves deeper into Alfie's bag. "One metal tin," the officer opens it up and says, "containing, a packet of large rizla, several cigarettes, and what would appear to be some form of vegetable matter." Again Alfie thinks, 'fucking knob, get the fuck on with it, the suspense is fucking killing me.' The officer pulls out the pair of shoes and says, "One pair of brown slip-on shoes." As he weighs them up he then looks into the shoe itself and removes a bag of pills.

A large smile creeps across the officer's face, he knows he's hit the jackpot and says, "One bag of unidentified white pills."

Alfie looks at his pile of stuff on the desk while the police are discussing their next course of action, but Alfie doesn't give a toss, he's just staring at his shit and the fact that the police have separated the drugs and the wine glass from the rest of his stuff. 'Really, the fucking glass, fucking pricks,' Alfie thinks. The police look at Alfie and give him the opportunity to shed some light on their findings but Alfie remains tight-lipped. He is then told, "You will remain here until a police unit is available to collect you and take you to the police station; on your arrival you will be processed and interviewed, do you have any questions?" Again Alfie just shakes his head; the police escort Alfie to a holding cell where he is asked to remove his shoes and leave them on the floor outside, they usher him in and close the door behind him.

Much to Alfie's dismay the experience of being nicked has done a very good job of sobering him up. He can't help thinking about the box of wine potentially only feet away in the other room, what a fucking waste. He looks at the bed thinking the time must be getting on for midnight, so with little else to do or think about he decides that he'd best get some kip in order to prepare himself for the pending police interview, which he knows is going to be a real eye-opener. Alfie grabs the shitty mattress that doesn't look particularly inviting but even so remaining fully clothed he unfolds it and lies down. The blanket provided can either be used as a blanket or be folded to make up a makeshift pillow. Alfie opts to use it as a blanket; not even considering if it's clean he just throws it over himself and closes his eyes. There's quite an eerie silence about this place. All Alfie can hear is the sound of the odd door being opened or closed, certainly not the usual chaotic sounds of a police station, nevertheless he eventually drifts off and falls asleep.

Without warning and what feels like only seconds after he's dropped off, he hears the cell door being unlocked. A voice says, "Your transport has arrived sir, if you'd like to get yourself together." Alfie swings his feet around and plants them on the floor; he rubs his face and looks towards the door where he can see a different policeman, this time he looks like a real one. Alfie gets up and walks towards the cell door, he's beginning to feel a bit anxious as the sleep he's just had however long it might have been has sobered him right up. He's even feeling the edge of a slight hangover. Alfie slips his shoes on and looks towards the custody desk, where he sees the same officer manning the desk; Alfie is ushered towards the desk where the desk sergeant says, "You are now being transferred to another police station where this investigation will be continued, do you have any questions?" Alfie remains silent and simply shakes his head.

Two uniformed police stand next to Alfie and secure his hands with cuffs, while a third one appears carrying a couple of large sealed clear plastic bags containing Alfie's stuff. Alfie casually glances at the two bags where he automatically zooms in on the wine, he can't see the pills, but he does just clock his pot tin. The three police look at each other and one says, "Okay let's go." Alfie is gently nudged as they all move off towards the exit. As they move out of the station Alfie notices a clock on the wall indicating that the time is just after one twenty in the morning, "Fuck me, an hour's kip is that all I had." He is taken through a double door and out onto the car park.

All things considering, it's a fairly pleasant night and the fresh air comes as quite a welcome break. Alfie looks across the small car park where a couple of police cars and a van are parked up. Alfie is escorted towards the van and as he looks at the van he can see across the car park exit and out towards the main entrance to the train station which is now completely deserted. Quite a stark difference to when he was dropped off several hours ago by The Boy. Alfie is led towards the rear of the van where one of his escorts opens the back doors revealing a cage. Alfie is immediately asked to get in and he complies. Alfie takes a seat and looks out as the officer slams the door shut. 'No need to slam the fucking door,' Alfie thinks. Alfie then turns his attention to the front of the van, where he can see through the clear panel positioned between him, the cage and the interior of the van. The three coppers take their seats and the driver starts up and pulls out.

This journey means nothing to Alfie. It's just one step closer to a prison sentence. He's pondering about what comes next whilst frantically trying to remember the name of his solicitor. After a short while the van slows down and stops. Alfie can see a large set of gates in front of the van; the driver mutters something into an intercom and the gates begin to slowly open, the van pulls forward and into what must be a secure police car park. The van manoeuvres around and reverses into a space. As the driver shuts the engine down, Alfie puts his head in his hands and takes a deep breath; he hears several doors being opened and closed at the same time. The next thing he realizes is the back doors being opened and sees the three of them standing there. If Alfie were the sort of person to feel intimidated this might come across as intimidating, but not Alfie, not in a long shot – things like this don't even register. He looks them all square in the eye, not in a threatening manner but just to put the message across that he isn't going to be intimidated or threatened.

The door is opened and Alfie climbs out, the officers take up their positions and escort Alfie into the police station, this one's much bigger and is more than likely the main central police station. Alfie walks along a long corridor towards the custody desk; this is more like it, he can hear pissheads kicking doors, people shouting at each other from cell to cell. As he passes a row of cells, most of which seem to be occupied for one reason or another, all of them have some kind of footwear placed outside of them. They approach the custody desk, the cuffs are removed and Alfie is asked to confirm his details and he is asked if he wants legal representation to which Alfie responds "yes" and as if by magic the name of his solicitor pops back into his head. The desk sergeant takes the information down and then says, "Okay, I'll chase them up. I see from your records that you were with us just a few months ago so there's no need to do your prints again. Have you had any more tattoos done since your last visit?" Alfie shakes his head. "You'll now be secured here until we've conducted an interview, do you have any questions?" Yet again Alfie just shakes his head. He's then taken to yet another cell where he kicks off his shoes, goes in and gets straight on the bed.

Alfie's trying to sleep but he's just staring at the ceiling. The gravity of his predicament has now begun to set in but he still refuses to stress about it – what's the point, his path is set, he's going to jail, he'll be charged and remanded tonight and sent to the big house in the morning. He's led here contemplating if he should have a shit or not. He doesn't like the look of the toilet but he is bursting. Fuck it, he gets up heads towards the toilet which has no door and is a metal stainless steel item with no seat. It looks clean but looks can be deceiving; fortunately there's toilet paper available, he takes a seat and offloads. Alfie finishes up and heads back to his bed, he's now hoping that the police come to his door as the whole cell fucking reeks of shit; it should be enough to make their eyes sting, the thought of this is enough to make Alfie chuckle to himself.

Alfie has no idea of the time. He knows it's still the middle of the night as there's no natural light coming through a small rectangular window located at the top of a wall to the rear of his cell, and with it being the middle of the summer it starts to get light at about half four so, if he were to make a guess, he'd say it's about half two, but that's just a guess for all he knows it could be four. He doesn't know if he should try to sleep or not. He could be dragged out for his interview at any time. He opts to just lie there looking at the ceiling, curious if the cell will still smell of shit when the door is finally opened.

It's hard to say how much time has passed when Alfie finally hears a click as the cell door is opened. The officer in charge says, "Your solicitor's here." Again Alfie swings his feet around, gets off of the bed and heads towards the door. He slips his shoes on and is taken to a small interview room. Alfie walks in to find his solicitor sitting there, looking extremely tired. Alfie takes a seat opposite him and the officer closes the door and locks it. Alfie spends the next half hour or so discussing his options, and they are limited. He is advised to go "no comment", standard stuff for drugs charges. His brief makes it quite clear that he'll more than likely be charged with "possession with intent to supply". None of this is news to Alfie, he just hasn't thought about it until now. His brief does advise Alfie that if he is in a position to provide any information that may help the police with their inquiries, any judge would look on this quite favourably and Alfie may be offered a deal. Asking Alfie to even consider this has the same effect as telling him his mum just died, there's not a hope in hell that he'll ever grass. Alfie's brief looks at Alfie and says, "Are you ready?" Alfie quickly replies "yes". His brief gets up and knocks on the door to alert the police that they have finished talking and are ready to be interviewed.

The door opens, Alfie gets up and follows his brief out and into a small corridor, the police officer ushers them in the direction of another room only a few feet away; a sign on the door says "Interview Room 1 knock before entering". The police officer opens the door and gestures to Alfie and his brief to enter and take a seat on the left-hand side. It's a small room with four chairs, two on each side of a table; the table has a recording device stationed next to the wall, apart from that the room is empty. The officer asks, "Would anyone like a drink?" to which Alfie replies, "Coffee, white with one," and his brief says, "Just water please." The policeman locks the door and wanders off. Alfie just waits in silence as he isn't sure if the room is bugged so he just sits back and tries to relax. Inside he's getting nervous as hell; after all he is human, only just.

After a few minutes the door is opened and two plain-clothes men walk in. One of them is carrying one of the clear plastic bags where Alfie spots the bag of pills, his pot tin, wallet and the wine glass. They both sit on the two chairs opposite Alfie and his brief, placing the bag on the floor to their rear; they introduce themselves as Dave and Neil and inform Alfie that they are part of the drug squad. Again this brings little news to Alfie; he knows what's coming and does his best to remain calm. Not a lot is being said. The two coppers are just looking through paperwork, while Alfie's brief seems to be doing the same. It would appear that everyone in the room would seem to have an idea of what's happening except for Alfie – he's sitting here waiting for his coffee.

The door goes and in comes the refreshments. Alfie is handed a small light-brown take-away cup of coffee while his brief is given a clear plastic cup of water. The officer leaves and locks the door. Dave looks at Alfie and delivers a statement informing Alfie that he is now going to be interviewed and this is his opportunity to tell his version of events. To Alfie it's just "blah, blah, blah". He isn't remotely interested in anything they have to say, he knows he's banged to rights so they just need to get the fuck on with it. Dave takes out a small packet of tapes, removes them from their packaging and writes some information on them both, he then inserts both of the tapes into the recording device and presses record.

The interview begins, Dave begins to reel out a list of generic questions, things like "can you confirm your name?" and on every occasion Alfie says "no comment". As the questions progress in a direction that becomes less generic and more relevant to Alfie, the nature of the questions take on the tone of things like "where were you travelling to?" and Alfie is faced with some questions that he really would like to answer but once you go "no comment" that's it you're committed. Neil looks at Dave, reaches into the evidence bag and produces Alfie's pot tin, placing it on the table they ask, "Can you explain to us what this is?" Again Alfie says "no comment". Dave opens the tin and begins to remove the contents of the tin listing them as he does. Alfie sits there, alternately staring at Dave, Neil and the contents of the tin. Alfie's thinking, 'get to the fucking point, bring out the pills and let me get to sleep.'

The line of questioning continues and skirts around why Alfie was at the station and where he was intending to go. As Alfie is not complying, the interview continues to hit a brick wall. Finally the pills are produced by Dave and they are placed on the table, sealed in an evidence bag. Neil asks, "Can you tell us what these are?" Alfie says, "No comment." Neil then says, "I believe they are ecstasy and it looks like there are a few hundred – is that about right?" Alfie says nothing. The questioning continues focusing on the pills and Alfie's answer is always "no comment". "Where did you get the pills from?" asks Dave. "No comment," says Alfie. "Who are you running for?" asks Dave. Alfie looks him square in the face and says, "No comment." This continues for quite some time – credit due, they're trying hard to crack him, but Alfie's solid, he doesn't have a breaking point.

Neil takes the pills and replaces them back into the evidence bag, he then produces Alfie's wallet and puts it on the table. Dave opens the wallet and begins to remove its contents, laying them all out on the table – money, train tickets and a few receipts. Dave then flicks through the money counting it out, "You have here three hundred and twenty pounds in cash, quite a lot isn't it?" Alfie says, "No comment," but he's thinking, 'not really'. Dave then takes a look at the train tickets and enlightens Alfie of his intended destination. Alfie looks at him and says nothing. Dave moves onto the bits of paper and receipts, in amongst them is an A5-sized piece of paper folded up to make it fit in Alfie's wallet. Dave begins to unfold it and Alfie's heart skips a beat.

Without warning, Alfie leaps across the table knocking what's left of his coffee everywhere and snatches the paper out of Dave's hand. Neil immediately presses a button on the wall to raise the alarm, then along with Dave, runs around the table and makes an attempt to restrain Alfie. Alfie quickly stuffs the paper into his mouth and begins to frantically chew it up but the filth are on him. The door swings open and in flood several officers. Alfie's brief has fucking shit himself and is cowering in the corner, while Alfie is wrestled to the ground. Alfie tries like fuck to swallow the paper but it's just too much and his lungs are on fire. The police pin him down, hold his nose and shout, "Spit it out." Alfie just continues to try and chew the paper up but this is proving impossible as his lungs are now at bursting point. The police start to poke their fingers into various pressure points around Alfie's jaw in an attempt to get him to open his mouth, and this has a degree of success as Alfie has no choice but to open his mouth if only to take a breath. The police react to this and hold his mouth open and remove the paper. Alfie does his best to take their fucking fingers off as he snaps his jaw closed, but it's not enough – the filth have retrieved the paper.

Alfie is cuffed and bundled back into his cell; he's fucking fuming, he can't believe what's happened. He can only hope that he's managed to destroy any information written on the note. He's pacing up and down the cell absolutely seething, coughing his guts up in the process. The cell door is unlocked and Neil looks in and says, "Have you calmed down yet sir?" Alfie looks at him and says, "Fuck off." The door is slammed. Alfie continues to pace up and down slowly trying to compose himself. Time passes and his coughing fit subsides. The door is opened again. This time it's Dave. "Sir, would you like to continue the interview?" Alfie looks at him and reluctantly says, "Yes go on." Alfie once again is led from his cell to the interview room.

Alfie enters the room to see his brief sat in the same seat as before. He still looks quite shaken, not that Alfie gives a toss as he fucking hates anyone to do with the legal profession. He sits down and the smell of the coffee that was spilt during the chaos reminds him of what he's just been through and what may be to come.

Dave and Neil sit down and look at Alfie. They begin to deliver a statement, "Can you tell me who Jeff is?" And they produce the paper that Alfie had tried so hard to destroy which is now looking pretty sorry for itself but has now been reconstructed and laminated to protect it from any further attacks. Dave goes on to say, "This is a bill of sale for a BMW five series, sold a couple of months ago by someone called Jeff, and guess what, we can make out an address on here, which is what I presume you tried so hard to destroy, so we will be applying for a warrant to search these premises as well as your own for anything linked to the drugs industry."

Alfie just looks at them with utter contempt, the gravity of what's happened has finally taken hold of him, the dominoes will now begin to topple and there's fuck all he can do about it.

10. DARK TIMES

Last night was tough. I achieved little sleep in a feeble attempt to try and figure out a game plan but all I could think of was how much I owe Cliff. Eighty grand, so breaking it down, once I've rounded up all that's owed, combine that with the twenty I have tucked away I can probably get the debt down to around fifty and in my mind that's nearly half of it. This should make the prick happy as I can almost guarantee his profit on the four boxes will be about twenty, so this will only leave thirty bags outstanding. That may seem a lot but when you weigh up that he'll probably have that covered he shouldn't stress about it, but this is Cliff and he likes to make a lot of noise so no doubt he'll be on my case regardless of how much is left to pay, and no matter how I dress it up it's still eighty bags.

Once again I'm back in that fucked-up zombified state. I get up and get myself ready, for fuck's sake it only felt like yesterday when I had all that shit with Murray and Si. I can't be arsed with breakfast. I'm going down to the stall to break the news to Lance and Carl. They need to know that everything's gone tits-up and if I'm brutally honest, I can't be fucking bothered with the stand. I'm just gonna fuck it off and give it to Carl. It'll be one less thing to worry about and thinking ahead it's something on the back burner for a bit of laundering should I ever need to, but that's fucking miles off yet.

Trying my best not to wake anyone, I just get on my way and quietly slip out of the house. As I sit in the car and look at my burner I can't even begin to get my head around how I'm going to start letting people know what's happened. It's a catch twenty-two. If I tell them the truth they might bail on me, if I lie and it all comes on top I'll lose any respect turning my name to shit and they'll bail on me, but the way my mind is at the moment I need to look at the bigger picture. I have to be honest and tell them the score, if they jump ship then so be it.

One mile out and I reassembled my phone. My anxiety hasn't really changed from yesterday, it's maxed out, so whatever happens once my phone's on will have little effect on my state of mind, but this doesn't stop me stressing. I push the on button and place the phone on the passenger seat so I can see the screen. The phone powers up and moments later it goes fucking mental, text after text coming through, I can't see who the messages are from so I'll just let it run its course. Sometime later it finally stops beeping. I daren't fucking look. I only have about ten customers and one of those is now in jail, someone's eager to get hold of me, no guessing who. I pick the phone up and scroll through the names, some of the texts are from my customers acknowledging my new number, I have three from Flash, one from Skimmer and nine from Cliff, fucking knew it.

I pull over and have a proper look at the messages; looking at the times they were sent it would look like Flash and Skimmer have updated Cliff. Subsequently Cliff's lost the fucking plot and decided to text me, had no luck, then got Flash and Skimmer to try me, and that's just going on the times the messages were received. I haven't even read them yet. I'm not sure where to start – do I start from the beginning and entertain myself as the messages slowly get more threatening or shall I just read the last one and get it over with?

I start at the beginning, filtering out the texts from everyone else. I opened text number one from Cliff received at eleven o'clock last night. See what I mean – he has no regard for anyone; the text says "trying to call u, switch your phone on", okay that's not too bad, fucking stupid, but not bad. The next one reads "call me when you get this message". Well that's pretty much the same as the last message just worded differently. The next two texts read exactly the same as the others, they've just been resent. Cliff's next text number five is sent after Flash and Skimmer have sent messages from their new numbers saying "Cliff is trying to get hold of you". Cliff's message says "we need to sort something out as I need to pay the rent on the garage and those cars that you wrote off will need to be paid for", now we're getting somewhere. The last few messages were the same but once again just worded slightly differently with a couple of fucks in them, so not that bad especially for Cliff.

I text Skimmer "got your message, call me when you get 5". I'm gonna deal with Skimmer, Flash doesn't have the mental capacity to manage the level of negotiation needed to close this deal. No sooner than the message is sent my phone rings, it's Skimmer and he asks, "How did you get on?" I reply, "I'm just getting on it now; I'm off to work to hand over the business so I can focus on getting this debt paid." Skimmer pauses for a moment then says, "Can we link up straight after?" My response is, "Yes mate where to?" Skimmer says, "The market's not too far from me so I can see you near there if you want." That suits me just fine so I say, "Yes mate I'll give you a heads-up when I'm done."

I pull into the market car park, get out of the car and head for the stall; it's still early so the market is fairly quiet. As I close in on the stall I can see the lads hovering around with a brew in hand. They notice me approaching. I try my best to smile but I can feel the cracks are beginning to show. Surprisingly Lance looks slightly concerned, maybe the lack of a heads-up has caught him off guard – who knows, maybe he's put two and two together and clocked on that something catastrophic has happened.

The next hour is spent explaining how much shit I'm in and what lengths I might need to go to in order to get myself back on track. Lance genuinely looks and sounds worried; he knows that I've just recovered from a shit time and he knows the lengths that I'll be prepared to go to in order to pay the debt off – this concerns him and for once he's quite vocal about it. I do my best to reassure him that I'll be okay and that I'll try not to do anything stupid, but this is just a case of lip service and I'll do whatever it takes to get this done. On the plus side, the news that I want to relinquish the stand and all its stock to Carl seems to go down extremely well. He's managed everything quite well so far and I see no reason to change it.

Once again I walk away from the stall, my mind is back in neutral, I don't even look back as I call Skimmer and let him know I'll be available in a few minutes; a convenient time and place is agreed. I sit in the car and although Skimmer is good as gold it's almost guaranteed that if Cliff is in a piss he'll be breathing down Skimmer's neck applying pressure on him to apply pressure on me. The shit will be rolling down hill and it's coming in my direction. I pull out of the car park and head for the meeting place which is a small retail outlet about a mile away.

I pull into the outlet still being extremely mindful that the filth could be on my case; with this in mind, I park up at the far end of the car park, leave my phone behind and using the cover of vehicles and people I walk the relatively short distance to the agreed meeting point. As usual I'm a good five minutes early. I can't help it as this was drilled into me during my service – "five minutes before parade" – and if you're really on point you'll be five minutes before that. If you're as much as a few seconds late then the shit hits the fan, and when I say late I mean later than five minutes before the actual time the parade is scheduled to start. It's not a bad way to operate as it gives me a few minutes to assess the area and that's quite handy considering the current state of affairs.

I'm plotted up in a fairly busy doorway of an electrical outlet. Looking across the roofs of the cars I see Skimmer's van pull into the car park and park up. He gets out and walks towards me, I acknowledge him with a discreet nod and he returns the greeting. We shake hands and Skimmer says, "Shall we go for a wander?" I reply, "Yes, let's pop in here and have a look around." We both walk into the store, and as we enter I look in the door's reflection to see behind us; as far as I can tell there doesn't appear to be anyone following us.

The shop is quite big and surprisingly busy for the time of day, but then again it is the school summer holidays so there will be more people floating around than usual. Skimmer gets to the point and asks, "How are we looking? Cliff's been given the update and to be fair he's not too stressed, well he didn't sound too stressed, but you know how his moods can switch." I look at Skimmer and say, "I know how many have been nicked but we aren't sure how it came about, so we just need to wait for any feedback from their girlfriends who should be arranging visits in the next few days. As to money,

I'm going to start ringing around to see what I can realistically raise – if you can give me a call maybe later, better still tomorrow morning and by then I'll have a good idea of where I stand."

At this point of the game a degree of tactics needs to be deployed. If Cliff becomes aware that I have twenty large ready to go he'll take it and that's it gone, then he'll apply pressure on me regardless. What I need to do is find out what my customers are doing then depending on where I stand with them will determine on what I do with any money that I have access to. Put it this way, that twenty grand could be a lifeline for me to purchase goods cheaper from another source allowing me to pay the debt off a whole lot quicker, plus if Cliff does lose the plot this twenty gives me a bit of money to calm the prick down.

We walk for a short while, Skimmer mulling over my predicament and if I know Skimmer he'll be trying to think of an amicable way to conclude our meeting. Skimmer says, "Okay mate, I'm gonna tell Cliff you need some time to let the dust settle and speak to your customers face-to-face – do you think you'll be in a position to pay anything tomorrow?" I reply, "Yes, there is money to round up and I'm gonna call on a few old debts to be paid up; if everyone plays ball I'll have about ten quid. I'm going to call on some favours to see if anyone can help bail me out, but there's no guarantee so don't hold me to that." I have a little think and then say, "On the off chance of anybody wanting anything, what I may do is cash-only deals – this might help me bring the debt down a bit at a time. Do you have any stock just in case?" Skimmer says, "Yes, that's not a problem, but it will have to be cash back on the same day." I say, "That's fine mate, for now I'd prefer to work this way." I look at Skimmer and ask, "Bit of a long shot, but do you have any pure in stock?" Skimmer smirks and says you know I do but you also know that Cliff only sells bashed." Feeling slightly deflated I say, "That's a shame because I could pay the debt off a lot quicker if I could bash it myself, plus I do have some cash-paying customers who only buy pure." Skimmer says, "I know mate but you know what Cliff's like, he's a greedy fucker."

I can't help but feel a bit pissed off, not with Skimmer but with the situation. I say to Skimmer, "Okay, I guess if that's how he's gonna play it then this'll be a long haul; if he changes his mind then let me know because I could get this debt paid in a few months rather than years…" I pause and try to think of how long it'll take to pay off eighty grand the slow way. I say, "I don't know how long, probably fucking ages." Skimmer holds his hand out and we shake. I say, "I'll be in touch tomorrow at some point; a face-to-face would be better for me, shall we link up here again?" Skimmer says, "It would be better at big Tesco's as I'm seeing Flash tomorrow morning and he's up near there." I quickly respond by saying, "Right mate, see you at big Tesco at about ten." Skimmer agrees and heads back to his van and I head back to the car.

Right, there doesn't seem to be any major pressure yet, this would be down to Cliff shitting himself and not wanting to be caught. This is a perfectly normal reaction and part of my plan is dependent on Cliff's greed and instinct for self-preservation to kick in, and believe me he has a massive sense of self-preservation. Some would call it selfishness, others would call it narcissism, personally I would say all of the above and then some. Cliff will be having a massive internal battle, his overwhelming sense of greed will want all of the money now, but his self-preservation will want to stay out of jail – after all, what good is having loads of nice things when you're banged up, his head will be fucked. One thing's for sure, I can guarantee at some point something will change, I just need to be ready when it does and whatever he throws at me I need to be able to deal with it.

It's approaching lunch time and as much as I'm dreading it, the time has come to call my customers. Part of me hopes they remain loyal but in turn this brings a conflict of interest, I have to ask myself "would I remain loyal?" That's a tough call, I think I would still crack on trading but would definitely keep a safe distance for a short while, maybe do a few dry runs to draw out any surveillance that may be in place. This is one option I could offer, I'll just have to see how the calls develop. I look at my phone and scroll through the names; the first one I see is Alfie – it pains me to do so but I delete his name and number from my phone, while I'm at it I also delete Jeff's. It feels like I've just been to a funeral, because when you delete a good contact that you haven't fallen out with from your phone it means something's gone badly wrong. It brings on a sense of guilt, they are now potentially looking at some proper jail time but out here life just goes on. Saying that, I wonder if they will be feeling the pain that I'm likely to be going through in the coming months, years even. I make the call to my first customer.

* * *

Forty minutes of bartering and negotiating later, I've finished giving everyone the heads-up and to be fair it wasn't that bad; a couple of my smaller customers have had a bit of an arse twitch and said that they will shut down for a bit but thankfully my main customers are still on board. What I have done is aim to go and see all of them over the next few days for a chat, just to suss out the lie of the land. My intention now is to gather any outstanding money for Skimmer and get this bill started on. The customers that owe the money have confirmed that it isn't a problem, as have some of my slower debtors. This is gonna keep me occupied for the rest of the day because none of them live near to me or each other and the way my finances are going to be I can't really afford to get any of the lads to do the running. So it looks like I'm going back to the shop floor, it's not like I haven't done it all before. Besides it'll give me the opportunity to discuss any plans that I can put in place for when Cliff eventually loses the plot.

So the last day hasn't exactly gone to plan. The majority of my customers had a change of heart and have decided to jump ship. I can hardly blame them and part of me wishes I'd just fucking lied and not told them it was on top. On the flipside, if there is such a thing, I've inherited a couple of new contacts from Alfie's leftovers – these are yet to be tested and knowing Alfie's lot they will more than likely bring me more headaches than being good customers. I'll need to be cautious with any credit that I give, that's if I can get any; I haven't asked for anything on tick yet, in fact I haven't asked for anything, full stop. Part of me doesn't want it until I see how the dust settles. I could still be nicked at any time. All I've done is focus on getting this bill down in order to keep Cliff off of my case.

All my debtors have come through and paid in full, this is hardly surprising given the alternative is to be bundled in the boot of a car and taken for a drive out into the sticks. On top of that everything that was owed from the previous week has been paid; some of these payments felt like a golden handshake as they were intent on moving on to new suppliers. They did say, "it's only until things settle" but once they've gone it's fucking hard work to get them back on board. This gave me the feeling that my ship was slowly starting to sink, and it is – with a lack of decent reliable customers, how the hell am I gonna pay this debt. It's down to just over sixty-nine grand, and even though I've held on to this twenty for now, I still owe the better part of seventy large.

I have to get this wheel spinning and, by my calculations, at best I can shift is about a key a week – this is a significant reduction on what I was shifting but if I'm clever about it and do everything myself then I ought to be able to earn about two grand a week, minus what I need to live on. There's still no sign of The Boy, but I do have Spice and Red on standby, and I am in no doubt that they will be needed at some point, as my wife will begin to question what the fuck is going on. She is aware that I've handed the stall over to Carl so that I can focus on my security work and as usual I think or hope this has washed, but this will begin to wear thin when a lack of money is on the table. I'll cross that bridge when I get to it. I hate lying to her but the last thing I need is her stressing about the sort of shit that I have to deal with on a daily basis.

Talking of stress, Cliff is still out of the country and the longer he's away the better. If I can just get this bill down to about forty bags over the next few weeks, then when he does come back it won't seem as bad, well that's how I see it anyway, but Cliff being Cliff he'll only care about the forty that's left and not the forty that's been paid. I can't stand this part, this is the time when my nerves, anxiety, call it what you want, they peak. I can't put my finger on why, they just do and it starts to grind me down. I've got to make the call, there's nothing worse than having to swallow your pride and literally go fucking begging, stroking the egos of people who only care for the dollar, but I don't see there being many other options – if Cliff wants his dosh then he'll need to supply me. I do have another supplier on standby so I can do some juggling, and as much as I hate juggling it will be a necessity to get things moving quick enough to not notice this seventy grand hole I'm sitting in.

As I stare at the phone, scrolling through to Skimmer's number, it becomes quite clear that the majority of numbers in my phone are now surplus to requirement, redundant; the customers that have jumped ship will eventually change their numbers, all I can only hope for is that they forward me their new contact details when they do. The other thing that has become painfully obvious is the lack of phone calls I'm now receiving from anyone. None of this is good news or unexpected besides there's fuck all I can do about it now, what's done is done and I have to focus on what's happening right now. I call Skimmer, the phone rings several times and connects, "Hello mate," Skimmer says. I reply with a simple, "How's things?" Skimmer says, "Not good mate, Cliff's having to cut his holiday short to come back and sort this mess out." For fuck's sake, this is not the news I needed to be hearing, bang goes my plan of getting this bill down before he gets back. Cliff is going to be hard fucking work, he'll now be blaming me cos he's had a shit holiday. I wouldn't put it past him to up the bill in order to compensate for the inconvenience he's suffered.

I take a deep breath and ask, "When is he due in?" Skimmer replies, "He's on his way now, the plane's due at Heathrow later tonight." He then says, "These are his words not mine – it would be in your best interest if you had some more money ready for him when he lands." I like Skimmer too much to have a whinge, plus it's quite clear that Cliff is calling the shots. Again I take a deep breath and say, "Mate, you know I've got fuck all left to give. I'm ready to work again. I just need to know if I can get any credit." Skimmer replies, "I'm sorry mate, I don't know, Cliff will decide on that when he gets back."

Well that's me proper fucked then, I can't get any credit to make any money and Cliff's expecting to see some form of payment when he lands, but I know Cliff, he's just fishing to see if I have any money, he'll apply as much pressure as he can and I know for a fact his greed will overcome his urge to have me kidnapped or killed. He knows I'll pay, what he also knows is that I won't be pushed. Hands up, yes I accept I owe money, and I'll pay it back, all of it, what I won't accept is being bullied – if he wants to go down that route he can go fuck himself. I pause for a moment and then say, "Look there is one option, I've picked up a new customer from this mess and he's cash paying, if I get the money off of him in advance can I then get some work off of you?" Skimmer goes quiet then says, "Mate, it's a funny one, we have got work in but Cliff wants to hold on to it till he's back. I think he's got some kind of plan to sort this out." I don't know if this is good or bad, you know what – fuck it. I say, "Okay mate, I'll sit tight for now; as it stands I'm not gonna have any cash for him when he gets back as I think the best thing is to sit down with Cliff face-to-face and come to some kind of arrangement. Believe me I don't like owing the money and the sooner I get it paid the happier I'll be." Skimmer reluctantly agrees and wishes me good luck.

I'm so torn, on one hand I know that twenty grand will make Cliff relax enough to be happy to start working again, but on the other hand if I play that trump card now I'll have nothing left to give except my car and I really don't want to give that up. All I know is when he lands he's going to be worn-out and pissed off or pissed up – either way he'll be calling me as soon as he lands, regardless of the time. I'm gonna text him now, knowing he's on the plane and will get this when he lands. I text "sorry to hear you're coming back early, it's not how this should have panned out. I've got to pop out of town tonight and won't be back until tomorrow morning, a friend of mine has stepped up to help lighten the load, see you in the morning, text me when you're ready to meet up". I send it. Right, hopefully that'll get him off my back. I've decided I'm gonna give him half of the money and use the other half to work with, fuck it I have to do something, I've got more at stake than a debt – if he starts sending dickheads round to my house that's my marriage over, kids gone, the lot.

This is becoming a lot harder than I thought. My original plans have gone to shit. I'm lacking both suppliers and customers. I'm not even gonna go there with Si, and not that I would bother but Murray's back in jail on a recall, his drugs empire fell off the cliff and he was forced to start trading with younger people, really young – prison turned him into a bully, a juiced-up bully. Some kid owed him a few quid, so he decided to kidnap him and give him a few slaps in his car and dumped him in the middle of nowhere, sounds familiar. Anyway, this poor kid eventually gets home and is given a bollocking by his mother, on that he spills the beans on Murray, not about the drugs but about the kidnapping. Murray gets nicked by the filth, they search his car finding the evidence needed to secure his recall. The silly prick knocked one of the kid's teeth out, which was found under the passenger seat, some people will never learn. My point being, my options are becoming extremely limited, I honestly think I'm going to have to sign up to whatever Cliff throws at me and take each day at a time, I really don't see any other way.

* * *

Another rough night, you'd think I'd be getting used to it by now but I'm not. As I lie here in bed, my head is fucking banging with the stress. I really can't be arsed to get up but Cliff will be on my case. I'm dreading putting the phone on, I just know it's gonna be shit, pure fucking shit, I haven't done anything that would warrant good news. All accounts have been settled and ordinarily this would be good news, but just for once I'd love to still have some money due in, about seventy grand would be nice. I'm just delaying the inevitable, I decide to get up. Usual drills – it's still early, I'm not sleeping that well and I'm back on the cheap fucking beers. I have to neck a fair few just to get off to sleep and have the desired effect sending me off sharpish; but I soon wake stirring throughout the night, trying to figure a way out of this mess… next thing I know the sun's up. I've been lying here stressing for most of the night, the reality being I've achieved fuck all because my mind has just been spinning the same thoughts around, and none of them are good. I can't help thinking life would be so much easier if Cliff was dead!

I quietly get out of bed, I'm not sneaking but that's how it feels, because I am being deceitful because everything I do or say is a fucking lie, that's why I'd rather be up and gone before the Mrs or kids are awake. The kids have recently broken up for the summer holidays and that brings a whole new set of problems. The lack of money being the obvious one, and yes I feel guilty that I've got a stash of doe that would give them the best summer ever, but if I start dipping into it I'm fucked, besides I'm never here and if I am here I'm quietly sat in the corner stressing, supping on shit lager. I can't talk about how my day has been because that means more lies. My wife doesn't work as the youngest isn't at school yet, so apart from bringing up the kids there is absolutely fuck all going on in our lives that we can have a meaningful conversation about. Look, if I told my Mrs how much money I owe and how interesting all of these characters are that I see on a daily basis, I'm pretty sure the next thing I would hear is the sound of bags being packed and the door slamming as she fucks off up her mum's taking the kids with her.

I pop out to the back garden and carefully walk down to the far end where I have a little hole dug under the neighbour's fence, mindful that the sun is up and it's quite bright. I remove a large rock which reveals some loose soil, I scrape the top of it away to reveal two packages, both containing ten grand. I take one, look it over just making sure it hasn't leaked in any way. Fortunately, it hasn't so I carefully replace the soil and rock back over the remaining package, hoping that I won't need to grab it anytime soon. I go back into the house and clean it off ready for transit. I pop the package into a small rucksack, along with some gym kit. I have no intention of going to the gym, my days of training stopped when I left the army – gutted really as I'm fucked, the only prolonged fitness I did do was dancing whilst off my tits on pills and I haven't done that for years. I just wanted to pad the bag out a bit, I grab my keys and phone and head out to the car.

I haven't really got anywhere to go, I don't regret handing over the stall, but it did give me a sense of purpose and now it's gone I don't have that anymore. However, I will drive towards the stall. It's too early for town, it's too early for anywhere. A few minutes pass and I make a conscious decision to get my phone up and running. I'm actually feeling okay about this, Cliff has my contract number and if he was that hacked off he'd have called me on that one, but I have no missed calls from him or anyone. The phone powers up and I look at the screen, waiting for it to light up and start beeping. The phone beeps a couple of times. I look at it and, as suspected, I have a message from Cliff at 23:48 and one from Skimmer at 23:55. I open the message from Cliff, it says, "OK, Skimmer will be in touch tomorrow". That's brief and very hard to gauge – does he want to meet up or not? What's the point in flying all that way back from the States just to send a fucking text, he could have done that from over there, so there's a time difference but not enough to be a problem. I look at the text from Skimmer, "C is back, can you call me in the morning, cheers". I am none the wiser, I was up all night stressing, for what – two random texts; if I've spent the majority of the night awake, stressing, I would appreciate some kind of fucking grief to make it worthwhile, otherwise what's the fucking point, I guess that's the difference between someone who gives a fuck or not.

    I call Skimmer and he promptly answers and says, "How are we doing?" I reply, "Pretty much the same as yesterday – do we have a plan as I need to get things moving?" Skimmer says, "Yes, he's got a way to get you up and running and back to work, but we'll need to discuss it with a face-to-face, what are your plans?" This sounds good, I say, "I'm all yours mate, just let me know when and where." I slow the car down awaiting an answer; it's a case of do I turn left or right. Skimmer says, "Big Tesco in about an hour. I've got to pick up Flash as he needs to be in on this as well." We end the call. This sounds interesting, I make a right turn; I may as well start heading into the area. Now if I am to read between the lines, Cliff is now trying to show force by adding Flash into the equation. Skimmer is more than capable of managing this on his own and if I'm honest he'll achieve so much more with me without having people tagging along just to make up the numbers.

    A short drive later I arrive at the so called big Tesco, it earnt this name because there are so many of the fucking places cropping up, so that those who weren't in the know had the likelihood of gong to the wrong one, not good if one happens to be loaded up with drugs or money. So big Tesco was aptly named because it's fucking big, and although it's not my preferred place to conduct a clandestine meeting, it works if you bother to go in and actually buy something; this makes your visit there plausible, plus there is an abundance of free carrier bags to be accessed for sticking all the drugs in! The car park is fairly quiet but then again it is early; based on this observation I decide to just have a recce around the car park and then fuck off out of the area to plot up and wait for the heads-up from the lads.

An hour passes and still no call, this will be down to Flash dragging his fucking heels, Skimmer is on point and is rarely late. Flash, well he's cut from a different cloth, nice guy but he's just fucking slack. Look, if I respect you I'll listen and reciprocate on the same level, if I don't then I'll just fucking glaze over and pretend to care. So, when Skimmer advocates for Cliff I listen because it's Skimmer talking not Cliff; the same message will come from the likes of Flash or even the horse's mouth and I just will not care. If Flash tries then just forget it, waste of fucking time. So, I ask myself again why bother complicating matters, this is typical bully-boy tactics, it won't work, this was tried on me in the past by another firm, and it all went south, quickly.

Another twenty minutes pass and finally the phone rings. I look down and sigh, it's Flash, great. I actually debate on whether or not I should bother answering, almost in some kind of passive form of protest. I let it ring a few more times, then pick it up. Flash instantly starts gobbing off, "Where the fuck are you?" he shouts. What the fuck, I respond in kind, "Look, you jumped-up prick, I'm not fucking deaf, you can stop playing the loud-mouthed gangster and talk to me like a fucking person, if you can't do that then fuck off." I eagerly await his response; Flash then says in a more acceptable tone, "We're here, where are you?" My answer is brief, "What happened to a heads-up, my balls are made of flesh not crystal and besides you're fucking late?" Flash then says, "I didn't realise I was supposed to call you." I then hear Skimmer in the background saying to Flash, "I asked you to call him when we left, but you were too busy fucking about with the stereo." Flash then says, "See you when you get here," he then puts the phone down, fucking rude, he learnt that from Cliff.

I arrive at the meeting point, and as usual opt to park some distance away from the entrance and walk the short distance; this gives me a little breathing space and it doesn't do any harm to let Flash wait a bit longer, maybe he'll learn something from this, it's idiots like him is what gets people like me caught. The car park is slightly busier providing more cover for me but on the other side it also does the same for anyone that may be trying to watch me – bit of a double-edged sword really but it puts my mind at ease knowing that my countersurveillance is probably on par or maybe slightly better than the police who may or may not be watching me. Truth is, I won't know until I get nicked and then it's too fucking late to worry about it.

For fuck's sake, Flash sticks out like a sore thumb, he's got his shirt off, fuck knows why – it's only just gone nine, it's summer yes but fuck me it's England not fucking Greece. Skimmer understandably isn't standing next to him, totally ignoring Flash. I approach Skimmer, on realising this Flash quickly joins us. I look at Skimmer, he knows me well enough to know what I'm thinking, and just subtly shakes his head, all of which goes right over Flash's head. I briefly look at Flash then back to Skimmer and say, "So what's the crack?" Flash starts to open his mouth but is quickly overruled by Skimmer who replies, "Basically Cliff won't meet up as he thinks you're a bit hot at the moment, but he does think he can lighten the load to get things moving again." I frown, look at Skimmer and say "Okay, what's he thinking?" Yet again Flash attempts to speak and once again is overruled by Skimmer who says, "Cliff can borrow some money for you to help reduce the debt and get it right down, but there will be interest on top."

I look up and just casually look around the car park, not sure why, I just do, plus it gives me time to think. "How much can he borrow and how much is being stuck on top?" I ask. Skimmer says, "He can access thirty grand but wants forty back." I look at Skimmer, I'm not sure how to feel, I say, "So my bills just went up another ten bags!" Flash pipes up and says, "Yes, so you now owe eighty grand." Eighty grand!? Trying my best to contain my anger I look at Flash and say "I haven't said yes yet." Skimmer says, "Mate, if you go for it we can get you working this week, I know it's not ideal but it will get you up and running, what do you say?" I know I've got no choice, if this is the only way I'm going to get things moving then I'll have to commit.

Flash moves his position and stands next to Skimmer, I look at them both and say, "I don't have a great deal of options do I, how long do I have to pay it back?" Skimmer replies, "Cliff thinks he can get you six months on it." I'm frantically running the numbers in my head. I say, "What about the forty left, how does that come into play?" Skimmer says, "Cliff can do some juggling at his end plus he can get rid of a few bits, based on that he thinks he can cover it; he did mention that you might have some on you as well." Reluctantly I say, "Yes, I've got ten that I borrowed last night." Skimmer smiles and says, "Nice one." Flash holds out his hand as if to collect the money, I look at him and say, "It's in the car, you fucking tit." Flash just lowers his hand and like a pet that has been told off just looks at Skimmer. I don't know if I'm worse off or not; on one hand I'll be back to work but on the other this ten grand I'm about to hand over will be swallowed up by the interest of this loan Cliff claims he's sorted.

Fuck it. I state, "Okay, tell Cliff I'll go for it, as far as I'm concerned if I take on this loan and the interest, Cliff has to supply me, that's the only way he'll get the money back. If I can shift the minimum of a box a week then I can make between fifteen hundred and two grand, less a few hundred for costs and I've got to live on something." I then say, "Anything earnt on top I'll pay towards the other forty that Cliff has covered." Flash says, "Fifty, you owe Cliff fifty." I look directly at Flash straight in his fucking eyes and say, "If this is too complicated for you then let me know, I've already deducted the ten I've got with me." Skimmer quietly laughs to himself and says, "Sounds good, I'll grab that off of you now then we can go from there." Feeling a bit relieved, I look at Skimmer and say, "Are you ready to go today?" Skimmer replies, "No but we will be tomorrow." Actually that makes perfect sense, it gives me the day to get everyone ready – everyone, that's a fucking joke there's hardly anyone left.

Skimmer asks Flash to get the car while he accompanies me to grab the money. We don't really talk, my mind is preoccupied with what's going on, I know I can earn the money to pay the debt, it's just that I can't help feeling that the piss is being taken. Not by Skimmer, he's not like that, but Cliff he'll squeeze as hard as he can, if he can find an angle to monopolise on this then he will. My thoughts are, he hasn't borrowed the money, he's got it covered, what he's doing is fucking bullshitting me and bumping up the bill by ten grand, I hope I'm wrong, but I know what he's like.

As we approach the car I once again scan the car park; I unlock the car, reach in and rifle through the bag, I grab the money and subtly hand it to Skimmer. He thanks me and promptly heads off back towards Flash, I don't envy him having to work with the likes of Flash it must be a constant drain. As Skimmer disappears from sight I get back into the car and sit tight, what I don't want is to leave at the same time, so I just plot up and wait for them to leave. I can see the exit clearly and it's only a short while before I see them drive out of the car park.

* * *

It looks like I have got the rest of the day to prep everyone up for a potentially busy day tomorrow. I'm not even thinking about getting caught, that ship has now sailed, my focus is on this debt and nothing else. I do have the option to take on runners to lighten the load but this will make a dent in my profits. What I need to do is cover as much as possible myself and only employ people if I go over a certain threshold. I'll only take on what I need and fuck it off out the door immediately. Bollocks, I don't have anywhere to stash the coke. I hadn't even considered that. I've got no scales, fuck all. Fuck, this is yet another dent to my operation. No safe house and no kit, there's no guarantee that everything I take on will go, well not straight away. I can't put it at home, not a chance, I'm not having it in the house or anywhere near the Mrs or kids. The money is enough and that gives me fucking headaches. I'm gonna run it by Red or Spice to see if they have any ideas, but this is unlikely. If I remember correctly, Alfie used these guys as runners and not for storage and there's usually a good reason for this. I'll ask anyway, never know I might get lucky.

Comms with these guys is hard fucking work. Red works all day, which does look good plus he's a biker which is even fucking better. When I say a biker I mean he rides a bike, he's not one of the Angels, big difference. Spice, as far as I know, does fuck all and plenty of it, but I'm really not sure about him. I've had very little interaction with him apart from when we had to put Jeff's door through the other day and even then he was shaking like a shitting dog, so I do have concerns about his integrity to get the job done. Remember, Alfie didn't do coke, so far as I can tell his lads haven't been exposed to this end of the market. They've done a bit of running for me via Alfie but that's about it.

Red is my first point of contact, although he works he's good at answering the phone. The only issue I do have is that like Alfie, he doesn't use a burner. He's still got the same number, so if the police are looking at starting an investigation his number will be logged from Alfie and Jeff's contact list, scanned and monitored. So, the minute I call on my brand-new, clean burner, it immediately becomes contaminated by his phone which means that every fucker I subsequently call will also have their new burners picked up and so on and so forth. That's how people get caught. But there's fuck all I can do about that, so I call him anyway.

The phone rings several times and Red answers, "Hello who's this?" I answer, "Yes mate it's me." The other end goes quiet while Red is clearly trying to work out who's calling. I don't ever use my name on these phones, and nor do I call anyone by theirs. If they don't have a handle or a nickname when they start working with me then they soon fucking get one. A few more moments pass and Red says, "Oh hello mate, I didn't know if you'd been nicked or not!". That's a strange statement. I ask, "Why do you say that mate?" Red replies, "I take it you haven't spoken to The Boy yet?" Feeling a bit perplexed, I say, "Not yet, do you have a contact number for him?" This is ideal as The Boy is a good runner, he's always available and is a bit of a blender. I ask Red, "Can you send me his number please.

I'll give him a call and see how he is – oh, and I'm giving you the heads-up, it looks like we're back to work tomorrow, are you about?" Red replies, "Yes but not until after six." I know this from old so I say, "Yeah that's alright, I'll be in touch tomorrow once I have some timings."

11. THE BOY

A few days ago.

The car door closes and The Boy looks at Alfie as he slowly mingles with the commuters and disappears into the train station. The Boy, still stoned, looks across the car park at the so-called fake police, who are parked up just a couple of cars away with no occupants in them; besides it's not like he gives a shit and even if he did he's in no fit state to care or do anything about it. He tentatively pulls away from the drop-off point, drives towards the main road and away from the station. In a feeble attempt to ensure his liberty, he checks his rear-view mirror just in case the police do follow him, but they don't, so he continues to casually drive down the road towards the station exit.

He pulls up at the traffic lights which are currently red and patiently waits for them to turn green. While he's sat there he ponders. He knows he's meant to be doing something but for the life of him he can't remember what. Whilst pondering, the lights have turned green and continued through another sequence from red, amber, green and eventually back to red. The Boy's sitting there like a complete fucking idiot, deliberating on what he's supposed to be doing. The sound of a car horn eventually snaps him out of his trance and on seeing a green light he casually pulls away totally oblivious to the person in the car behind shouting, "Wake up you fucking dickhead." All this and he's still none the wiser of his destination. So as if to be in some kind of semi state of autopilot, The Boy heads home. He's not local so it won't be a short trip. He lives around forty minutes away, which translates to about three hours with The Boy in his current state. Fortunately for him and other road users he's not in any fit state to roll another joint, so as he gradually recovers he should progressively get a little quicker.

A few miles later he approaches the city limit. A degree of clarity begins to return; this doesn't help as he begins to feel a little uneasy as a touch of paranoia slips in. This is normal but isn't helping the situation as he knows that there's something he was supposed to be doing. Trying his upmost to recollect, he attempts to think back and figure it out but it's no fucking good. His head is battered, he's at a complete loss. He just continues on his way, hoping that whatever he was supposed to be doing will just come back to him in some way. This is usually prompted by a phone call or a shitty text of some kind, or not, depending on who it is and how desperate they might be for their drugs.

Another hour passes and his phone doesn't ring. He's finally on the home stretch, all things considered he hasn't done too badly, he didn't crash or get pulled; granted the journey took considerably longer than it should have, but he made it home in one piece and that's all that matters. Now feeling much more coherent he drives into the parking area and manages to successfully reverse his car into a space, he gets his shit together, exits the car and heads towards the communal doors to his flat. He lives on the top floor of a three-storey building. His head has straightened out nicely and in the nick of time; in the past these stairs have been a fucking nightmare especially when pissed or stoned.

There's one particular occasion that plagues him still. Several months ago he arrived home in a right fucking mess, only to find that he was locked out. Naturally he begins to knock on the door but with no response he progresses to kicking the door until it's barely hanging on its hinges. He pulls it off of the door frame and steams into the house in a right fucking mood only to find out he was on the wrong floor! He had just smashed his way into an elderly neighbour's flat who was sitting in her bedroom fucking shitting herself. The police got involved and a whole ton of shit was thrown at him including a caution for damaging property and subsequently he was hit with a bill for the door and fittings. These sort of things do happen, but it brings unnecessary heat into our circles, elevating the risk of fucking it up for everyone.

The Boy lives with his girlfriend, who like most normal people actually has a real job, a nine-to-five, but unlike most she tolerates The Boy's activities. And tolerates being the most fitting description. She pays the bills, and the cash he brings in is for fun, it's more of a symbiotic relationship – he needs her for a roof over his head, and without him her overheads would leave her broke. I'm not saying they haven't got feelings for each other of course they have, it just means that at times the relationship can be dominated by the illegal activities of The Boy. Many of us and I say "us" because we are a certain strain, many of us graduate from the clubbing or party scene – this scene has an eclectic mix of people, some of whom just party on weekends and work hard during the week and some don't. Relationships naturally form between these partygoers, and this is one such relationship.

The Boy unlocks the flat door and walks in, his other half is ready for bed; unlike The Boy she has to get up early for work. She's quite used to him getting back at all hours and she's also used to him being in a fucking mess. She's quite partial to a bit of a smoke so is fully aware of how The Boy will be feeling. Talking of feelings, The Boy who is now a lot less paranoid and relatively normal, heads straight for the fridge, hunger has set in, also known as the munchies. It's a common misunderstanding, some think that smoking pot makes you hungry – this isn't the case, smoking pot supresses the hunger so whilst stoned you don't feel hungry or are in no fit state to address said hunger, so can end up not eating for quite some time, then when you eventually come down the hunger returns with a vengeance, and you hit the fridge and eat the fucking lot.

The Boy opens the fridge door, supporting himself by placing one hand on the top of the tall fridge and the other on the fridge door. He partially leans forward to get a better view of the contents, if he was still stoned he would be at risk of falling in; fortunately he's not in too bad a state. He gazes in at the contents looking for something that will satisfy his hunger. He has to weigh up a couple of things – does he go for something quick that doesn't require cooking or reheating, the trade-off with this will be flavour and overall enjoyment, or does he exercise some patience and go for something hot? He reaches in, passing the stuff he needs to heat up and grabs a small four-pack of yogurts, then as he closes the door he has a change of heart and reaches in and takes out a pasty. He hastily removes the plastic wrapping, grabs a plate to put the pasty on and slings it into the microwave. He fumbles with the controls and the microwave starts up. While the pasty heats up he ploughs through the small packet of yogurts, not even bothering to snap them apart, a few moments pass, and while keeping one eye on the microwave timer he peels open the last yogurt. He starts to lick the lid when the microwave beeps. On this signal he automatically discards the whole pack of yogurt, including the one he was just about to eat, into the kitchen bin and removes the hot steaming pasty from the microwave, then retreats to the lounge.

He slumps into his usual chair while simultaneously his other half gets up, gives him a kiss and says "goodnight". She simply wanted to know that he had returned safely. She's fully aware of what he does and as a result of this will always carry the burden of waiting for some form of bad news to arrive. He smiles and looks at her as she disappears into the bedroom, thinking how lucky he is to have someone that puts up with him. He looks down at the pasty and begins to eat it, while watching the television. There's fuck all on and he's not really concentrating on the television. It's providing more of a background noise as opposed to entertainment. It's all about the food. He's fucking starved and tired. It's been a long day and he wants to have a munch then get his head down…

The Boy wakes with a sudden jerk – yet again he has fallen asleep in his chair; he looks at his watch and the time is just after seven in the morning. His Mrs is literally going out of the door. He hears her shout "Goodbye, see you later." He responds but she doesn't hear him as she closes the door behind her. He leans forward, reaches down between his legs and under the chair he's sitting on, he can just about reach the edge of a tray that's been pushed under the chair. He slides it out with the intention of making his breakfast – the smoking kind. He looks at the various materials scattered about the tray and much to his dismay he has everything except the main ingredient. Bollocks, he thinks, this fucking sucks. He gets out of the chair, has a good stretch and heads for the bathroom to clean himself up.

The Boy eventually emerges from the bathroom, washed, fresh and fucking sober. He grabs his keys, phone and exits the flat, sheepishly walking past the elderly neighbour's door. He hasn't seen her since he took the door off its hinges and hopes he never does. He's so embarrassed, mortified would be a better way to describe it. The Boy isn't a bad guy, like a lot of us he's just a bit naughty and when "on one" doesn't particularly think straight. We live in a lawless society, or we like to think so, we run drugs that's what we do, so breaking other laws to some is more than acceptable and is usually of a lesser offence, so therefore feels like its okay. This however is not my way of thinking, breaking the lesser laws puts you on the radar and that's never a good thing. I only break one law – supply of class A drugs, nothing else, period.

The Boy exits the small block of flats and approaches his car, it's a nice day, hot, and although it's just before eight he can feel the heat of the sun on his face giving him a positive feeling. The only thing missing is a big fat joint, something for him to smoke enabling him to relax and make the most of it because he's quite sure that Alfie will have him running around like a blue-arsed fly later. His first port of call is to catch up with Jeff and get a bit of green sorted, in fact it's his only port of call, so either way he's going to Jeff's.

Out of courtesy, and of course to avoid being hit with an axe, he gives Jeff a call to inform him of his pending arrival. The phone starts ringing. The Boy patiently waits for it to be answered; granted Jeff's a pisshead, but he's on the ball when it comes to comms. The phone rings off. The boy continues on his way, gives it a few minutes and tries again, nothing, he tries again, still nothing. Unfazed by this, The Boy continues towards Jeff's. He gives it a few more minutes then sends a text, "on my way to yours, be with you in about 30". The Boy is now satisfied that he has done all he can to prep Jeff for his arrival and not risking having an axe embedded in his skull.

The trip to Jeff's is a fairly uneventful journey. It always is when you are clean, this is a time to relax and drop your guard, take in your surroundings and not worry about the police pulling you over. This doesn't stop your arse twitching if the old bill are close by, but you just have to take it all in your stride and this is what The Boy does, this is what he's good at, not giving a flying fuck. The only time he stops is to fuel up on the edge of the city.

Another twenty minutes passes and he decides to call Jeff again. This time the phone is engaged, this is as good as a green light for The Boy, it means Jeff must be using the phone, maybe a tad bit early for Jeff, but The Boy's wishful thinking is paying off. He doesn't fancy driving all this way and Jeff not answering the door. Okay, worse case The Boy can plot up locally if need be and just wait for Jeff to answer, but he's sure Jeff will be up and about, so continues on his way there. The Boy glances at the time on his phone and it's approaching 09:10, he pulls off of the main road and down the side street towards Jeff's place. It's so fucking tight down there, normally there are a couple of spaces outside of Jeff's but it's not looking too good at the moment and with it being a dead end road, The Boy normally doesn't risked getting blocked. Today as his head is straight and he's feeling confident in his ability to not get blocked, he heads down to the end of the road. He pulls onto Jeff's street and slowly crawls along the line of cars looking for a gap big enough to fit his car into. Fuck all here, he gets to the end, and now regretting his decision opts to reverse back out.

As he gradually backs up he has a brainstorm. He calls Jeff again to see if he can just run the green out to him, perfect, and he won't even need to get out of his car. There is no traffic, so The Boy just stops in the middle of the road and calls Jeff – it's ringing. The Boy winds down his window to get some air and with a bit of anticipation readies himself to receive a small package. The phone rings off, so he calls it again, this time it's engaged. In sheer frustration The Boy gets out of the car leaving it in the middle of the road, walks towards Jeff's house and bangs on the front door. He can hear some noise inside and the door is slightly ajar, on this is he proceeds in being mindful that Jeff might come running at him brandishing some kind of weapon.

He doesn't get far, as he's greeted by several police officers, some in plain clothes and others in uniform. Fuck, he thinks and turns as if to make a break for it but he's got no chance – they're on him in seconds. They cuff him and immediately escort him outside to an unmarked car parked outside of Jeff's. The Boy now realising why there was a lack of spaces. The police place him in the back of their car and reel off a set of questions like "What's your name? Where have you come from? Why are you here?" All standard stuff. The Boy who is now relaxing thinking, 'they've got fuck all on me', just says, "I was just popping in to say hello." The police respond by saying, "We will be detaining you for the purposes of a drugs search. Do you have anything on you that you shouldn't?" The Boy is feeling a bit smug and thinking how rare an occasion it is that he can actually say, "No." The police usher him out of the car and proceed to empty the contents of his pockets onto the roof of their car and give him a thorough frisking down, revealing nothing incriminating, a bit of cash, his phone and car keys.

The officer conducting the search takes the keys saying, "Your car I presume sir?" The Boy can hardly fucking deny it as it's double parked outside of Jeff's, plus the keys he's got in hand were taken out of The Boy's pocket during the search, so based on that he acknowledges this with a polite nod, triggering the officer to begin searching the car. The Boy still feeling smug gazes around the street, looking up at the houses and trees gently blowing in the summer breeze. He begins to wonder how this all came about, and strangely enough it's this moment of clarity that brings a sudden yet very real sense of utter dread. His sphincter actually loosens, his legs go weak, his heart starts to pound and he immediately breaks into a sweat. He's just remembered what he was meant to do last night. He looks up into the air and lets out a sigh as the searching officer turns around, and looking even more smug, waves a little bag of green at him and says "Is this yours sir?" The Boy says nothing as he is placed back into the police car.

12. THE NEW FIRM

Looking at the new number for The Boy fills me with confidence. Yes he's a stoner, yes he looks young, hence the nickname, but he's a fucking good runner. Alfie always sang his praises, saying he has the potential to do extremely well and with all of Alfie's faults, and he has plenty, I always trusted his judgement. It's around midday and this will be my first direct contact with The Boy, not only since the loss of Alfie and Jeff but it's the first time we've actually spoken, I always ran everything through Alfie.

I initiate the call, and The Boy answers sounding extremely bright and coherent, almost fucking singing "Hello mate". I have to presume that by his initial answer he knows who's calling him or he's very polite, either way I like his telephone manner. I ask, "What you been up to, nobody could get hold of you for ages?" The Boy replies saying, "Oh I got nicked outside of Alfie's." He then goes on to explain in great depth how stupid he feels forgetting about the green in his car but he also did his utmost to ensure that he didn't give anything up and that he was safe to continue working.

The clever bastard was down as living at his mum's, so she got a knock from the filth and The Boy's bedroom was spun – nothing found as he operates from his girlfriend's house. He's a very lucky young man indeed. He's right in the shit with his mother but from his flippant attitude I get the impression he isn't particularly bothered. I'd be absolutely mortified if that were me. I honestly couldn't think of anything worse. This is another reason why I keep what I do a secret.

There is however a slight problem that The Boy has disclosed. He's awaiting sentencing and has been advised that he will be looking at a community order along with some kind of home curfew. I have to look at this from an angle of calculated risks. His name may possibly flag up with the police as known for drugs, initiating a stop and search, so he cannot carry drugs or money, not the sizes I'm doing. That's not going up his arse, well I fucking hope not anyway plus he's limited on movement and availability. I take a moment and say, "Okay, looking at your situation I think we all need to meet up and hammer out a plan. Are you able to pop over later?" The Boy replies, "Yes no problem, what time?" I respond, "Well Red doesn't finish until six, so how about half past, I'll let you know where later." The Boy acknowledges this and sounding surprisingly grateful thanks me for giving him the opportunity to continue working despite his apparent restrictions.

I call Red back to see if he's available to catch up after work. He's all good and is happy with the time so we agree on a location. I call Spice. The phone rings and while it's ringing, part of me isn't that keen on working with him. I can't put my finger on it yet, but I have concerns. Credit is due though, he was there with Milly and I when we had to get into Jeff's, so for now he gets the benefit of doubt. The phone continues to ring and then rings off. I give it a few minutes and decide to try again, and once again the phone just rings – this is the problem I'm facing. I honestly don't know these guys well enough to really see how they will be. They're not used to running with stakes as high as mine. The phone again rings off. He's got my number so I just send him a text "call me ASAP" that should do it.

My next task is to see who is still on board and what they want, this is yet another time when my anxiety can get the better of me. If nobody wants anything or they've decided to jump ship, I'm fucked. I'll have no way of clearing the debt. I'm looking through the names and I'm counting about ten names, six of which are customers that will buy the product I am or will be supplying; the others, Jay for example, will only buy pure or no less than a seven out of ten. The other couple of names are mutual suppliers, guys in the same or similar level to me so if I need to start juggling and I really hope I don't, I can look at sourcing goods from them. I've always got my back-up plan with Terry if I need any pills. The problem is Alfie used to sell most of them and there's not a lot of money in them; but if push comes to shove, if I can get some bigger sales going and inject some collateral into the business, it may be of benefit. I have to remember just because my world has turned to shit, it can't have any knock-on to the chain of customers that want their drugs. Life goes on.

Several calls later and I'm feeling a lot fucking happier, all six of them want loading up. I need about one and a half keys, with the potential for more towards the end of the week. There is a demand for pills but I'm gonna wait for now. I need to see if Terry is happy to work with me, then maybe I'll get a few thousand in. Fuck it. I'll call Terry now. The phone rings a couple of times, he answers and says, "How you bearing up with all the shit? I see you're still around." I reply, "Hanging in there. I've got a bit of an overdraft facility in place but it's temporary so I need to catch up with you if that's okay?" Terry, who is rarely fazed, says "Of course, usual?" I reply with honesty, "Mate I don't know how long it'll take; I don't want to fuck you about." Terry says, "I understand your dilemma and I also know that you'll do your best. If it takes a bit longer to complete the contract I'm not going to lose any sleep over it." On that a little spark of excitement runs through me, not because of an earner but more so that some people aren't just out for the doe.

It's approaching three and Spice still hasn't responded. Feeling quite worked up I try to call him again; the phone rings, "Hello," Spice actually answers. I'm about to fire some fucks into him when he says, "Sorry I didn't call you back, I was out of credit," that explains a lot. I immediately calm down and say, "Nah that's okay, bud. I'm getting Red and The Boy over for a meeting this evening. I start back to work tomorrow and am gonna give you some work." Spice says, "Fuck me, yes please, I'm broke." I ask, "Are you still mobile and in a position to get credit?" Spice answers saying, "Yes just about. I do have fuel but only enough for local work." This isn't ideal as most of my lot are out of town, the only one that isn't is Billy and I'm not sure about Spice going round to him. Reluctantly I say "Okay, we can figure it all out later, see you at half six."

* * *

I've kind of got an open book with my hours when it comes to explaining my whereabouts to my wife. She's now well and truly under the impression that my security work is up and running again, so my hours will be random and at times long. Plus because of the nature of the work I'm supposed to be doing she doesn't really ask any questions. This meeting tonight won't raise any eyebrows, the downside is I'd better start producing some money.

This is the first real meet I've set up since the arrests. I'm not quite sure how I'm supposed to feel. I've got a new work force that hasn't been properly tested with supplying coke, yeah they've done some bits but they haven't been fully exposed to it. And this is my concern. I've opted to meet up somewhere central. It's the middle of summer, plenty of people around with a myriad of bars and locations to sit and blend in. And if I'm being really honest, meetings like this aren't normally a problem as there's nothing tangible being exchanged. However, this meeting then rises to a whole new level creating a conspiracy, and that's something I don't want to be getting lifted for. When I first got into this, my first supplier who had done a brief spot of time inside said, "If you get nicked they will arrest you with one of the following – possession, possession with intent or conspiracy to supply." He then went on to say, "You do not want to be getting done for the last one, trust me it's a nasty charge," and this has always stayed with me.

So with all of this good advice in mind I operate in a certain way, evaluating my runners and staff, gauging their levels of awareness and basic common sense, and this is their first test. It's about ten to six and I'm on plot. I can see the pub but I'm parked up observing, not for the police but for the lads. I need to assess how they are, where they will park, will they have music blasting out of the car windows drawing attention to themselves. All of these things matter to me, they will be carrying thousands of pounds' worth of coke, I need to know that I can trust and rely on them to fucking behave and be professional about it. That's what I liked about the Russian. He was fucking good at his job, he just got greedy.

The first to arrive is Red. I know it's him as he's on his bike, no real problem there. He pulls over, removes his helmet and takes a look at the time on his watch – good fucking skills, he's five minutes early. I remain where I am, just seeing if he clocks me, but so far he's just sitting tight. The next to arrive is The Boy; once again I'm pretty happy, no music, he doesn't look as if he's stoned but then again maybe his encounter with the police has shaken him up a bit. He clocks Red and goes over and appears to be chatting. The logical thing for them to do now would be to go in and get a table, preferably outside and somewhere relatively discreet, that's why I chose this place, it lends itself well for a good old clandestine meeting. Two minutes to six and I get out of the car and approach the lads. They see me approach and as I join them we all head into the pub. As skint as I am, I have to get the drinks in. I take the orders and suggest a suitable table for us to retire to.

I walk into the bar, hypervigilant, always on the lookout – exits, toilets, windows, fire doors, stairs, any way in or out, I have to know, I need to know everything. The interior smells old, not a bad smell just like old timber tainted with alcohol. These smells weren't noticed prior to the smoking ban, back then everything smelt the same, stale smoke and ash. I have no idea what Spice wants to drink as he's not fucking here so he can wait. I just hope he's joined the lads at the table, but if I have to be brutally honest, if he doesn't show I'll not be that fussed. I order the drinks and look at my phone for any missed calls, there are none. I can't see outside from here as my line of sight is blocked by some fuck-off wooden posts. I keep looking around – any sudden movements catch my eye, paranoia, call it what you want, but it's people like me who notice things that could be out of place and potentially harmful. Not sure if it's a good or a bad thing, I'll never be able to fully switch off. Good for everyone else but a fucking ball ache for me.

The barman places the drinks onto a tray, which slightly bends as I pick it up. I can almost guarantee the tray will be sloshing with half the contents spilling from the glasses placed upon it – who in this world designs pub trays out of bendy metal? The brewery selling the beer no doubt. Still it would be worth grabbing a fourth glass for the slops on the tray. That'll sort Spice out, the scruffy fucker. I walk outside, look over at the table and much to my disappointment, Spice is sitting there, smoking. I take a seat next to The Boy and hand out the drinks. Against my better judgement I ask Spice, "Do you want a drink?" And he surprises me by saying, "No I'm okay ta, don't worry about it." Feeling stunned at this I ask again, "Are you sure?" He takes a deep inhalation on his cigarette and says, "Okay, yeah I'll have a pint," for fuck's sake. I chuck him a fiver and say "Help yourself mate." Spice gets up and ambles off towards the pub entrance.

I look at the lads and ask, "What time did he rock up?" The Boy responds saying, "He's literally just sat down, said he'd had a blow-out with his bird." I look at my phone, it's ten past and say, "Well at least he's here." What I'm really thinking is, 'he's fucking late'. I say to them, "I won't go over anything yet as Spice needs to hear it as well." The lads agree and we engage in meaningless chit-chat. The truth is none of us have anything in common. The only thing that has brought us together is drug dealing, and that's not really any way to form a friendship. It's false and anyone who says it is, is wrong. You may meet the odd person that you get on with, but we are all driven by this industry and what it has to offer. Friends are hard to find, and you will rarely find a good one here.

Spice exits the pub sporting a pint and a bag of fucking nuts, the cheeky bastard. He sits down and lights up another fag. I stare at him for a while, I want my change back, this isn't a matter of money it's a matter of trust, reliability, and principle. If he's capable of fleecing me for a couple of pounds then he's more than capable of skimming the top off of the odd bar, this will upset my customers and put me in a difficult position. I continue to stare at him as he takes a gulp from his pint, he then proceeds to light up a cigarette. I shake my head and say to all of them, "Okay, thanks for coming down. I appreciate things are a bit fucked at the moment but I've been given the all clear to get resupplied." Spice says, "That's good, I need the work desperately." I just look at him as he rips open the bag of nuts and pours them directly into his mouth. I'm really starting to dislike this guy. I go on to say, "There is an immense amount of pressure on me to get this debt down. It's fucking huge and I need to get a fair bit through the door which means you should all get plenty of work."

The lads all seem pretty attentive, so I carry on; either Alfie's got them well trained or is it the fact that they are a little unsure about me, fuck knows. I look at The Boy and say, "Mate, because of your recent arrest I can't risk you carrying anything, not until I'm sure you're clean, so if you're happy you can store and weigh it up – is this okay for you?" The Boy looks delighted and says, "Yep, cool with me, thanks." I then look at Red, "Because you don't finish until six you can see the customers that aren't ready during the day, the evening shift, but it won't be any later than nine, I don't want anyone out later than that." Red agrees. I half-heartedly look at Spice who's almost nailed his pint and say, "You'll be doing the day shift about midday till whenever – happy with this?" Spice smiles and nods.

I look around the area, then looking at Spice and The Boy I say, "The first lot is due in tomorrow, not sure what time but I'll be giving you both a heads-up," Spice just nods. I clear my throat and say "Everyone wants nines so there won't be any fucking about with weighing it up, it will come prepacked and it will be delivered exactly as we received it, 'intact'." As I close the statement I look directly at Spice – he doesn't react, he just finishes off the nuts I've just bought for him.

My next statement is clear. "All money given will be in a sealed envelope or envelopes depending on numbers. Do not open anything up, fucking leave it as it is, this is to protect you from any shortfalls. If I get a package that's open or has been interfered with and it comes up light, you will pay the fucking shortfall. Understood?" I again look more at Spice rather than the others, they all nod in agreeance. I then say, "If they give you a package that isn't sealed, fucking pull 'em for it." They all look a little concerned so I say, "Look, I'm not being a prick about this, but I have to make sure you guys are protected against any piss-takers. I wouldn't be giving you the work if I didn't trust you." I actually look at The Boy and

Red when saying this. Red says, "I'm happy with that and it makes sense, thanks." I look at the other two and say, "Any thoughts, are you happy with this so far?" They both nod.

I look at them and decide that while I'm laying down the law I may as well do it properly. I say, "I know we've not worked together yet, but all I ask is that we communicate clearly and by that I don't mean talk in clear sentences, what I mean is if I call, you answer. If you miss the call then call me back ASAP. I do not want to be in a position where I can't get hold of you." I look at The Boy and say, "You may think you have an easy ride but you need to be on the ball. I need to be able to get hold of you twenty-four seven, no excuses." The Boy frowns and says, "How come?" I answer, "It's because you will be sitting on top of tens of thousands of pounds' worth of kit. I'll need to be able to access it during the day. The only time I'll call at night is if there's a problem and you'll need to clean up, so have a secure place outside where you can stash it if need be." The Boy smiles, nods and says, "Yeah, that's fine. I know where I can put it in the event of an emergency." I respond quickly saying, "Don't forget while it's in your care, you are responsible for it, that's what you get paid for."

Well I think that went well. They all appear to be happy with their given roles, and despite my reservations with Spice I'm fairly confident in their abilities to get the job done. I'll be happier tomorrow once the first lot has gone out. I look at them sitting there, not talking, there's no sense of team here, they aren't really clicking as a group. This is a concern because there will be a lack of loyalty. We may not be friends but we are a group with a common goal and for this to work there has to be synergy, without this my job is made harder. I have to come up with a much more hands-on approach, sorting their shit out for them, but this is a new team and untested. I'm just going to have to bide my time and see how they work out.

Simultaneously Red, The Boy and I finish our drinks off. Spice has been staring into the bottom of an empty glass for a while now, he looks vacant, lost. I say, "Well if nobody's got anything else to add then I'm gonna fuck off." They all look at me and apart from Spice seem quite content to get on their way. I choose this moment to attempt to build a bridge. I grab Spice and say, "Have you got a moment?" I look at the other two and say, "I'll call you with timings when I know more." They simply acknowledge this with a nod as they head off towards the exit.

I ask Spice, "Are you okay?" With a blank stare he looks at me and says, "Yeah, why?" I reply, "You don't seem to be with it – if you're having problems I need to know you're good for this." He looks down at the ground and says, "It's my bird, she's doing my fucking nut in." Trying not to show my amusement I say, "Is it major or just a tiff?" Spice says, "Not sure. I've only just met her but she's fuckin nuts." This is raising red flags for me, so I say in as a caring way as possible, "It's probably nothing major, just get home and patch things up." Spice looks at me and says, "I'm on my arse mate, can you sub me some money until I get paid?" For fuck's sakes, he's not even started and he's asking for dosh. I look at him, hard in the eyes and say, "I'm not exactly flush. I can probably chuck you a score, maybe thirty quid, but you'll need to make sure you got fuel and phone credit for tomorrow." Spice says, "How much for fuel?" This is not going well. I breathe in and out then look over his shoulder. I'm feeling uneasy about the whole thing. I squint and say, "If I chuck you thirty quid, you'll need about twenty for fuel as you will be going over the bridge and down the road, so about ninety miles give or take." Spice looks at me and says, "Okay. It'll have to do," and holds out his hand. I look at his dirty hand stained with tobacco; this is a whole new level of blatant greed, this is not a good sign. Every fibre in my body is saying "fuck him off, bin him now" but the humanitarian part, the annoying part that wants to help others regardless of how it ends for me, nearly always gets the better of me. I give him the thirty pounds which he takes and says "cheers". Spice sticks the money in his pocket and simply fucks off.

I casually walk out of the pub, looking around as I do. The lads have gone but I still have to be mindful that there might well be some kind of op being conducted. So as usual I deploy all my standard counter surveillance techniques in an attempt to draw any would-be pursuers out of the shadows. Not that easy on foot but when in a car it's a piece of piss. I reach my car and, while opening the door, I have a good long look at the pub entrance for any suspicious activity. No one else has really moved so I get into my car and head out of the area, constantly checking my rear-view mirror for anything, nothing. Feeling fairly at ease, I head home for the night. There's no point calling Skimmer as I'm quite sure they'll be on the blower as soon as the coke lands.

* * *

Yet another restless night. I'm feeling way too apprehensive about getting back to work. These guys all have their pros and cons, except for Spice, he unfortunately only has cons, but as it stands he's mobile and willing and that will have to suffice for now. The other two, yeah I'm sure they will be fine, but time will tell; my main problem is I can't afford any fuckups. The slightest mistake has the potential to be extremely costly and could throw me further into debt. Even if I can stick to the proposed amount of paying about a grand a week, it'll take me well over a year to recover, that's if everything runs smoothly. This is a hell of a mountain to climb. I just don't know if it can be done, what with an untested group of lads and having the likes of Cliff breathing down my neck. The temptation to get rid of him is so fucking strong, but as it stands he's not actually done anything severe enough to warrant a hit.

I take the usual drive out of the area as my phone comes to life. I have no reason to expect any bad news, so far as I can tell an arrangement is in place and if everyone does their job right, all parties should be satisfied. Noting the phone is silent, no messages, that's a first in quite a while; with the silence comes a feeling of being slightly at ease. This is nice, I don't feel stressed, I actually feel a bit positive and my reservations about the lads just fades away and now I'm filled with confidence. However, it is only half seven, and generally speaking things don't go wrong first thing in the morning, unless your door's gone through; most issues happen at night when everyone is active and running around.

I don't even bother to text anyone, there's no point they'll contact me, so I opt to take a drive into town just to kill a bit of time. The drive helps me focus, it helps me to process my thoughts and plans for the day, I already know who's doing what. My role in this group is to organise the lads and ensure that they get to their destinations on time. This sounds easy, and it should be, but you throw an untested team together and have new faces delivering to regular customers and the customers will be a little sketchy, and quite rightly so, they don't want to be getting caught as a result of some newbie fucking up. It's like being an air traffic controller, precision timing is crucial. If the drivers are running late, the customers will normally call me to get a sitrep. It's then down to me to find out what's going on and mediate between the driver and the customer. This is great for getting the job done but fucking horrendous if we all get nicked.

The next couple of hours are spent taking in the morning sun, down by the river. When under extreme stress it's hard to appreciate the simple things in life, even more so when you're about seventy bags in the red. My phone rings, it's Skimmer and the anxiety starts creeping in. I just hope Skimmer's got good news for me. I say, "Morning, how are we looking?" Skimmer replies, "All good, are you ready?" This is the news I've been waiting for, so I say, "Pretty much, I'll fire the lads up and get back to you." I then say, "Mate, can you double check that the cars have well-fitted seat covers." Skimmer chuckles and says, "Trust issues?" I reply, "No mate, just a new team – start as we mean to go on and all that." Skimmer says, "I'll make sure the seats are well protected." "Thanks mate, I'll be in touch ASAP." We end the call.

13. NOT EASY MONEY

Okay, so it's just after eleven. Spice should be awake and I'd like to think primed, because I would be, but yet again this is another call that fills me with anticipation, because I'm expecting a problem of some kind. The phone rings for a while and I can already feel my frustration sneaking in. I'm thinking, he'd better fucking answer, but as soon as this thought manifests itself Spice answers, simply saying "Alright." I can't help not liking him, he's just not my bag. With a slight feeling of contempt I say to him, "Ready when you are, are you all sorted?" Much to my surprise he replies saying, "Yes, I'm good to go." Okay, so now I'm feeling slightly better about this, "Where are you? I'll head up to you, then I'll give you all the details," I say. Spice gives me his location. I cut the call short and head his way.

On route to Spice's, I call The Boy and warn him that there will be work arriving in about an hour and to be ready. He suggested he get a bus closer to me to save Spice going out of his way. I knew The Boy was good, he could have quite easily sat on his arse and just waited, but I guess he's got a little bit more about him. We decide on a suitable meeting place and agree for Spice to be there in about an hour. I approach the area where Spice lives and much like the area that Alfie used to live in, it's a fucking shithole. Carrying the burden of hypervigilance comes in handy at times like this, but is a pain in the fucking bollocks when I try to relax. I park at the end of his street with my arcs covered and drop-call him.

I've got my eye on the whole road. I didn't ask Spice for his address but I intend to eyeball where he's living. It's always worth having some kind of insurance policy in place for runners that can't be totally trusted, and unfortunately Spice is one such runner. I clock him as he emerges from a house only a few feet away. It's the large plume of smoke that gave his location away. I remain in situ, again testing him for awareness and, just as I thought, he walks straight past me, like a fucking steam train leaving a cloud of smoke behind him. He stops at the end of the road, literally feet away and he still hasn't noticed me. I wait, patiently watching him in my mirrors, this has now become more of an exercise of curiosity. What's he gonna do? Fuck all, he just stands there smoking, sticking out like a sore thumb, and his big fuck-off head of orange hair isn't exactly helping – ginger prick.

This is getting silly now. I drop the window and discreetly call to get his attention. He looks over, casually wanders over and gets in the car, still fucking smoking. I look at him and politely ask him "Please don't smoke in my car," and like a scolded child he opens the window, takes a big puff and throws what's left out of the window and in a feeble attempt he exhales out of the window. As expected, the majority of the smoke finds its way back into the car. Shaking my head I pull away and begin to slowly drive around the local area; I spend this time giving him his instructions, contacts, locations and amounts. I even give him a bit of a brief on the customers, what to expect and how to interact. Spice just looks at me, he doesn't have to say anything. I know what he's thinking, he's thinking, 'why do I need to know all this?' So without him having to open his fucking gob I tell him, "This is important, some of these customers have been with me for a long time, they've stuck around because they know I respect how they operate and in turn they reciprocate the same respect." I look at him and you can tell he just doesn't get it. He's got his orders and as far as I'm concerned he can just fuck off, so I drop the useless prick off. He gets out and while I drive off, I can't help thinking, 'he's gonna cause dramas.'

I call all my customers and use a variety of codes. I give the heads-up and potential timings of a pending delivery; apart from one that doesn't answer, they're all ready for either Spice to see them soon or Red at some point in the early evening. The guy that didn't answer was Mick. I know he's hard work and does at times need chasing, but he can shift a bit so he's worth holding on to for now. My only reservation is his ability to operate as effectively with coke as he does with pot, time will tell.

That's the bulk of my work done. I'm now on standby to oversee Spice doing his run; it's hard going and can be stressful, especially with a new runner and even more so with a runner that I don't have complete faith in. Here's how it works: if I hear nothing for ages it means he's either got everything bang on, and has managed the whole run without any delays, or, and this is the one that creates the stress, has dropped a massive bollock, then I'm more likely to hear from an irate customer wondering what the fuck is going on and where's their coke. So, when briefing new runners, I have to be quite clear about my methods. The guys need to let the customers know how they are getting on. When you leave, you say, "on my way ETA in one hour", or whatever, then you call them when you are arriving. If you hit a delay, let them know, don't keep them guessing, it's not rocket science.

Fortunately it's not long before I get the much anticipated call from Skimmer giving me the heads-up. In turn I pass this info on to Spice who will be then left to his own devices to contact The Boy so he can arrange offloading Red's workload for later. This all sounds straightforward, and it is if you're not a complete fucking idiot, but the very nature of a drug runner usually means that they're not always the sharpest or most dynamic of characters, if they were then they wouldn't be in the job in the first place. I have to show faith though, I can't run the guy down for being willing to take risks on my behalf, so I'll just have to wait out until the job is done.

The next few hours pass with zero comms, and as mentioned this has the desired effect of fucking my head right up, but I don't want to start calling people, they'll call if there's a problem, and so far so good. I know how long it takes to do this run, fuck me I've done it so many times I can visualise the whole route in my head, just shy of three hours and that's allowing twenty minutes for a coffee with Bill, unless I hit traffic, but during the working day this rarely happens.

It's getting close to four and the phone goes, I can't help having a little arse twitch, as I look at the phone and see it's Spice. Timings are on par for a job-done report, so I answer, "You all good?" Spice immediately replies saying, "Yep all sorted." I breathe a large sigh of relief and say, "Nice one mate, that's you done for the day – did you have any issues?" Spice says, "No." Short answer but good enough. Feeling slightly relieved I say, "Okay, I'll give you a shout towards the end of the week to sort wages." Spice says, "Can I get paid today as I'm skint?" For fuck's sake here we go again, has he forgotten how much I owe, but then this isn't his problem is it. I reply, "I'll see what I can do later. Red has a couple of cash deals so he might be able to drop yours off later." Spice says "Ta" and hangs up.

One run down and one to go. The Boy will be the one carrying the baton at the moment so the burden in a way is with him, but it's not, it's with me, it's always with me and I will always be responsible for the goods until they are paid for. Red finishes at six so all being well he'll be done by half eight; he's got the other three to cover, but they are out of town. I've called Red and let him know the score and Red is a seasoned runner for Alfie. He's been collecting my coke in bulk for a couple of months now, and so far he's given no dramas.

I try my best to switch off and let them get on with it. I must have faith, but I've taken so many knocks in the last couple of years, I just can't help feeling a tad beaten. I can't even go home, I need my burner on at all times, I just have to sit it out, waiting patiently for it to go tits-up, fucking great life. Easy money – my arse.

I look at the time and it's approaching six. Red will be getting on his way now, and there will be some cash to collect in as well, but this will be left for the last drop. I don't want him carrying cash unnecessarily, I got to think about damage limitation at all times. I spend the next hour and a half driving from one place to another, periodically looking at my phone for any missed messages or calls, but there aren't. Another hour passes and the phone goes – it's Mick, this doesn't look good, so I answer and say, "How's it going, have you seen him?" Mick replies, "No I've heard nothing." I say, "What, nothing at all?" Mick again says, "No, is he still coming down?" Well that's it, my head has just fucking gone, what the fuck is going on? I quickly say to Mick, "Leave it with me, I'll chase him up." I hang up and call The Boy who answers immediately in his usual chirpy way, "Hello mate." Feeling quite unsure about how to feel I say, "Has Red seen you yet?" The Boy answers saying, "No, but he said he'll be with me at about nine." "Nine, why so late?" The Boy says, "Don't know mate, he just said he was busy." What a fucking prick. I say, "Okay, thanks I'll call later," and hang up.

Red is supposed to be the reliable one, I call him, he answers in a blasé tone, "Alright what's up?" What's up, what's fucking up, is he for real? I compose myself and say, "Are you still okay to work tonight?" Red says, "Yes mate why?" I say, "Well, I've had a call saying that they've heard nothing and it's getting late." Red says "Yeah, well my Mrs needed to go shopping and she needed the car." I'm not being funny but what the fuck has that got to do with me, so I say, "Could you not have taken the bike?" Red replies "Suppose." Is that it, "suppose" that's all he has to say "suppose"? I've been stressing for the last two hours for nothing, this is putting fucking years on me, just so he can take his Mrs fucking shopping. I say, "Don't you think it would have been a good idea to inform everyone of your delay?" To that Red says, "Yes I suppose." I can feel my blood boiling and I never thought I'd say this, but I'm tempted to fuck Red off and give all the work to Spice. I say to Red "Do me a favour, can you call all the lads and give them a heads-up and some idea of your timings?" Red acknowledges this and feeling quite deflated I say goodbye. I'm fucked, ordinarily I'd just fuck him off or give him a proper bollocking, but I have a serious shortage of manpower, so for now, I'll just have to suck it up.

All things said and done, the next few hours pass without hitch and despite Red's lacklustre approach everyone gets seen and Spice gets paid. It's gone eleven and I'm Red's last drop as he offloads the rest of the money to me. This time of night is way past my comfort zone, such a high risk of being pulled. I know it's only a few grand tucked neatly into an envelope, but neat or not the police will still have a field day if they find it. I look at the time and it's approaching midnight. I slowly allow myself to relax and slip into a daydream state, still hypervigilant but chilled, for me this is a must. It's the only way I can happily carry money or drugs, because if I am pulled, I don't give off any signs of someone shitting their pants with a car full of drugs, cash or both.

* * *

Surprisingly, the last couple of weeks have run extremely well. I've gotten used to Spice being needy, Red being slow, and The Boy – well from time to time he does go on a bender, but as yet it hasn't created any problems. I've stayed on top of my running debt and paid three grand off of my bill. Cliff has behaved and his boys have been on the ball with the supply of coke, and I've had no complaints. Although I'm under extreme stress, I don't actually feel it, maybe I've got used to it, but then again when I think about the sixty-odd grand I still owe, my heart sinks like a lead balloon.

Another month has passed and the pressure for some reason has become relentless, regardless of my faultless repayments, Cliff has gone fucking bonkers. He's screaming down the phone on a daily basis, "I want my fucking money, you need to work harder," and all that bullshit. This change of mood is usually a sign that something has changed in his life and he's squeezing every fucker. Unfortunately this pressure has caused significant problems on my end, as I've had to up the pressure on my runners and as much as I hate to do it, some of my customers. So inevitably the cracks have started to show. They aren't used to me applying this level of pressure. My customers are beginning to back off and buy less, which in turn reduces the amount I earn. I can feel a downward spiral and once this starts, it's extremely hard to recover.

The nights are drawing in as autumn is upon us. This brings the added benefit of the cover of darkness and poorer visibility and would have played well into the hands of the lads doing the running but regrettably everything has gone tits-up. I've lost all three of Alfie's lads. Thankfully not to the police, but they have been chewed up and spat out by the hostile and unpredictable world of cocaine, every last one of them gone.

Let me start with Red, his blasé approach got the better of me, he was consistently late, and his comms were fucking atrocious, he created his own problems. He'd take his Mrs shopping or something like that, keep the lads hanging around for hours with no rhyme or reason. He'd then turn up on plot and be sat in a meeting place for fucking ages loaded up with coke, wondering why the customers aren't ready, they're not ready because you're fucking late – I lost a potentially good customer and because of this, you're fucking sacked, fuck off, I'll do it myself.

Spice, he began to show promise, until The Boy let something slip about Spice's Mrs. His words were, "Spice has got his Mrs with him again," so, my thoughts are if they're old enough to know the score then it's up to them, plus having a couple in the car can create a better impression, that's until The Boy said, "Yeah, she's a crack whore, rough as fuck." Oh, that's just fucking perfect, so my guard is officially up. You cannot have a crack head around coke, no, no, no, not gonna fucking happen. However, I didn't sack him because as it stood there were no complaints of the packages being light or interfered with.

But it's inevitable, a crackhead will eventually exhaust every avenue for a supply, and when the money runs out they will then start dipping in, it's just a matter of when, not if. So, Spice was due into work, he'd collected a couple of bags the previous night, and it was a bit late to meet so I said I'd see him in the morning. I was ringing his phone and getting nothing, it was ringing but just ringing off. I needed that fucking money; Cliff was throwing his dummies out of the pram and needed sorting.

Eventually Spice answered the phone. He's bumbling like fuck, and as far as I was concerned it's just noise. I said, "Where the fuck are you? I need that money now," so the stuttering fuck just said, "I'm doing a job out of town." I replied, "Out of town, what do you mean, you know I need that money, where, where are you?" Spice said, "Cornwall." Fucking Cornwall, what a load of bollocks, so I said, "Okay mate, no problem, do me a favour will you?" Spice by that time seemed to compose himself and said, "Yeah sure, what?" what he didn't know was that I was about to dig him out.

I said, "Go to a public call box, the first one you see." Spice then said "Why?" I simply answered, "Because mate, I want you to call me from a public phone from Cornwall, and, if I don't see a Cornish dialling code you're fucked." The phone went quiet for a while and if I wasn't so pissed off this would have been funny. He then said, "Okay, I'll try and find one." Predictably my phone didn't ring, and Spice did a fucking excellent job of ignoring all my calls. I eventually received a text from Spice, "Sorry mate, my Mrs stole the money and has fucked off, I've been trying to find her, I'll have to pay it back." Fucking right you will, you're sacked, fuck off, I'll do it myself.

The Boy, such a shame as he showed so much potential and although he did go on the occasional bender, he seemed to function well – fuck me, all he had to do was babysit the drugs. But life being as it is, his relationship became somewhat volatile and this was yet again down to coke. His Mrs wasn't happy with it being in the house, I'm sensing a common theme here. So, he had to begin stashing it in his designated emergency place, the one that was outside. This carries its own set of problems. If left unattended it runs the risk of it being found, it happens, and it'll be found by someone conscientious and that will lead to the police being involved.

So, The Boy being equally conscientious, for different reasons took it upon himself to continue the babysitting service, by parking his car up by the chosen bush and setting up camp. This wasn't necessary, every day as generally speaking it might only be there for a couple of days. But nonetheless he did it anyway. So, you might be thinking, 'so, what's the problem?' The problem starts when The Boy tucked into my fucking coke and had parties in his car to keep himself entertained while the long cold nights drew in. He would happily plough through half an ounce a night, he was absolutely smashing it. I couldn't get hold of him for days at a time, and as much as I hated to do it, fuck off, you're sacked, I'll do it myself.

These three have set me back over a month as I'm now coming up short by another three grand. Cliff has gone fucking nuts. I've lost a customer, I have no staff, nowhere to keep the coke, my pill sales are dead because they're shit so nobody wants them. In a word, "I'm fucked."

14. MAN DOWN

Well you know what they say, "if a job is worth doing, don't employ anyone that's hanging out the back of a Crackwhore", or something like that. As an indirect result of this I'm officially back on the ground, and have been for a couple of weeks, yet again taking all the risks. Yes, on the plus side I'm saving money on runners, storage and I know exactly what's going on. The understandable downside is that I will be covering a lot of ground; too much ground for one man plus I'll be forced to store any excess drugs at home or at least close by. The fact of the matter is, I no longer have the luxury of choice, that was taken away from me when Alfie's lads couldn't deal with the extra stresses put upon them from the coke industry and to top it all off Cliff is going berserk – dummies and toys everywhere. There's no talking or reasoning, he just fucking screams, even Flash is getting too loud and as far as I'm concerned totally unnecessary. I might have been a tankie and used to loud bangs but I'm not deaf, so please, stop fucking shouting because my greatest fear is, that a time may come when my self-control will no longer be enough, my hand will be forced and I will go and put one in him.

Running drugs isn't my concern, my problem is that I keep ending up back at square one, and rarely is it my doing. It's nearly always a backlash of someone else dropping the ball, the difference this time is that virtually every penny I earn is to be handed over to Cliff. I'm not averse to this. I just don't care for his tiring noisy gangster attitude, screaming and shouting like a banshee. He gets paid either way so why be so emotional, it's almost childlike, but regardless of his demeanour I owe him and he will get paid.

Despite the amount of grief I'm getting, my focus must remain on the job in hand and that is to keep this wheel spinning, keep the customers on board, that's what gets the bills paid. This shouldn't be a problem, so long as the supply is good and consistent; then the only problem I'll have, should have, to be aware of is the obvious one – getting nicked. If only that were true, the reality is much worse. I'm constantly lying to my family, I never see my kids and when I do I'm too busy stressing about the next day. I'm carrying a huge debt over my head, as well as a constant running debt for a new supply – talking of supply, there are always issues linked to the distribution of the stuff and that's putting it mildly. The customers are the most important part of business but they are usually the biggest problem.

As it happens, losing Mick as a customer has been a bit of a blessing. Miles has increased sales by nicking his customers, the difference is, Miles is on point and is never short or late with payments, which is great, the backlash of this is, Mick has an outstanding bill that needs to be settled. Repayment of this is hindered with a lack of customers stolen by Miles; either way, trade will be coming my way, they can fight it out between themselves. Not my problem, and if this comes across as selfish or greedy, that's because it is.

Some of the issues I have to contend with, aside from the debt of course, issues that are potentially damaging for business are customers that consistently fuck up. Boe, who I inherited from Alfie is one and Mick is the other; a certain amount of disruption is to be expected, but these two are hard fucking work. Boe will take on between a half and a whole key at a time, which on paper looks great, but when it comes to payment he's either got the majority of it left or moans like fuck that the quality was poor and he's had loads of complaints. This of course totally fucks up my repayment plans for Cliff, the goods need to be paid either way. I know for a fact that the coke's shit, I also know that Cliff will be stepping on mine a little harder than usual, as he's trying to recover funds lost. Then there's Mick who is now nothing more than a depressing mood hoover. He constantly whines about how difficult his life is and that he's trying his best. So, between the two of them I'm using most of my energy stressing about whether they will have any money for me or not.

As a result of these two causing such headaches I'm having to cut deals with my good customers to see if they can turn things around a bit quicker, giving me funds a little sooner than usual, the problem with this is they want a better price which then reduces my profits even further. So, what eventually happens is I run around like a fucking idiot all day and night sometimes to just cover the cost of the coke that's been laid out that week. The result of this is my debt doesn't go down, it just sits there stressing me out. So, Cliff screaming at me, giving me unrealistic targets, is fucking up my repayments. I know something has gone wrong for him; he only gets like this when he's under pressure.

* * *

It's November and I've been grinding this bullshit out since the summer, and so far I don't see an end to it. I've got no choice and with a heavy heart I have to give up my car and the ten grand, just to take a lump out of the debt. Cliff wants the car, he always has. I'm hoping to get around twenty-five grand, truth is he knows it's worth a lot more, and if I add that to the ten grand I've got tucked away, that's a fucking good lump.

I call Cliff, he answers and surprisingly sounds quite civil, "Yes mate what's up?" I take a deep breath hoping that this will be the answer to some of my problems and say, "Look mate, I'm doing my best to get the rent paid but I'm hitting brick walls all the time. I've got an offer for you." The phone goes quiet for a bit then Cliff says, "You want to give me your car don't you?" I replied, "Yeah, how did you guess?" Now sounding somewhat smug, he says, "Because it's all you got left." Feeling defeated I then say, "Yes you're right, and you know how much that car means to me." Cliff then says, "I'll give you ten for it." My reply is swift, "Go fuck yourself, I can sell it privately for thirty all day long; you can have it for twenty-five, plus I can give you ten grand cash as I have some parts to get rid of – take it or leave it."

Normally if someone tells Cliff "to go fuck himself" he gets quite irate, but he knows that I know he's always wanted that car. Cliff says, "Drop it to Skimmer today, when can you get the ten?" Suddenly feeling a lot better about things I say, "Should be a couple of days, I have a buyer interested in these bits." Cliff then says something quite disturbing, "Thanks mate, speak later," and hangs up. As if by magic, I feel good, the stress has totally been lifted, I've just paid thirty-five grand off of my bill. Okay, I still owe twenty-seven, but I've just halved it. I feel a mass sense of euphoria, it's been months since I last felt like this.

But the euphoria doesn't last long, just a few days as I'm back on the tools, and now this twenty-seven grand seems to loom up on me like a bad dream. I now have nothing left to bail out with, I've used my trump cards, if I have problems now I will be proper fucked. The relentless running around spinning the wheel, the circle of debt just hovers around the twenty-five mark, it's just not shifting. The coke is getting poorer and my customers are beginning to back off, they are taking less and less and returning more and more. I have to resale the shit that comes back in at a lower cost just to cover the bill, and yet again I make nothing, my debt remains the same.

So much for Cliff loving the car. He's decided to flog it, he only had it for a couple of weeks, fuck knows what he got for it, but the pressure from him is so fucking intense it's beginning to fuck with my head. I can't think straight anymore. I just spend what little money I do have on shit beer and drink myself to sleep, waking up hungover and under extreme pressure. The daily drive out of town becomes a grind, it's an effort, my customers have all but jumped ship. I'm literally driving around to collect pennies; at times I spend more on fuel than I manage to collect. It's fucking soul-destroying, I can't look my Mrs in the eye anymore, I don't even have the mental capacity to be a dad. This is seriously wearing me down.

Although I try to vary my route as much as possible it's hard to avoid the fact that I have to visit the same people in the same areas, consequently I'm doing the same kind of journey every time. Once I leave the city I immediately hit the countryside, it's beautiful, rolling hills and lovely winding roads, but my head is so fucked I don't notice any of it. The only thing I do notice is that every time I pass a certain point, I turn onto a road that winds up a steep hill bordered by a small stone wall and at the bottom of this hill is a small river where standing alone is a large tree. Every time I pass this spot and on my return journey I wonder how easy it would be to just crash through the wall and hammer it down the hill and into the tree. Surely this would take the pain away; this would solve everything. Every fucking time I think, what would it feel like, going through the wall, down the hill – would I die or would I be unlucky and just be seriously injured or worse still just write the car off and walk away? I just want a way out, a means to escape the constant pain and suffering, the endless stress and anxiety. I can't fucking take it anymore, I wish I was dead, dead would be so much easier than the pressure I'm putting on myself to get the job done and pay this fucking debt.

But I can't, I love my kids too much, I can't punish them for my mistakes, I have to be strong for them, they need their dad and my wife needs her husband back. This is the only thing stopping me from smashing through the wall and to a potentially miserable death. But the pain won't go, it's there when I go to sleep and it's still there when I wake, I can't continue like this. I can feel my mental stability beginning to crumble. I've been down before but this is different, this is serious, if I don't do something about it I'm gonna lose my head. As if something inside of me clicked I do something totally out of character – I switch off my phone and, despite the job in hand, I turn around and head back towards home. If I'm going to get through this I need help, I can no longer function well enough to deal with the stresses inflicted on me from this world that I now live in.

I'm not thinking about anything now, I don't care what happens about the debt, all I care about is my fucking sanity. Fuck Cliff, I know he'll be going off his nut but I can't face it, not any more, I've tried so hard but I finally feel that this life has defeated me and I've joined the mass of people that the cocaine industry has pulled in and spat out, ruined and beaten. All I feel now is a strong pressure inside my head, bubbling away, it's so intense it hurts, seriously hurts.

The drive back seems to pass by in slow motion, I'm not really taking anything in, I'm just driving, one set of lights or roundabout at a time. My new destination is the doctor's, I'm not a religious man but I pray the Doc can help me, I don't even know what I'm going to say, or do. I just need help, but I'm fucking terrified if the Doc fucks me off. As a squaddie it's hard to accept defeat, I thought I could handle anything, but I can't, not anymore, I'm broken.

Pulling into the doctors' surgery car park feels weird because I still don't know what I'm supposed to say – I'm not ill, well not in the traditional sense, I'm just losing the plot. It's late afternoon and fortunately the doctors' waiting room is quiet, just two other people sat minding their own business. I approach the reception desk and the receptionist asks if I have an appointment. My answer is vague at best. I just say, "Please can I see my doctor." The receptionist asks for my details which I provide, and she verifies who I am. I guess they can operate with a degree of discretion because she didn't ask anything else, she just said to take a seat.

I slowly wander over to the part of the waiting room where nobody else is sitting and take a seat with the exit clearly in sight. I lean forward and grab a magazine from the rack in front of me, I don't know what it is and I don't really care as I have no intention of reading it. No sooner than I open the magazine and start flicking through the pages of pointless bullshit, I hear the receptionist call my name and say, "Can you please go to room number two." I carefully place the mag back where I found it, squaring off the small stack of magazines as I get up, old habits and all that. Still clueless about what I'm going to say, I leave the waiting room and walk into the corridor where I can clearly see room two with the door open. It's at the far end of the corridor and as I proceed along I pass several other rooms, the doors of which are all closed. This feels odd, I honestly don't know what I'm going to say, I can't exactly say, "I owe a ton of money for a shipment of coke that was seized," or can I? I'm not sure how far doctor-patient confidentiality goes.

I look at the door and head straight in to see a familiar face, he's been my doctor for a few years, so I guess it'll make this easier, whatever this is. He swivels around on his chair and looks at me through his glasses and says, "What can I do for you today?" My only thought is 'fuck' but what actually happens is quite the opposite, I burst into tears. I don't mean quietly sobbing, I am fucking going for it, I'm crying so hard I can't even speak. Am I breaking down, is this what it feels like? The doctor continues to look at me, patiently waiting for me to get my shit together, but I can't. I've got my head in my hands and I'm bubbling like fuck, but you know what, it's helping so I keep going for a good few minutes.

After what feels like ages I look up at the doctor, my eyes are fucked, I take a deep breath and before I speak he says, "Take your time," and I'm off again. Shit what the hell's going on here, it's uncontrollable. I try again and sounding like a child that's had a proper bollocking, my bottom lip quivering, I attempt to start speaking and thank fuck the bullshit begins to flow. I go into a lengthy explanation about how I was robbed at my stall and since then I've been terrified of returning and consequently my finances have been hit and I'm in debt. I can feel the Oscar already having my name engraved in it for best male actor. But you know what – every good lie is based on certain truths. I then say, "I can't take any more, I've been thinking of killing myself," and again when I think of the reason why I don't, it sets me off again.

All the bullshit aside, I'm here for a reason. I need help so I tell him how I can't face life or my family because I'm a total failure, and I feel that if I don't get help now and I mean right fucking now I will kill myself. The doctor looking genuinely concerned says, "Can you get to the hospital to be further assessed?" My answer is, "Yes, but what will it involve?" The doctor smiled reassuringly and said, "It's likely they will keep you in overnight for observations." Basically, it's to keep an eye on me to make sure I don't top myself. I like this, it means they must be able to help me in some way. The doctor makes some notes on his system and prints off a piece of paper which he seals in an envelope, which he then hands to me and says, "Hand this into the receptionist on your arrival."

I thank the doctor for his help and, feeling embarrassed, apologise for crying all over his carpet. Clutching the envelope, I get up and head out of the surgery. I don't even know how much time has passed. I take a deep breath and I can feel the emotions deep down, it's weird because I feel numb, I have zero emotion, nothing, no happiness but no misery, so this is definitely an improvement. Having a good old cry seems to have got a few things out of the system. I get into my car and place the envelope onto the passenger seat next to my phones; without any delay I head directly for the hospital. It's only a quick ten-minute drive. On the way I look down at my phones, the burner is silent as it's off, my other is still on so I take the opportunity to call my wife and managing to get my words out – I tell her I'm working away and it might get quite late so not to worry about me if my phone's off, utter bullshit. I can't even be bothered to give a plausible reason for my pending absence, but it's the best I've got, so off goes my other phone, I am officially off the grid.

I drive into the hospital, clueless of what dept to head for, so I aim for A&E, it only feels like yesterday when I was here getting my face put back together after the Murray saga. I find a car park – pay and display – they can fuck off, I'm in no mood to dick around with tickets. I'll cross that bridge when I get to it. I park up and head directly to the A&E dept. In I walk, red-eyed and broken. With a sense of déjà vu, I approach the desk and say, "My doctor suggested I come in," and I hand her the envelope. She reaches out, takes the envelope and opens it, she looks at me and can clearly tell I've been crying. Normally I'd feel embarrassed about being in such a mess, but for some reason I don't, maybe I'm getting into character, fuck this is real, yes the story is bollocks but the emotional instability isn't. She looks at me and asks me to confirm my name, DOB and address, which I do. The receptionist asks me to take a seat, I guess it's the waiting game now.

I'm shut off from everyone, and the stress levels that had dissipated when I think of my world slowly falling apart. My concern is if Cliff or his boys can't get hold of me, they might and quite rightly, so presume the worst. The questions will be asked, "Has he been nicked? Or has he done a bunk?" They won't give a fuck about my welfare; Skimmer will but the others, not a chance. If they believe I've been nicked then they will spend the night shitting themselves, but if they think I've done a bunk they might be inclined to visit the Mrs, and although Cliff threatens this on an almost daily basis, it's unlikely that he will. That's the sort of thing that gets you shot, and he knows it.

While I mull away, still in a semi-state of numbness, I hear my name called, again I don't know how much time has passed. I've admitted defeat, it feels like I can almost shed my concerns for feeling responsible, like a case of fuck it, I no longer care if I live or die. And that's a dangerous but slightly liberating place to be, especially if certain people are made aware of my instabilities; if I can find a way to cope with stress, this whole ordeal could play into my favour. I get up and approach a set of double doors that lead out to the consultation rooms, there is a nurse standing there waiting to assist.

We walk out back, and I am ushered into a small cubicle bordered by green curtains, there is a bed and a couple of chairs. I take a seat and the nurse takes the other, she does offer me the choice of lying down but I choose to sit. She goes on to say, "Okay, we have a direct referral from your GP and he's given a brief assessment of your mental health, he believes you are suffering with a breakdown and possible depression." She then looks at me and says, "How are you feeling right now?" For fuck's sake, why did she have to ask me that, and I'm off, crying, again. This emotional stuff is hard fucking graft, it's draining, I never thought that it would be this hard, my whole body aches. I didn't even know this was possible.

This feels like a rerun of my performance in the GP's, only this time I can just about get my words out. I think the nurse can make out what I'm saying, she's not taking notes so I don't know if I'm being assessed or not, best keep crying though, just to drive the point home. So I continue to let the emotions get the better of me, simultaneously explaining how shit my life is and how I can't cope anymore. This goes on for a while and she then says, "If I bring you a questionnaire are you able to complete it?" I reply, "Yes I should be okay." She gets up and as she walks out asks, "Do you want a drink – tea, coffee or something cold?" I reply, "A cup of water please." She acknowledges this and leaves the cubicle, closing the privacy curtain behind her.

I take a look around my new surroundings, not much going on really, there's no equipment in this room, just the bed and chairs. I can hear other people in the area although it's hard to pinpoint exactly where they might be. Is this me for the night, what happens now, will I suddenly be confronted by the men in the white coats as I get nutted off? This is definitely new ground for me. I don't really care what happens next, I just want the pain to go away, so I can function again, is that too much to ask? I look at the bed and it looks quite inviting, for a moment I consider getting on it and having a quick five minutes.

Without warning the curtain is flung open and for a moment a sense of panic sets in, only to be calmed by the nurse returning with a cup of water, a piece of A4 paper and a pen. She passes me the water and then goes on to explain what the purpose of the questionnaire is. It's kind of sinking in but my mind is wandering, I'm finding it quite hard to focus on reality, very surreal, almost an out-of-my body sensation. She hands me the pen and paper, I take it and have a quick look over it as she gets up and leaves, again closing the curtain behind her.

It's about three pages long and appears to be asking a number of questions related to my mental health. I begin the arduous process of ticking boxes, it feels like a test, so unlike my school exams I care if I fuck this up. I think honesty is the best policy here. I gradually move down the list, ticking off the answers as I go; page one done, page two done, the last page, nice it's only half a page, but it does have an open box at the bottom giving me the opportunity to elaborate on my condition, and I can definitely elaborate.

Feeling relieved, I finish it off and place the pen and paper on the bed. I take a drink from the water, lean forward and put my head in my hands. I can feel my temples pulsing, my heart still hurts, and I can still feel this huge emotion as I breathe in, anxiety mixed with an overwhelming sense of sadness, failure. I sit back, hands still cupped over my face. What the fuck am I doing here? I ask myself, surely I'm better than this. I'd have laughed about this a few years back, but things were different back then, I wasn't alone, I had the lads to pull me through the bad times, I wish they were here now.

The nurse re-enters the cubicle and collects the paperwork, she then says, "It's approaching ten, so we're going to keep you in overnight. The doctor will be with you shortly to talk about what happens next. I suggest you get some rest." She looks at the bed as if to make a point. I thank her for her help and climb onto the bed as she leaves, everything goes silent.

Lying here, looking up at the ceiling, my mind is totally blank, I think about my wife and our kids, and this once again brings a tear to my eye, but this is out of a sense of guilt, pure guilt. What the fuck am I doing to them? My wife is basically bringing those kids up alone, I can't even provide anymore. I'm fucking useless, if I get out of this mess, I'm done with it, I'm going back into security, properly. Pay the debt and get the fuck out of it.

I can feel myself drifting in and out of consciousness. The room remains silent, it feels like I'm the only person in here, I can't even hear the footsteps of the nurses coming in to attend to anyone. So, when I do hear footsteps it's almost a guarantee someone is coming to see me. The curtain is gently pulled open and in walks a tall thin man, presumably a doctor, or specialist, he smiles, says hello and takes a seat next to the bed. He then says, "Okay, we've had a look at your paperwork – going on what your GP says and what you've explained to us today, we believe you are suffering from moderate to severe depression." I look at him, feeling slightly relieved that they've given me an explanation as to why I feel the way I do. He then says, "This is made manageable with medication, but unless you deal with or manage the problems that have caused the depression you will be prone to it returning or not going in the first place." The doctor asks, "Do you know what has caused the amount of stress you are under?" I look at him and say "yes", he then says, "Well that's good, at least you have a starting point." He continues for a while describing the condition and how it affects the brain, but I stopped listening a while ago. It's not really going in. I'm trying to look interested, this is becoming quite painful, I just want to go to sleep.

Eventually the doctor finishes talking and leaves me alone. Again I look up at the ceiling, this time the lights go out, it's not pitch black but dark enough to get some shut eye. I slowly drift off to sleep, visions of my kids without their dad keep creeping in. This is distressing, but I can't stop thinking about them. I can't stop thinking how much I've let them down. My youngest is only one, and hardly knows me. The oldest is six and needs a dad, but I'm not capable of being a dad and this is what kills me.

The curtain opens up and in walks a new face, he says, "Good morning, we have your paperwork ready, you just need to go to the pharmacy to collect your prescription." Wait a fucking minute mate, I'm thinking, I've got to leave the safety of this bed? Nah mate I don't want to, the stress comes back hard and fast, the reality of my situation has just smacked me straight in the face. Fuck, Cliff will be going fucking mental, my Mrs won't know where I am, this is too much, what the fuck have I done, nothing has changed. I've still got to pay the debt, I've still got to collect money, deliver drugs, it's all the same, only now I've been MIA for a night. I've fucked things right up, for what, a restless night in a hospital.

I head out of the room, towards the counter to collect my paperwork. There's no queue and the person hands me my prescription. I take it, thanking them as I do. I walk out of the building, it's bright and sunny, the warmth hits my face so I stop and close my eyes soaking up the rays, this is nice, I slowly drift off into a peaceful place; however, this is short lived as the thought of what awaits me when I switch on my phones is overwhelming, plus I still don't know what time it is. I can just about make out my car in the distance, the car park is relatively full.

As suspected when I get to my car there is a ticket on the windscreen. I just shake my head and look around to see if I can see the wanker that stuck it on there. No such luck, standard hit and run, fuckers. I climb into the car and close the door. The car is warm, it's been cooking in the morning sun. I stick the keys in the ignition and power up. The first thing I noticed is the clock, it's 07:52, thought it was later than that. The next thing I do is look at my phones, I can't do it – which one do I switch on first? Does it really matter? I grab the burner, and consider switching it on, but I can't face it. I look at my other phone, I can't face that either.

I start sobbing again, this is killing me. I lean forward and pop open the glove compartment, it's hard to reach all the way in but I manage to rummage around – ahh, there it is. I remove a small black-handled folding knife. I look around the car park, it's very quiet. Still sobbing I open the knife, the sun reflecting off of the razor-sharp blade, it's never been used. I look at the blade which is slightly serrated and press it up against my wrist. I'm crying uncontrollably, but I'm not really sure why but it feels like the answer. I push the blade harder against my skin, it doesn't hurt as I slowly draw the knife across my wrist. I see a few little spots of blood appear, then I see a vision of my kids crying, my wife comforting them. I immediately throw the knife onto the floor and look at my wrist, it's bleeding but not bad, I grab some tissues from the door pocket and apply them to the wound. Fuck! What am I thinking?

As if something just clicked inside I decide to face the music, things can't possibly get any worse for me right now. I switch on my burner and wait, it comes to life, but there's nothing, no messages, no beeps. I switch on my other phone, again nothing. What the fuck is going on, this isn't expected at all. Right fuck it, I'm calling Cliff and telling him the score, I don't care what he thinks but he needs to know what he's dealing with. I make the call and it rings for a short while; he answers, "What happened to you last night?" That's a fair question, so I say, "I ended up in hospital." Cliff doesn't do compassion, so how he reacts to this will at least be interesting. He says, "Oh what happened?" I simply say, "I've been diagnosed with depression so they kept me in for tests." Cliff goes quiet for a while and says, "Look, this debt is taking a while to go down and it hit me quite hard, I do have a way you can pay it off a bit quicker." At this point he's almost sounding civil. I say, "Okay, what are you thinking?" He says, "You can bring it over." My answer is quick and without hesitation I say, "Fuck it, why not!"

TO BE CONTINUED…

Glossary

A & E	Accident & Emergency
ANPR	Automatic numberplate recognition
Arcs	Military term for an area covered for laying down fire or observation.
Bag/Bags, "a bag of sand"	Grand/s money
Balance the books	To take the edge off of being under the influence.
Bangs out	Sells
Bashed	Cocaine that has been adulterated or mixed to reduce purity and increase volume.
Bass	Pure Amphetamine
Blender, A	Fits into a crowd and is very unassuming.
Bog roll	Toilet roll
Bollocking	A good telling off
Bollocks	Testicles
Bought	To be believed
Breakfast	Early morning joint
Brew	Hot drink
Bugle	Nose
Burner	A mobile phone used for illegal activities that can be disposed of.
Car parts	Drugs
Casing	Watching
Charlie	Cocaine
Class A's	Class A drugs such as Cocaine/Ecstasy
Clean up	To get rid of or move any drugs or money from the warehouse.
Cloner	A car that has had a set of false plates fitted to mimic the identity of a similar car.
Comms	Communication
Cop shop	Small police station
Copper	Policeman/Woman

Different kettle of fish	To be in a different league
Dig him/her out	To catch someone out for lying
DOB	Date of birth
Doe	Money
Drop call	Let a mobile ring once without being answered.
Dry	Drug and money free
Expensive parts	Cocaine
Fags	Cigarettes
Filth, The	The Police
Fiver	Five pound note
Fullscrew	Corporal
Getting on it	Getting drunk/drugged up
Going down	Sent to prison
Goods	Drugs
Got the hump	Angry/annoyed with something
Gurner/s	Ecstasy
Hammered	Very much under the influence of some kind of substance
Handle on it	Under control
Hanging out the back of	Having sex
Hardware	Guns
High power	Good quality
Hinge, to the	To take something to the maximum.
Hot	Potentially under police observation.
Hot as fuck	Very blatant in criminality, potentially risking exposure to the authorities.
Hundred pound wraps	Where you have a hundred pounds in notes, fold the last note and slip it over the top of the others.
In, An	To find a route or 'way in' to a business, source or closed circle.
Juice	Steroids
Key/s	Kilo/s
Kip	Sleep
Lady of the night	Prostitute
Laters	Goodbye

Lay on/Laying	To get drugs on credit
Licence conditions	A set of rules that the probation service impose on someone released from prison.
Lifed off for a 20 stretch	To receive a life sentence of at least 20 years.
Loaded up	Carrying drugs/money
MIA	Missing In Action
Modified	Cocaine that has been adulterated or mixed to reduce purity and increase volume.
Mood Hoover	A person that will kill a positive atmosphere within seconds of entering a room/Depressing attitude.
NAAFI	Forces shop/bar
Natter, to have	Talk/conversation
Nicked	Arrested
Nine	Nine ounces of drugs AKA Nine bar
Nose bag	Sniff coke directly from the bag
Nut down, To get your	Go to sleep
Nuts and bolts	Ecstasy
Nutted off	Sectioned under the Mental Health Act.
Odds and ends	Drugs
Off your nut/tits	High on drugs
Offy	Off licence
Old bill	The Police
On a Para	Feeling paranoid
On top	Very blatant in criminality, potentially risking exposure to the authorities.
Parade	Military term for a meeting
PC brigade	Politically Correct
Persy	Personal drugs supply
Pete Tong	Wrong
Pills	Ecstasy
Piss, in a	Not very happy; pissed off
Pissed up	Drunk
Plonk	Cheap wine
Plotted/plot up	To wait or hang around in a designated area.

Pot tin	A small container used to hold materials and equipment for rolling a joint.
Powder	Cocaine
Power outout	Quality or percentage of drugs
Proper one, The	Cocaine of a very high purity
Prossy	Prostitute
Puff	Smoke Pot
Pulled, Get	Stopped by the Police
Pure	Pure Cocaine 90%+
Put one in him, To	Shoot someone
Put the kids to bed	Store the drugs
Quid	Pounds/Money/short for a thousand pounds
Rack one up	To prepare a line of cocaine
Recall	Sent back to prison for a breach of licence conditions.
Recce	Reconnaissance, to have a sneaky look around and gather intelligence.
Reliable motor	Consistent supply of coke
Repress	Cocaine that has been adulterated or mixed to reduce purity increase volume.
Rizla	Cigarette papers
Runners	Drug couriers
Safe house	Somewhere to store drugs, money or to just stay if it's on top.
Sale or return	To get drugs on credit
Shagging, To Shag	Have sex
Shithole	Rough place
Side burns	When a joint only burns on one side, potentially spilling its contents.
Skiddies	Dirty or well-worn underpants
Skin up	Roll a joint
Skunk	Strong herbal Cannabis
Smashed	Very much under the influence of some kind of substance.
Solids	Cannabis resin
Sparrow's fart	Early morning

Speed	Amphetamine
Spunk	Spend without care
Stamped on	Cocaine that has been adulterated or mixed to reduce purity increase volume.
Sticks, The	The countryside
Straight goer	A person not involved in criminal activity
Straight phone	Contract phone/phone not used for illegal activities.
Stuck the nut on	Headbutted
Tankie	A soldier that served in The Royal Tank Regiment
Tenner	Ten pound note
Tick	To obtain drugs on credit. Tick list, list of people that owe money.
Trolley, off of	Under the influence
Twatt	Derogatory term for a vagina
Twatted	Hit/Punched
Valeted and serviced	Drugs have been prepared
Work mode/Work	Selling drugs

Printed in Great Britain
by Amazon